25
PERFECT
DAYS

PLUS 5 MORE

Mark Tullius

VINCERE
P R E S S

Published by Vincere Press
65 Pine Ave., Ste 806
Long Beach, CA 90802
25 Perfect Days: Plus 5 More
Copyright © 2016 by Mark Tullius
All rights reserved.
For information about permission to reproduce selections from this book, write to
Permissions, Vincere Press, 65 Pine Avenue Ste. 806, Long Beach, CA 90802
Printed in the United States of America
Second Edition
ISBN: 978-1-938475-37-5
Library of Congress Control Number: 2015961013
"Five Minutes Alone" originally published by Devil's Work/Mountain Voodoo
Company
Also appeared in Star-Spangled Zombie, published by Maniac Press
Front, back cover, and all interior photographs and produced by Karl Dominey (c)
DOMINEY Photography
All Rights Controlled and Administered by DOMINEY Photography, LLC.
All Rights Reserved International Copyright Secured Used by Permission
DOMINEYphotography@gmail.com
Model in photograph titled "13th on the List" – Allie Marshall
Cover graphic design by Florencio Ares aresjun@gmail.com
All Hope Is Gone
Words and Music by Slipknot
Copyright © 2008 EMI APRIL MUSIC INC. and MUSIC THAT MUSIC
All Rights Controlled and Administered by EMI APRIL MUSIC INC.
All Rights Reserved International Copyright Secured Used by Permission
Reprinted by Permission of Hal Leonard Corporation

For Jen who helped create this twisted world,
and who always reassures me it won't become reality.

"We have made the present obsolete
What do you want? What do you need?
We'll find a way when all hope is gone."
– Slipknot

TABLE OF CONTENTS

Thank you for joining me on this journey, a trip to a world I hope never materializes.

Thirty interconnecting stories over a forty-year period can lead to quite a few characters. I know how confusing it is trying to keep track of all them all, so I've included a cast of characters at the back of the book. I've tried to keep spoilers to a minimum, but I make no promises.

Since the stories in *5 More Perfect Days* were written to enhance the original novel, I placed them in chronological order. Hope you enjoy the ride.

FIVE MINUTES ALONE

August 19, 2036

How much damage could Michael really do in five minutes? It's not like he was launching a nuclear attack or sitting behind the wheel of a semi, plowing into pedestrians. He just had to stand in a room. An 8x10 concrete cell. It'd be over in a blink. Conference calls at his office allotted more time for being on hold. There was nothing to worry about. If this meant closure, it was worth every second. That's all Sarah wanted, after all, for the twins, for the family. They needed to move on.

Sarah's voice came barreling up the stairs saying breakfast was ready. Michael couldn't remember the last time he'd heard that, couldn't remember the last time he hadn't awakened to her staring at the wall, lying there until the day was nearly done.

Michael threw off the covers. He smelled bacon and coffee. Bypassing his work suits, Michael slipped on a pair of jeans and a Polo and headed downstairs.

Sarah was behind the stove in an apron, her hair pulled back in a ponytail. The way Michael remembered her. Looking like a mom.

"It smells great," he said.

Sarah scooped sizzling strips onto a plate, blotted them with a paper towel to soak up the grease. "You talked to your boss, right?" Sarah set the plate onto the kitchen table.

"Yeah."

"I just really don't want anyone calling today."

Michael took his seat and poured a glass of orange juice. "They won't. And I talked to the boys' principal too. It won't even count as a sick day."

"Good." Sarah wiped her hands on her apron. "Boys! Come on, we're going to be late!"

Like they were waiting outside the door, the fifteen-year-old twins walked in and took their places, Justin to his father's left, Jeremy to the right. Black pants, black shirts, no words.

Michael started to think the family might not be ready for this, but as if she was reading his mind, Sarah pointed at his shirt. "You're not really wearing that, are you?"

Michael realized he was the only one in white, not exactly an appropriate color for the occasion. "I'll, uh, change after we eat."

Sarah pulled off her apron, took a seat. She was wearing the black dress she wore for Jenny's eighth grade graduation. The dress Michael teased her about because she was just like the other parents acting like it was some big deal. Sarah asked the boys if they liked their eggs. They gave little nods. Sarah didn't respond, didn't touch her food, she just sat there, staring at her empty juice glass. Michael told himself it'd get easier.

After breakfast, the two-hour ride to San Angeles was quiet. Only Sarah spoke, and only once. She said, "This is good, this is going to be good."

When they got to New Parker Center, Michael kept the doors locked.

"There's something I have to say."

Sarah pulled on the handle. "We've already discussed this. Open it."

"Yeah, Dad." Jeremy sat up and glared in the rear view, his eyes the size of golf balls. "You promised."

Michael didn't know if that was true. He couldn't remember promising, but he couldn't remember not promising either. It had been like that lately, Michael's recent memory had become a thick fog and as always, he was too exhausted to try to cut through it. Instead, he just wondered what kind of father would promise his children something like this and unlocked everyone's door.

The cop at the desk signed them in, told them to be sure to keep track of the time. Five minutes each, not a second more.

Sarah grabbed the pen, signed her name. They had agreed she could go first. A uniformed officer led Sarah away.

The desk cop pointed Michael and the boys across the hall. "Someone will come for you."

The waiting room was cold and small, the floor and walls a dull white. The boys were on the little couch. Jeremy sat with his fists pushed together, his steel-toe boot tap, tap, tapping. Michael wondered if Sarah had bought them just for today. Justin sat hunched over too, but different, like there should be a bucket between his feet.

Michael felt he should ask if they were okay, give the boys a chance to back out. But Sarah said they had the right. What if it'd been his sister? Michael didn't have a sister, but he understood what she meant. This would give them a little control, help them move past this.

Michael locked eyes on the clock. Four minutes past nine.

A cop called Michael's name from the doorway. He got up without saying a word to the boys. The elevator took him down to an unmarked floor and a long hallway, the fluorescent lights and ceramic tiles part of the original building.

They turned right at the next hallway. Sarah was down at the end. An officer led her by the elbow, her face speckled red, the same color dripping from her clenched fists. Sarah didn't even glance at Michael as they passed, ragged breaths seeping through her plastered smile beneath a vacant gaze.

Michael's officer nudged him toward the door. "Mr. Adams, you've been advised of your rights. Do you have any questions?"

He did have questions. What would he see on the other side? Did he really want to know what his wife was capable of? And what about the boys?

The officer unlocked the door. Red globs covered the floor, fragments of Sarah's footprints. Michael started to ask if it could be cleaned then realized how ridiculous that would be.

"Mr. Adams, clock's ticking."

Michael stepped inside. The dimly lit room smelled of blood and sweat. That's what he remembered about Jenny's birth. The complications. All that blood.

It was three days before the doctor took Jenny out of the NICU bed and said they could hold her. Michael was scared because Jenny was so small, but once she was in his arms, he swore he'd never let go. He'd protect her from everything.

But Michael failed.

The monster who raped and murdered his baby girl sat naked, his hands cuffed to the top of the table. Sarah had kept her word, but just barely. Olsen's eyes were swollen, but he could still open them.

For a second, Michael thought this was the wrong guy. Olsen looked nothing like the family man with five adoring kids. Each of them had written Michael and Sarah at least once a week begging them not to come today. They asked for mercy. They said none of this would bring Jenny back. Sarah burned every letter.

The cell looked like the interrogation room from an old cop show. Three bare metal walls, a fourth with the one-way mirror Sarah said she'd be behind. The only light flickered from the 60-watt bulb hanging over the table, where the naked monster looked like something out of a horror movie. Olsen's face oozed blood. His nose flattened and mushed to the left. The whites of his eyes were clouded red. His left ear hung on by a few ropes of skin.

Michael sat across from Olsen and stared at his hands. The top of the right one was a dark purple mass, the cuff smashed into the skin, looking like someone had slammed an anvil on it. Even if Olsen lived, it'd have to be amputated.

But Olsen wasn't going to live. If he made it past today, they'd still fry him tomorrow. That's what Michael kept telling himself.

An electric timer was mounted on the wall next to the mirror, thirty seconds already gone.

Olsen's attack on Jenny lasted a minute and fifty-three seconds. Some coward on the third floor caught the whole thing on video.

Below the timer was an iron stand that held a sledgehammer, a fireplace poker, and an aluminum baseball bat, smudged red on the end.

Olsen made a noise. It came out all mumbled through his broken jaw. Two teeth poked through his bottom lip. He was trying to speak, but Michael had heard enough of this prick's voice. During the trial, Olsen made a full confession and cried the entire time. He said Jenny had smiled at him. He said he couldn't help himself. He was sick.

Olsen finally got out his words, clearer this time. "Finish it," he said. "Please."

Michael closed his eyes and took a deep breath, tried to remember the last time he'd held Jenny. She was only thirteen.

"Kill me," Olsen begged.

Michael banged the table and drove it into Olsen's chest, pinned him to the wall. Michael jumped to his feet. "You don't get to decide."

The timer said Michael had three minutes.

He walked over, told himself not to pick up the poker, but there he was, pulling it out of the stand, careful not to cut himself on the razor-sharp hook and pointed tip.

Olsen moaned and Michael watched the seconds tick away. If Michael hit him once, that would be it. There'd be no stopping.

At two-forty-two, Olsen said, "She cried for you." Olsen cocked his head, raised the pitch in his voice, mimicking some ditzy teenage girl. "My daddy, my daddy…"

Michael spun around. Olsen leaned into it. But Michael let go of the handle and the poker flew past Olsen's face, clanked off the wall.

The timer hit Jenny's minute fifty-three. The head of the sledgehammer was as wide as Michael's fist. One hit is all it would take. Finished. The boys wouldn't have to step foot in this room, lower themselves to this piece of shit. They wouldn't have to hear Olsen's goddamn voice.

Michael reached out, picked up the sledgehammer and faced the mirror. The man staring back looked nothing like the man Michael had awakened as.

The mirror thumped. It thumped again, Sarah pounding it over and over until Michael let the sledgehammer fall to the ground.

The timer was down to one-fifteen, the moment Jenny had stopped fighting, and Olsen slammed her head into the concrete.

Each passing second was one less for Olsen, a little closer to the death he deserved.

Michael concentrated on the mirror. He saw the timer in the reflection. The buzzer rang. His boys would get their five minutes alone.

Fourteen Angry Marchers

October 11, 2037

Kenneth Murphy refused to fidget. He sat alone in the front pew, his sparkling white suit jacket too big, his fingers peeking out pale and stubby. The shoulder pads did little to add confidence, did nothing to stop him from picturing all the families at home watching and wondering how a scrawny, pimply-faced eighteen-year-old could take over for his glorious father, who was commanding the altar like God's personal general. Sunlight poured through the stained glass windows and streamed over the Reverend's crimson locks, creating a fiery halo worthy of the archangel Michael. All that was missing were wings and a sword.

It was often said when the Reverend spoke, the world stopped, and when the Reverend asked his flock to join him in prayer, Heaven rumbled from the thunderous sound.

Kenneth and his father were the only ones wearing white, the sacred color of the Chosen, but Kenneth just felt like a fraud. This was the day he was to take his first steps toward becoming the leader of the Church of the American Way, the largest ministry in the world. The Reverend had baptized the current president, countless senators, and two Supreme Court justices. Kenneth's reign would forever reside in the shadow of his father.

The Reverend raised a golden book to the rafters. His amplified voice boomed, "The Only Way!" The congregation echoed his words, each member showing off his copy to the angels above.

"For too long we have allowed selfishness to poison this glorious land. But no longer will we turn our backs on our brothers and sisters. We will no longer stand by as this country falls into the hands of the few, while the rest suffocate in death."

Kenneth joined in the applause. His father smiled for the cameras. "This book, inspired by the Almighty, shows us the Way, but a book cannot make our decisions. It is only a tool, a guide. It is up to each of us to accept our role, to take up the burdens of those in need, to elevate the least so we can all be given seats at the banquet of God. For how we treat the suffering souls of this earth defines our kingdom. And come election day, we will usher in an era of prosperity for all, not just those willing to lie and cheat their way to the top, but for those courageous enough to play by the rules. For we are all in this together. One people. One Way!"

The crowd leapt to their feet, praising God and the Reverend, who made his way down to his flock.

"I look around this room and I still see the faces of fear. At least a hundred of you have over a million dollars in assets. Some of you even more. And you've worked hard for that money and you're concerned. How can you trust it will protect the ones you love? How can you be sure it will care for those in need long after you pass on?"

The Reverend leaned against the second pew, just a simple man of the people. "I'm afraid I cannot take away those fears. But I know someone who might..." He looked to the rafters. "I suppose you might call it faith."

The plump woman in a floral dress sitting three feet from the Reverend, held her heart with both hands, had the biggest smile. The Reverend smiled back at her then continued.

"When November 3rd comes around and you step inside that ballot booth, I want you to see beyond Proposition 867. I want you to see the faces of the children you'll feed. I want you to see the roofs over families' heads. See the shoes, the highways, the dignity and self-respect each of us deserves." He turned his back to the crowd, returned to the altar. "Vote no and your family keeps ninety percent of your money when you die." He spun back. "Sounds like a great deal, right?"

A few couldn't help but nod.

"Sure. Who cares if children starve? Who cares if the whole country burns?"

No one moved.

"How much is enough?! Tell me!" He took out a handkerchief, dabbed his brow. "Proposition 867 isn't about taking everything, and don't let anyone tell you different. If you're making more than a million, it's half, not a penny more. And if you're making over a million and you cannot get by on half, then you need an accountant."

A sliver of laughter sliced through the tension.

Wayne, the lead usher and bodyguard, stood watch at the side door, his long hair slicked back in a ponytail. Kenneth could tell there was something going on outside. Shadowy figures seemed to be gathering on the other side of the stained glass.

The Reverend continued. "Think of the changes we can bring. The good we can accomplish if we'll simply join together. Heaven on earth, where everyone gets a seat at the table."

The applause came crashing and everyone was stomping and hollering hallelujah. Everyone except Wayne and a few other bodyguards.

The Reverend said, "Difficult decisions are part of life, but they will always be rewarded when the correct path is chosen. And today, God has blessed us with a special choice of his own. Before us is a young man who has been called to serve the Lord and His people."

Kenneth's cheeks grew warm. He needed to calm down. Having to approach the altar with his white suit and red hair was bad enough. He didn't need a red face to match.

The Reverend began listing Kenneth's accomplishments, but he was soon drowned out by the violent shouts outside the doors.

Most of the congregation swiveled their heads toward the back of the church. The Reverend spoke louder.

"As the Church of the American Way's first youth minister, this wholesome young man will guide us through the Word and the Way…"

The voices outside grew louder and echoed through the building. Their angry message was clear: the Reverend was leading his flock toward damnation.

But the Reverend would not be interrupted in his own house. "It is with great pride that I call forth my son, Kenneth Murphy the Second!"

Nervously, Kenneth rose. He was greeted with a smattering of applause inside the church and angry chanting outside. He stepped toward his father, but not too quickly. He'd learned his slick white shoes turned the carpet into an ice-skating rink. Slowly, he knelt before the altar.

The Reverend placed his hands on Kenneth's head and told the congregation to help usher this child into the light of the one, true Way.

Kenneth slid his thumb over his heart, stood, and took his place at the right hand of his father. He tried to look confident and strong, like his father wanted, but he couldn't help but notice the congregation glancing everywhere but at him. No one admired his fine suit. No one noticed his hair parted to the right just like the Reverend's. No one cared a single bit. They were focused on the rising chants from outside the doors.

Wayne and the other bodyguards shifted positions in the perimeter aisles, looked to the Reverend for the command to take action. The Reverend shook his head and said, "There is only one Way to salvation. The people outside are confused and bitter. They deserve our pity, not our condemnation."

Kenneth had never seen his father show such restraint, but he knew it had to do with the cameras. The world was watching, and the Church of the American Way had developed a reputation for harsh retribution.

The Reverend reclaimed his flock by returning their focus to the special occasion at hand. Then from outside, a man shouted, "No! Don't!"

The crash made Kenneth jump back, but he was still showered with pieces of stained glass. A tiny shard sliced across his right cheek, but the rest bounced off his sparkling white suit and the ridiculous shoulder pads.

Kenneth opened his eyes as the last bits of glass floated to the sanctuary floor. He faced the crowd, hands covering their mouths. He tried to stay calm, certain they could hear his ragged breathing. The Reverend brushed off his son's suit, took out his handkerchief and wiped the blood from Kenneth's cheek.

Through clenched teeth, the Reverend said, "Stop shaking. There is no fear in this house."

The Reverend turned to the congregation. "Everyone, please take your seats." He picked up the dirt-encrusted brick, grabbed Kenneth's arm and dragged him down the aisle.

As they approached the giant oak doors, the Reverend motioned for the bodyguards to take position.

Kenneth said, "We should call the State. Let them handle it."

The Reverend spun, pulled Kenneth close, their noses almost touching. "There is only one authority on this earth. Ours." He pointed at Roger, a tall man with thick glasses. "Stay with the money."

Roger slipped behind the counter piled high with signed copies of The Only Way as the Reverend threw open the double doors and burst out into the mid-morning sunshine, brick in hand.

The ushers surrounded Kenneth and his father as they headed for the protestors, only fourteen of them, not a real threat. Most of the protestors wore bandannas over their mouths or full-on masks. There were even a few rubber ones of the Reverend. They held picket signs: The Wrong Way. Five Minutes Too Long. The Fourth Has Been Forgotten. One Way to Hell.

Two men in skeleton masks stood by the broken window.

The camera crew followed, and the Reverend slowed down to make sure they didn't miss this. An usher snapped out his baton, but the Reverend shook his head. They filed in behind the Reverend as he held up the brick.

"Who dares to throw stones at a house of God?"

A man in black, one of the few without a mask, whispered to a stockier, bearded man with clenched fists. The man in black turned to the Reverend and said, "We apologize for our actions. The window will be replaced."

"The cost is not the concern. The glass cut my son."

"Who gives a shit?" the bearded man said.

The man in black pulled back his friend. "I'll pay for it myself, if I have to. It should not have happened."

"Do you have any idea how much time and effort went into that creation?"

A voice from somewhere in the group called out, "Like you don't have the money!"

Another voice said, "Yeah, you probably get that from one appearance."

The Reverend inhaled through his nose and flashed that famous smile. "I do not deny my successes, and what I have made has been returned tenfold to those across this great land. But who among you can offer more than derision and scorn?"

The man in black unzipped his windbreaker, his white collar now visible to all. "I believe I can answer that challenge. I am Father Potter of St. Luke's Church, and I am here as a voice of gentle opposition to this abomination."

The Reverend held the brick to the cameraman. "If this is what they consider gentle opposition, I'd hate to see them angry."

"I don't condone what happened. I tried to stop it. But by His good name, this is no house of God. This is nothing but business, a shelter of greed."

"*Greed?*" The Reverend laughed. "Our money flows through the people of this country, not through your golden palaces in Rome."

Potter's face flushed red. Kenneth saw his father was staying true to their concept of never defend, always attack.

Potter said, "The money you donate to the government comes back to you multiplied by a number far greater than ten. You know it, even if your blind flock does not." The Reverend started to speak, but Potter raised his hand to silence him. "I've seen the provisions of this tax bill you're pushing. Your church is the only one to receive anything from the collected funds."

"Because unlike you, we guarantee it will be spent on the people."

A frail woman stepped forward, her grip tight on a picket sign. "You just want to take everything. So you can control our country."

"And what exactly is under control now? The traffic? The pollution? Corruption? Scandal? The education of our young?"

"My brother's dead because of the laws you support," a voice shouted.

"And my father," another announced.

Kenneth stared at the shell of a woman, a blond, thirty-something clutching an upside down picket sign to balance her withered leg. Her sunken eyes were dull gray like she'd been slowly poisoned. The sign read, "The Fourth Forgotten" in blood-red letters.

Potter put his arm around her and said, "Her husband was murdered in one of your raids for supposedly not turning in a registered gun. A gun they never found."

The protestors grumbled in anger, booed the Reverend, called him a charlatan.

"And what exactly would you call this so-called 'priest?'"

The bearded man lunged forward, his stick drawn. "Murderer!"

Potter and a young man, with a blue bandanna covering half his face, grabbed his arm, urged him not make matters worse for himself, for all of them.

"But worse is exactly what will happen," the Reverend said. "As long as the needs of the few outweigh those of the many, then suffering is all that awaits."

The protester, dropped his picket sign, took off his bandanna and stepped toward the Reverend. "And what would you know about suffering?"

For the first time, the Reverend stepped back. The protester was just a teenager, but his eyes looked like they'd seen years of death. It took a few seconds, but Kenneth recognized the kid. Justin Adams, the brother of that girl who had been raped and murdered. Justin's face had been splashed on every news station. That vacant stare, his chin dripping with blood after his five minutes.

Wayne stepped in, put his hand on Justin's chest, but Justin just kept walking. The crowd closed in. The ushers formed a line.

Wayne said to Justin, "You want to get sprayed?"

The protesters stopped. The blue dye took over a week to wash off and it was reason for any citizen to be picked up for questioning.

Kenneth said, "Do it!"

One of the protestors in the Reverend mask started for Kenneth, who nearly tripped as he backed up. The protester said, "Look at me, I'm Chosen, I'm Chosen."

Another one danced back and forth. "Me, too. Me, too."

Kenneth felt his cheeks flush. He wanted to shout, to tell these nothings they didn't deserve to live in this country, but he felt the stutter, the affliction he'd worked so hard to overcome, swirling around his mouth.

Several of the protestors shoved their camera phones in his face. One of them said, "Save us, Chosen One." They all started laughing.

The Reverend grabbed Wayne's hand, lowered it from Justin's chest. "No one will be sprayed." He leaned into Justin's ear, but spoke loud enough for the cameras. "I feel your anguish. But you don't have to carry this alone. We are here for you, son."

Kenneth watched Justin's eyes. The anger was starting to dissipate, but then Justin's hands drove into the Reverend's gut. The bodyguards snapped out their batons. The protesters drove them back.

Wayne pulled out a canister, shook it, pressed the button. A blast of blue sprayed Justin's eyes. Screams and the burning mist filled the air. Potter grabbed Justin and pulled him back, emptied a water bottle over the kid's face. Kenneth barely saw the woman pulling something from her purse, but he heard the shot. Saw the flash. The exploding hole. The blood sprayed across his face and dripped down his cheek. The Reverend collapsed, his head smacking concrete.

An usher pulled out his gun, returned fire, the woman a marionette dancing in the wind. Potter crawled toward her while the rest of the protestors ran, spread out like fireworks.

Kenneth fell to his knees, cradled his father's head. Their brand new suits covered in red. The hole gushed the contents of his father's heart.

The Reverend's mouth moved, but there wasn't a sound.

Kenneth took his father's hand. "Don't talk. It's going to be all right." Kenneth screamed for someone to help. He stroked his father's fiery hair and felt something gripping his jacket. His father's hand.

"You must lead them," the Reverend gasped. "Through everything."

"Dad…"

"It's all yours now."

Kenneth watched the brick fall from his father's hand and gave a small, silent prayer. He sensed the cameras zooming in, the world watching, waiting to see what he'd do next. Kenneth simply drew a deep breath and looked around at the scene. He saw the woman flat on the ground, her chest still rising and falling. He crawled over and bowed his head in prayer. He kissed her forehead to tell everyone watching she was forgiven. Then he leaned into her ear and whispered so only she could hear. "I doubt five minutes will be enough."

29-US89N4X

June 21, 2039

Walt Jaworski pulled up to the gate and lowered the cruiser's window. He slipped off the recog glasses recently banned inside HQ and faced the mirrored guard shack. When had he gotten so old? Fifty-one and still in the field, his dyed brown hair not fooling anyone. He gave his name and agent number to the small silver box, waited for the retinal scan. The gate rolled open. Walt drove through to the final security checkpoint, none of them manned by humans – Dreschner's latest efficiency reform. Walt wondered how long before he would be replaced by a machine.

The sun reflected off the massive, gunmetal gray building. Walt parked three rows from the entrance. It'd been six months since he'd been called into HQ, and that had only been to escort an analyst to the Retraining Center. This morning, dispatch said Dreschner needed to see him. Walt knew this couldn't be good. Rumor was that Dreschner no longer saw anyone.

Walt checked his smile in the rearview. "It'll be fine," he said. He got out and closed the door, the clenched fist of the Controllers' logo emblazoned on the side. He straightened his black uniform, reminded himself he was one of the best agents in the field. Maybe this was about his oldest son, Brian, who'd been submitting applications for almost a year. Maybe they were going to finally offer him a position.

The steel door slid open and snapped shut behind him. Walt stepped into the pristine, white lobby. Huggins, Dreschner's weasel of an assistant, was waiting, arms crossed. Talking as if he were the heavily muscled guard standing behind him, Huggins said, "Your guns. Both of them."

Walt watched Huggins' beady eyes. "Never had to before."

Huggins wasn't amused. "New policy."

Walt handed over the .45 at his waist and the snub nose .40 strapped to his ankle.

Huggins gave the .40 to the guard, kept his eyes on Walt. "You know you'll have to make the switch."

Walt nodded at the Huggins' particle pistol. "I don't trust those things."

Huggins headed down the hallway, finger on the .45's trigger. "Follow me."

Walt looked at the guard, "You a new policy too?"

The guard motioned with the .40's barrel for Walt to get moving.

Huggins said, "You talk too much."

Walt bit his lip. He wasn't about to throw this job away because of some power-hungry little prick.

Walt followed Huggins into the glass tube suspended a hundred feet over the building's Data Collection hub. Analysts in silver suits and matching headphones sat at their consoles, fingers scrolling through lines of encryption.

Becoming an analyst was even more grueling than the process for becoming a field agent. The agency couldn't afford to hire the wrong candidate. If a field agent went rogue, he could be tracked and eliminated. An analyst could spread a million secrets. Analysts had to be meticulous, loyal, and, above all, cold. If the information called for action, they had to follow protocol. They had to be above reproach. Even though Walt had handled some things he'd rather forget, he always had the assurance that it had been thoroughly researched and based on facts.

In front of the analysts below was a giant screen playing a two-year-old clip of the President behind his desk, his words piped through speakers and scrolling across his chest. Walt didn't have to read them or listen. He'd heard the speech a thousand times. He concentrated on his breath, tried not to think of how Huggins was walking, back straight, long strides. Walt had escorted enough people to know this wasn't a friendly visit. He tried to think if there was anything he might have recently done, something to raise a flag.

"Look around you, at your neighbors," the President said. "They can't even handle their own problems. You want them handling yours?" The President leaned forward, both fists clenched on his desk, looking like a true leader, not some figurehead who had bowed before the young Preacher. "We cannot allow this nation to fail. There is too much at stake. I will preserve order. Our country will triumph!"

The glass door slid open, revealing the rotunda – an arching dome, marble floors, and brilliant white walls. Huggins said to hold on and disappeared into Dreschner's office. Walt looked around the room. He felt dizzy. Huggins reappeared and held open the door, pointed to a silver chair in front of Dreschner's desk. "Take a seat."

Walt did as he was told. The chair was freezing and uncomfortable. He noticed the framed photographs were gone, nothing on the walls, no trace of what had been here during his last visit. Dreschner still looked sharp with his jet-black hair and winning smile, but something was off. Walt said, "I'm so sorry to hear about your daughter."

Dreschner nodded. "That's very kind of you." He pushed a button on the desk's console.

Strips of metal shot out from the arms of the chair. Walt couldn't move fast enough. They wrapped around his throat, chest, ankles, and arms. A mechanical claw crept out from between his legs and guided a syringe with an inch long needle to the side of his neck. He leaned as far as he could to the left, felt the sharp tip tracing over his skin.

Dreschner pressed another button. The needle stopped. "I have a few questions. Give me the right answers and everything's fine."

Walt tried to stay calm, didn't say a word. Maybe it was a test, some kind of new training program.

Dreschner turned to Huggins. "You two can go."

Huggins glared at Walt. The door opened. Footsteps. Walt couldn't see if the men had actually left. Walt said, "Sir, I haven't done anything."

"Really?" Dreschner studied him. "We've all done something."

Walt wasn't in any position to argue. He just tried to breathe.

Dreschner pressed his finger to the wall. The blinds snapped shut and his features disappeared in the darkness. "I want to believe you, but I need to be sure." He pressed the button again and the needle slid into Walt's neck. "I'm injecting you with P-604. Your answers better match what I already know."

The serum coursed through Walt's veins. He scrambled to think of what might be asked. He feared it was about rumors regarding Dreschner's daughter, why she'd taken her life. He'd heard the awful stories.

Dreschner sat on the desk, clearly waiting for the serum to settle in. "I hate bad news. Don't you, Walt?"

"Sir," Walt slurred. Everything slowed. Dreschner's mouth was moving, but Walt couldn't make out the words. He just heard his own heartbeat in his ears.

"Walt! When did you last speak with Vincent Morrison?"

"It was…Saturday. No, Friday. I picked up Todd after work."

"What was discussed?"

"Nothing. Nothing important."

"What was said?"

"Might've asked him how his day was going."

"And Laura?"

Shit. This couldn't be about that. They'd been so careful. "She was busy with dinner."

"But she came to the door?"

"Yes."

"Did you give her a hug?"

Walt's stomach flipped. He started to say he couldn't remember, but every time he touched Laura was permanently engrained. "I think so. Yeah."

Dreschner's smile disappeared. "I only want certainties."

It killed Walt to be talked to this way, especially by a hand-picked puppet for The Way. "Yes, I hugged her."

"Okay." Dreschner slid back. "Did you always know what Vincent was planning? Is that why you referred him?"

"Sir?"

"Answer the question."

"I referred him because he was an excellent Marine and my friend."

"So you knew him well?"

"Yes."

"And you expect me to believe you had absolutely no idea what he was up to? Even with all that time you spend at his house?"

"I don't understand what you're getting at."

"Okay, you might be telling the truth, but let's find out."

He pressed the button and another mechanical claw slithered out from the back of the chair. The needle plunged into the base of Walt's skull. The effects were immediate, and not like the last time when everything slowed. This time it felt like he was floating away from his body. His mouth was on autopilot. Walt answered each of the same questions. Thankfully, they matched, give or take a word or two.

"Your friend, Vincent, is a traitor."

Walt swallowed. "No."

"Yes, he is, and he needs to be brought in. We cannot have terrorists in our midst, especially one of our own. Now, you made this mess by bringing him in, and you will clean it up."

How could Vince have betrayed anyone? Walt didn't want to believe it. "You're wrong about Vince."

Dreschner stood and said, "October 24. Sacramento. Senator Humphrey's office." A screen popped up from the desk. The footage showed Vincent walking away from the building as people filed through the front doors. Three seconds later everything went up in flames.

Dreschner repeated his question. "Can I count on you to do your duty?"

The Controllers didn't make mistakes. And now he'd seen it with his own eyes.

"This is your last chance, Walt. Can I count on you?"

"Yes."

"Good. I want him alive. I need to know how far this has spread in the agency."

It calmed Walt to know Vincent wasn't already sentenced to death. "I will bring him in."

"And Laura too."

Walt nodded as much as the restraint allowed.

"And their daughter."

"Sir?"

"Relax. I want her brought in separately. I'll make sure to take care of her, place her in a good home."

Loralei, Walt's goddaughter, was only twelve. Dreschner's assurance he'd find her a home didn't offer any comfort.

Dreschner held his finger over another button. "You sure you can do this? Remember, we're all replaceable."

"I will do my duty and defend my country." The words every agent spoke on the day of graduation.

Dreschner hit the switch. The restraints zipped back into the chair, along with the mechanical claws. "I'm trusting you here. Fulfill your orders and Brian will have a job."

Walt didn't buy it. Dreschner was just bringing up his son as another threat.

The drive to Vince's was the longest and shortest thirty minutes of Walt's life. He exited the freeway, started down the route he'd driven thousands of times, but instead of turning at the corner, Walt went up a few blocks and made a right. He'd never been on this street before, half the houses with for sale signs, two teenagers with backpacks strolling down the sidewalk.

Another right turn. Different direction, same destination. He parked in front of the three-bedroom townhouse, a lot nicer than his own. Vince's unmarked black sedan sat in the driveway.

Walt checked his weapon, reholstered it, turned up the radio to drown out his thoughts. Laura was like a mom to his son, Todd, babysitting him every afternoon since his mom died when he was two. Walt first saw a picture of Laura in Afghanistan. Vince had said she was the only woman brave enough and dumb enough to put up with his crap.

Walt stared at his hand on the wheel. The chip embedded near his wrist made him get out of the cruiser. The Controllers were definitely monitoring, they'd know he was stalling. He put on his recog glasses, walked up the driveway, blew out a deep breath.

Before he could even ring the doorbell, Laura answered it. "I thought that was you in the driveway." She swept her blond hair from her eyes. "Vincent is actually downstairs. Should I get him?" Walt's recog glasses showed elevated levels of adrenaline. She was nervous. "I was just about to start dinner. Todd and Loralei should be home from school soon." Walt didn't need recog glasses to know she was covering something. This was her "happily married, everything's wonderful" voice. Vincent was probably in hearing range. "I didn't expect you so early."

Walt kept his tone friendly when he said, "I got off early. You said he's in the basement?"

"Yes." Quieter than before, she said, "Is everything okay?"

"Yeah. Boring work stuff. I just wanted to go over it with him before dinner."

"I'll get him then."

Walt stepped inside, grabbed Laura's arm. "Hold on a sec. I'll just go down."

"Really, it's no trouble. He needs to come up anyway. Been down there all day."

"I thought he had the flu."

Laura pulled her arm back. "Is this what happens when your husband calls in sick? Are you interrogating me with your glasses?" She moved toward the basement door, disappeared down the steps. Walt pulled out his gun, started for the basement then looked down the hallway, saw their bedroom. A suitcase and duffle bag near the door.

Vince came up the stairs. "You're a little early for Todd, aren't you? Don't they have art today?"

"Yeah, I came here so we could talk."

Vincent cocked his head. "Everything okay? What's with the gun?"

"I'm going to ask you some questions. Questions I don't want to ask."

Vince glanced back at the duffle bag by his bedroom, played it cool, walked into the living room. "If you don't want to ask them, then don't." He stood by the end table. There was an antique candleholder next to a TV remote. Walt's recog glasses registered them as a remote control and a weapon. Vince said, "What's on your mind?"

"You know why I'm here."

"No. But judging by the way you're all uptight, I'm guessing someone's pissed about me not showing up today. Either that or you want to admit to your affair with my wife."

Laura, now standing in the hallway, let out a laugh, but Walt didn't react. Vince looked like he was about to reach for the candlestick. Walt leveled the .45 with Vince's face. "Don't even think about it."

Vince put up his hands. "Whoa, what are you doing?"

"You're a goddamn traitor."

"A *traitor*? What the hell are you talking about?"

"Humphrey's office. I saw the footage. You blew it up. There were people in there, kids."

"Man, you've lost your mind. You're going to call me a traitor? In my house?" Vince headed for the hallway before the recog glasses could get a read on his vitals. Vince was walking toward the duffle bag.

Walt took aim at the back of his head. "Don't make me do this. Don't take another step."

Vince stopped. Walt told him to back up, to stand next to Laura.

Laura said, "This isn't funny, Walt."

Walt waved her over with the pistol, kept his eyes on Vince. "Did you have this planned from the start? Did you use me to get inside the agency?"

Vince shook his head. "You know I'm not a traitor. You know this."

"Then what's in the bag?"

"I have a disc, okay? I read something I shouldn't have, found out some things I couldn't believe. Just let me show you."

"Do not move."

"I opened an in-house message. You can see it for yourself."

"I don't need to see anything. You'll show it to them at the center."

"You're going to take me to the Retraining Center, huh? You know exactly what they do in there. Come on, man, this is me. I saved your life. I looked after your boys when you couldn't even get out of bed after Carrie died."

"Vince, I have to bring both of you in. I don't have a choice."

"Because it's an order? Do you know who you're even following? They're killing people, Walt. For their money. They're executing wealthy citizens and seizing their assets."

Walt had heard the rumors. He just never thought it possible. The recog glasses said Vince was telling the truth. Still, Vince had training to survive interrogation and had to be lying. Walt ripped off the glasses.

"They're setting me up, Walt. They are. Because I know too much."

"Not another word. I'm not your judge. Now put out your hands." Walt reached for his handcuffs.

"Come on, what about Loralei? Don't do this."

"The Director said he'd take care of her."

Laura screamed, "No! You can't do this. This is insane!"

He didn't respond. "Walt, please," Laura said. "Just look at me."

Walt glanced at Laura. "What?"

"He's not lying. I've seen the files. There are plans. It's social engineering."

Vince said, "Just let me show you."

Vince started toward the bag. Walt's finger tensed around the trigger. Laura lunged and grabbed Walt's arm, the gun swiveling. Laura tried to rip it away. A shot fired. Laura's eyes widened. She stumbled back against the wall, slowly slid to the floor, a trail of blood streaking down the yellow paint.

Walt looked down at his gun, his finger still over the trigger. It was if his hand belonged to someone else.

Vince fell onto his wife, her eyes staring straight through Walt.

The sound of brakes squeaking. A school bus pulled to the curb. Their kids would be coming out any second.

"Jesus," Vince said.

"I'm sorry."

Vince looked out at the bus. The door starting to open. "You have to kill me," Vince said.

"What?"

"You can't bring me in. They'll torture Loralei to get what they want. And all I have is the disc. You have to kill me now."

"No."

Vince got to his feet, yanked Walt's arm up, put the gun to his own chest. "Do it!"

The door to the school bus opened. Kids filed out.

"You have to protect her. You know what they'll do if I'm alive."

Walt did. They'd both be dead within the week.

"Please."

Walt swallowed, squeezed off a round into Vince's heart, watched him collapse onto his wife.

The screen door slammed shut as Walt walked into the yard. He cut off Loralei and Todd before they could see inside. "Come on, we have to go."

Thirteenth on the List

September 11, 2041

The sun inched over the mountain, and light slid across the massive facility nestled at the bottom of the valley. Forty yards up, Jeremy Adams lay motionless, blending in between two boulders, his tan cloak perfect camouflage against the desert rock. He counted sixteen men down below in beige fatigues, but Jeremy didn't have anything against them. He placed his eye to the Bushmaster's scope and panned to the heavily secured front gate, the one area not protected with electrified razor-wire fence. Six guards with light machine guns. Two more in the security booth. Another eight were spread across the grounds, moving along the perimeter and watching over the massive white silos Jeremy had been instructed to avoid.

There was no way of knowing exactly how many men were inside the massive storage area built into the mountain and the blue building in the corner, which served as the Bradfords' living quarters.

Jeremy zoomed in on the tallest guard at the front gate. For private security, the man was well-equipped. His precise gait and perfect posture meant ex-military. Jeremy tracked one guard after another. Most of them were in their thirties or forties. Their experience didn't worry him. Jeremy was only twenty, but in the three years he'd been in the field, he'd probably killed more men and women than these guards combined.

He took his first life at fifteen, and recruiters immediately recognized his determination and complete lack of emotion. While his brother and former classmates had fucked off in high school, Jeremy's handlers trained him in the art of death. Killing became his business and these days business was booming.

Jeremy adjusted his position against the rock and ran the numbers in his head. He earned one hundredth of one percent off each hit, but the combined net worth of the first twelve people on his list totaled fifty-three billion. The Bradfords added an additional eighteen, meaning Jeremy would clear over seven million, tax-free. Maybe if his family heard that they wouldn't be so quick to judge.

He needed to focus. The string of recent deaths had put the wealthy on alert. Some went about their lives hoping it was just a coincidence. Others hid. Most, though, hired security details like this one. But Jeremy knew that it was all false hope, no one was ever truly safe.

He checked his watch. If intel could be trusted, Jeremy only had to wait another five minutes. Every Saturday at that time, Kyle Bradford opened the living quarter's door, walked his wife down the short-walled path, kissed her goodbye, and watched her drive off to pick up their son. When Deborah crossed the front gate, Kyle would head into the mountain and begin work. Only today would be different. There would be no goodbye kiss.

Deborah's silver Hummer and Kyle's black Jeep were parked a dozen yards from the building's door, a mere seventy-three yards from Jeremy's position, no wind to deter his shot. He'd take out Deborah and then Kyle before she hit the ground.

Jeremy pulled his eye away from the scope and stared at the picture of his sister taped to the stock. Photos were forbidden on missions, but Jenny went with him everywhere. She started him down this path and it was to her he repented before every hit.

After a few silent words, Jeremy set his sights on the blue building. He ran the plan in his head. Two rapid shots, possibly three, empty the ten-round magazine on the closest guards, then retreat up the mountain. He'd be back at his car within five minutes, gone in fifteen.

Movement at the gate. A flashing red light at the top of the booth. A car approached on the lone road that sliced through the desert. A black bottom, red top town car, silver-tinted windows. Official car of the Church of the American Way.

Jeremy threw protocol out the window and clicked on his earpiece. He should've been alerted.

The car stopped at the gate and a guard approached the window.

In the quietest whisper Jeremy said, "We got company."

"It's just support." Captain Hayden sounded pissed. "Now get off the channel."

Jeremy didn't typically work with others, especially the Way. "Negative. Shake them."

"Do as you're told," Hayden said.

The earpiece went silent and the front gate rolled to the left. The town car drove around the blue building. It parked. Jeremy could only see one side. The passenger door opened and a young man in a silver suit stepped out. He combed his slick black hair, looked right at Jeremy's location and gave a little nod.

Jeremy ignored the goose bumps and the little voice telling him to fall back to the car and never look back. He told himself that having some help only increased his odds.

Silver suit stayed where he was. He spoke with the driver. A few seconds later, the building's front door opened. Jeremy laid his finger against the trigger guard and steadied his breath. With a twist of the scope, Kyle Bradford's profile filled the sight, the crosshairs rising and falling from the top of his thick eyebrow to the bottom of his ear. Jeremy zoomed out and watched as Deborah met the morning, the sun blasting off her long blond hair.

The Bradfords headed down the walkway. Jeremy hoped they'd say goodbye in front of their vehicles. Otherwise he'd have to deal with the waist-high wall. If he missed, the target could drop and hide.

The Bradfords continued down the path. Jeremy zoomed in on Deborah and relaxed his breathing even more. He cut the target area to the quarter-sized spot around her temple.

Deborah stopped and hugged Kyle. Jeremy's finger inched off the trigger guard and slipped inside it. The groove of his knuckle settled against the metal. As he was about to take the shot, Deborah bent down like she dropped something, ruined Jeremy's sight picture.

When she stood, the back of Deborah's head filled the sight. Jeremy held his breath and applied more pressure on the trigger. Deborah turned slightly, holding their two-year-old son in her arms. Jeremy jerked the rifle to the right just as the shot fired.

The boom echoed through the mountains and the bullet punctured the side of the Hummer. Kyle grabbed hold of Deborah and rushed her and the child toward his Jeep as the facility's alarm blared.

Kyle threw open the Jeep's front door and Jeremy squeezed off another round. The bullet struck Kyle in his side and knocked him to the ground. Kyle got to his knees and waved Deborah away. She disappeared behind the wall with the boy.

Jeremy waited to finish Kyle. He hoped the man's suffering would draw out his wife. Kyle started to pull himself into the vehicle, which forced Jeremy to take the shot. The fifty-caliber round splattered Kyle's head against the inside of the door.

Bullets peppered the mountainside as the guards blindly fired in Jeremy's general direction. He had to kill both Kyle and Deborah for the mission to succeed, but she was behind cover and if he took another shot, the guards would pinpoint his location. Some of the bullets had already come close.

The guards stationed around the silos were closing the distance. So were the ones walking the perimeter. The ones at the gate kept their posts, guns aimed at the mountainside. The tall guy loaded a rocket launcher.

Jeremy couldn't rely on the Way to finish the job and it was too late to retreat. He had one option and it wasn't good.

His first shot split the brow of the guard with the rocket launcher. His second knocked down the one running for the fallen weapon. The third and fourth shots stopped two guards rushing toward the base of the mountain.

The fifth missed the guy firing from the side of the living quarters, and Jeremy fell behind the rock as the gunfire found him. Dirt and chips of rocks filled the air. There were at least ten guards left, no sign of the Way, and a loaded rocket launcher. Time to move.

Jeremy freed a smoke grenade and rolled it down the hill. The heavy white clouds rose and Jeremy flipped down the face shield of the helmet hidden under his cloak as he ripped Jenny's picture from the rifle. He leapt to his feet and took off running.

A round hit Jeremy's chest, bounced off his body armor and staggered him. Before the smoke cleared, Jeremy pulled the M-14 slung across his back and dropped down behind a cluster of rocks fifteen yards from his original spot. They'd know he was in the vicinity.

The smoke was gone. The shooting stopped. Looking through a crack between two boulders, Jeremy could see Deborah crouched behind the wall, her blue shirt barely visible. There were two guards kneeling beside her with their guns aimed at the last place Jeremy had been. Another guard was positioned by the Hummer waving her toward him.

Jeremy eased the barrel of the M-14 into the crack and tracked the guard who had retrieved the rocket launcher. Killing Deborah was a top priority. Living to see payment, even higher.

The man fidgeted with the weapon, couldn't quite balance it on his shoulder. Jeremy's round punched through his forehead, dropping him and the launcher onto the ground.

All guns turned toward Jeremy's location and opened fire. He got off two more lethal shots before pulling back. Jeremy blocked out the deafening roar of guns and the piercing alarm and visualized where each of the remaining guards were positioned. The biggest threats were the ones at the fence line near the rocket launcher and the three by Deborah.

Jeremy took a grenade from beneath his cloak and pulled the pin. He couldn't throw it anywhere near the child and there was no way he could reach the fence line, so he lobbed it at the corner of the living quarters.

The grenade bounced to a stop by the feet of the firing guard, gave the guy just enough time to stare down before it exploded, shredding his body and blowing a hole through the wall.

Jeremy scrambled to the left, jumped over rocks, his feet sliding on the slippery terrain as bullets whizzed around him. A rocket slammed into the boulder he'd been behind and blasted him off his feet.

Jeremy flew through the air, his right cheek smashing into a rock, shattering with a loud crunch. If he stayed still, he'd be dead. He hugged his weapon to his chest and threw himself on his side, rolling down the mountain, his armor only providing minimal protection against the jagged rocks.

He tumbled down the last twenty yards, braced himself for the impact, and barely felt the sharp sting of a bullet rip through his calf. Several other bullets bounced off his armor as he banged down the hillside. His left forearm snapped when he slammed into the ground.

Staying down meant death. Jeremy got to his feet and brought up the M-14 one-handed, his aim unsteady. He pivoted toward the walkway and saw Deborah behind the wheel of her vehicle. Three guards surrounded her, fired at Jeremy and yelled at her to drive.

Headshot, headshot, short blast to one guy's chest. All three dead just as Jeremy got floored by a blow that felt like a baseball bat.

He rolled onto his back and looked toward the mountain. The massive foot-thick gate was stuck halfway open. A guard racked another slug into his twelve-gauge. Jeremy took aim, put the guard down then turned toward the squeal of tires.

Rubber spun on the warm concrete. The Hummer's rear snaked back and forth. Jeremy hobbled toward the jeep and stepped over Kyle as the Way car screeched around the corner. The silver suit on foot high-tailed it toward the silos with his pistol dangling at his side.

The keys waited in the ignition. Jeremy started the bullet-riddled jeep and floored the gas as the Way car flew past the Hummer and disappeared into the mountain.

The Hummer sped by the silver suit. The guy never even raised his gun. Instead, he faced Jeremy's jeep and aimed.

Jeremy flicked on his earpiece. "Support hostile. Repeat, support is hostile."

Jeremy swerved. A bullet smashed through the windshield, knocking out his rearview.

A thunderous explosion ripped through the day. The jeep shook as a blast of heat shot out from the mountain. The man in the silver suit kept his feet and tossed something small beside the silos. He smiled big. No fear of death, only expectation in his eyes.

Jeremy spun the wheel, but it was too late. Everything was red, the air an oven of fire. All four wheels were off the ground and Jeremy's world went black as he flew end over end.

The pain was so intense he had to be alive. Jeremy slid the vial from his collar, injected it into the unroasted side of his neck. The effect was immediate, although temporary.

Jeremy cracked the helmet free from his skull. He felt for the earpiece and instead found a lump for an ear. His right eye was stuck shut, but his left eye could open.

A fiery inferno rushed from the mouth of the mountain and merged with the silos. It seemed to Jeremy like a tongue lashing back and forth, its brilliant blue tip scorching the sky black with dark smoke.

Jeremy pushed onto his side and found himself on the concrete facing the gate. The jeep was a burning wreck, a permanent part of the guard house. Everyone was dead or gone. Except Deborah. Instead of racing off to Indian Springs or Las Vegas, she sat in her idling Hummer down the road. Then it moved, creeping toward him.

Jeremy took a grenade and held it close to his chest. The Bradfords had been smart enough to will all their fortune to a charity if something happened to their son. If Jeremy blew up both Deborah and Cody, the US government got nothing. If he could somehow get her by herself, his employers would get fifty percent instead of only ten once the new tax law took effect.

The Hummer continued to inch forward. Jeremy set the grenade by his side and reached for the forty-five in his waistband. His fingers wrapped around the handle when Deborah stopped fifteen yards away. The driver's door opened, and Jeremy slipped the gun from its holster and held his breath. He hoped he looked as dead as he felt.

Deborah stepped out of the Hummer. The opened door blocked most of her body. Her blood-speckled face peered through the window. No longer confident of his aim, Jeremy hoped she'd come a little closer.

She stayed there for several seconds then ducked into the idling vehicle. Was she going to run him over? That's what Jeremy would have done. A moment later, she came back out holding something in her hands. Even through one narrowed eye, Jeremy could see it wasn't a gun.

A flash blinded him. He raised the forty-five and fired one, two, three times, but she dove into the Hummer. Jeremy continued to fire as the SUV flew in reverse.

Jeremy got to his feet and limped out the front gate. He stopped where Deborah had been only a moment before. A small puddle of blood pooled on the concrete. With any luck he had hit something vital and she'd bleed out before she made it to town.

Either way, Jeremy was screwed. The Way had let Deborah escape and tried to kill him. He'd been set up and cut off. He should have known better than to trust the Controllers.

It wouldn't be long before jet fighters out of Nellis Air Force base responded to the explosions. The charred vehicles inside the facility were no longer an option, so Jeremy headed for the top of the mountain to retrieve the rental car with the documents tying this to the Muslims. Only Jeremy wouldn't be driving to the pickup location as originally planned.

He was on his own.

Nine Months Later

December 18, 2042

Maria Salazar's six hours were up and, although it would do little to ease her suffering, she wanted her Motrin. Last night, just before the midnight cutoff, she'd delivered naturally, refusing the epidural and narcotic offers she couldn't afford.

Ignoring the burning from her sutured tear, Maria steadied her cot and rolled onto her side, facing the doorway and the other women filling the small room. Just past the narrow aisle lay a gray-haired woman, her face wrinkled, her breasts sagging onto her cot. Next to the old woman was a young girl who was probably not yet in junior high. At first glance, Maria thought the girl was the granddaughter but they looked nothing alike. The girl's belly was still swollen, and the hospital would never allow a cot to go unused, even for a moment. The last two women were both turned toward the doorway, waiting for miraculous news to arrive or simply unwilling to face the rest of the room.

Maria wondered if any of the other women had planned to become pregnant. Maybe they'd been waiting because they couldn't afford a child. Maybe they hadn't been sure they wanted to bring a child into this world. Had any of them seen their baby before the nurses whisked them off to the nursery? Or been told what sex their child was, if it was healthy, if it was even still alive? She wanted to ask them how they were dealing with all of this, if they felt hollow, like someone had stolen part of their soul. Maria didn't need to say a word. The tears and muffled sobs said it all.

If she and Enrique hadn't been so careful, they could've been pregnant years before. There was no denying it would've been difficult to provide for a child on their measly salaries, but it would've been better in so many ways. For one, she would've been by herself in this room, not having to smell the soiled sheets, unchanged dressings, and sour stench of fear. She would've bonded with her baby after the delivery. She would've arranged a payment plan with the hospital. They would've made it work and there wouldn't have been a question of whether she would ever see her only child.

But they had waited and now here they were, 2042, the year of the baby. The year that man's foolishness had finally caught up with him. The year every woman with a uterus became fertile with one act of terrorism, the explosion in the desert changing everything.

Maria's gaze traveled from the door to the clock and back to the door. It was almost twelve-thirty. The nurse was running late.

A few minutes crawled by before a shadow crossed the doorway. It was Enrique. Black circles of sweat surrounded both armpits of his grease-stained jumpsuit.

Enrique treaded quietly across the room with his eyes on his boots. Maria could tell he'd been crying. Enrique never cried.

"Oh my God." Maria clutched the gown to her chest. "What is it? Enrique, what is it?"

Enrique motioned for Maria to calm down as he knelt at the foot of her cot and stroked her calf.

Maria didn't care if she upset the other women. Something was wrong. Not lowering her voice, she said, "Tell me. Tell me what's wrong. Is it dead?"

After shushing her, Enrique cleared his throat. "Everything's fine," he said, an obvious lie. "I just stopped by the nursery."

"The baby's okay?" Without giving him time to answer, she asked, "What is it? Is it a girl?"

"Maybe it's best not to know. That's why they didn't tell us."

Maria grabbed him. "Tell me."

"It'll make things harder."

"Damn it, Enrique, don't talk like that. I'm taking my baby home. Now tell me what we had!"

"It was a girl."

Maria's heart melted. She'd known it was going to be a girl all along. "Vanessa."

Enrique nodded then glanced at the clock.

"You're not going to leave already?"

"What do you want me to do? It takes me ten minutes on the bike and if I'm late again, I'll be fired."

"We only have until midnight." Maria struggled to remain calm. "How are we going to come up with the money?"

Enrique shook his head. "We can't. There's no way."

"We have to."

"It's too much. Where can we get the money? We're still three thousand short."

"What about your boss? Can't he give you an advance?"

"I already asked him, and even if he did, how would we ever make ends meet after?"

"I'll keep driving," Maria said.

"We already said this was your last year."

"We need the money."

"I'll work doubles," Enrique promised.

"On your salary you'd have to work four shifts a day." Maria hadn't meant it to sound mean. "There are three of us now."

Enrique started to speak, hesitated, then said, "Maybe it's better if it's just you and me. Better for her and us."

If he'd been closer, Maria would've slapped him. "Don't ever say that."

He stroked her leg a little harder. "You know I don't want that. I want a child more than anything." He fought back tears. "What can we do? Even if we could get the money, what kind of life could we give her?"

"A good one. We'd love her more than anyone else ever could."

"All the love in the world won't give her shelter if we can't pay our rent. It won't feed her if we can't buy food. If we let the Church adopt her, she'd have a chance at a better life."

Maria glanced a few cots away at a woman in fetal position, heaving, her face a frozen shriek.

"We are not giving up our daughter. And especially not to that cult."

"The Way isn't a cult. They're helping the government make the world a better place."

"You believe everything you see on TV?"

"I don't know what to believe anymore." Enrique held his head in his hand. "I don't know what to think."

"I'll die before I let them take our little girl."

"Calm down, Maria. You're still emotional because your hormones are messed up from having a baby."

"A baby I've never seen! A baby I carried for nearly nine months!"

"I'm sorry. I know how you feel."

"You can never know how I feel."

Enrique let go of her calf and stood. "Then where does that leave us?"

"What about the Family Support Specialists?"

"They're nothing more than well-dressed loan sharks. Thirty percent interest with an extra ten percent fee tacked on. How could we ever pay that? You know what they'll do if we don't?"

"We'll find a way."

"I don't even know if they'd approve us."

"We have to try."

Enrique looked at the clock. "Fine. I'll go after work."

"Thank you."

"Don't get your hopes too high, Maria" He headed for the door. "It may not happen."

After Enrique left, the old lady turned to Maria, her stale breath blowing into Maria's face, making her nauseous. "Is this your first?"

Maria nodded and pushed herself into a sitting position. Carefully, she swung her legs off the cot and onto the cold floor. She pulled the slushy ice pack from her underwear and set it on her sheet, gingerly got to her feet and hobbled over to the wheelchair in the corner. She needed the Motrin, but wasn't about to wait in this depressing room for it.

Maria eased into the wheelchair and rolled out of the room. Both sides of the hallway were lined with expectant mothers lying on cots. As she wheeled down the corridor, several of the women asked her questions. Maria pretended not to hear and headed for the lobby.

Vanessa's delivery was a few minutes before midnight, and Maria was one of the last natural birth mothers. All of the unfortunate women on either side of the hall would be having c-sections, the government's answer to the overwhelming surplus of pregnant mothers. Some of them might not even mind, but a c-section had been out of the question for Maria. Not only was it more expensive, it would've taken her longer to recover and get back behind the wheel. That's why she and Enrique had gone on all those walks, had awkward sex several times a day and, when all else had failed and they were running out of time, broke her water with the sterilized tip of a file he borrowed from work.

The cramped hallway led into a lobby crowded with swollen bellies and worried faces. Maria stared straight ahead and tried not to think of their fears. She had enough of her own.

Maria wanted to head to the nursery, but knew she wouldn't be allowed in. She veered right and pressed the button for the elevator and rolled inside when it opened. The bloodied nurse standing next to the control panel asked Maria what floor she wanted. Maria had no idea. She just had to get away from the other mothers. She said, "The top."

The elevator stopped at the third floor long enough for the nurse to get off. Maria continued toward the tenth, going higher and higher, trying to leave her problems down below.

She wheeled herself off the elevator and rolled past the sign for the mental health unit. The lobby was empty except for the sleeping security guard seated at the nurse's station. Maria rolled past him and headed down the quiet corridor.

The first two rooms Maria passed were empty. Giant suites with only one bed in each. The patients at the top could afford the best care.

Halfway down the corridor was a large window with steel bars across it. Maria parked the wheelchair beside the window and looked out at San Angeles, the city that had once been her home and was now her hell. The freeways down below were running smoothly, the only positive change that had been made. Crime hadn't been stopped or even slowed by the new laws, and people were losing rights every day. Maybe Enrique had been smart to question bringing a baby into this world.

Maria closed her eyes and blocked out the scene below. Vanessa was here now and they had to find a way to get her out of the hospital. If they didn't, Maria would end up in a place like this, only so much worse. She imagined the years of living with the pain and uncertainty. She wouldn't survive. She'd go crazy.

The tears came with such force that Maria couldn't keep her eyes closed.

A hand patted her shoulder and a woman's voice told Maria everything would be all right.

Embarrassed at her weakness, Maria stopped crying. She wiped her eyes with the back of her forearms.

"That's it," the woman said. "Just relax. Whatever it is you're feeling right now will pass."

The woman knelt in front of Maria, took her hand. "Would you care to talk about it?"

Maria shook her head, but deep down she felt grateful someone was taking the time to comfort her.

"Do they have your baby? They took mine."

Maria opened her eyes and saw the electronic wristband. She tried not to stare at the bright pink scar running across the woman's cheek. "They took your baby?"

The woman nodded. "And they're going to keep him as long as I'm in here. Maybe longer."

Maria thought the woman looked familiar. "I'm sorry to hear that. Is he with the Church?"

The woman's face grew harsh. "I'll get him back somehow. I don't care what I need to do. I'll get him out of there."

Maria began to cry again. "I can't let them take my daughter away. I haven't even seen her yet."

The woman smoothed Maria's hair. "You'll get her back."

"How? I have until midnight."

The woman smiled, her face familiar, but one Maria couldn't place. Maybe she was one of the wealthy Maria had cleaned for.

"I can help you," the woman said. "But I need you to do something for me first."

"The guard's asleep. You can walk right out."

The woman shook her head and held up her hand. "And receive a lethal shock the moment I cross the door? No thanks. And even if I didn't have this on, I wouldn't be safe. I'm not worried about the government killing me for my money anymore, but they're the ones keeping me here, all because I speak the truth. And then there's the public. With everything going on with all these births, people are going to hate me and Kyle a little more every day. There will come a time when everyone will want me dead."

Kyle Bradford. Everyone knew the name, the photo of the happy family always on the news. Maria said, "It wasn't your fault."

"Or Kyle's."

"Everyone knows it was the Muslims."

"That's just it," the woman said. "It wasn't terrorists. It was the Controllers."

Although she was a mental health patient and what she was saying was ridiculous, the woman didn't seem crazy. Maria did not have the same blind faith in the government that most of the country did. "Why would they do that?"

"They knew what we'd created, how powerful we'd made the clomophine. They didn't want to pay for it, decided to share it with everyone." The woman told Maria to wait then headed down the hall and disappeared into the last room. She returned a minute later and said, "Let me have your hand."

It was a photograph of a young man in black armor, the right side of his face a charred mess. "Who's this?"

"The man who killed my husband, one of the Controllers."

The man's ear was a black bump. His hair was gone. "What do you want me to do?"

"Spread the word to people not to trust the government. Tell them the Controllers lie and manipulate. Tell them the truth."

"And if they don't listen?"

"Then tell the next person and the next and the next. Tell everyone you meet, but be careful. The Controllers have eyes and ears on every corner."

Maria studied the woman's face and found only sincerity. She placed the photograph in her gown pocket and said, "I will. I promise."

The woman dug out a stack of hundred dollar bills. "They took away my boy, but they couldn't take away my money. I'm glad I can do some good with it."

Maria held up the money, barely able to speak. "Thank you, but I only need three thousand. This is too much."

"You'll need to take care of your little one. This will help you get by for a bit, make life a little easier."

The tears came again. "How can I ever pay you back?"

"I already told you," the woman said as she turned around and headed back to her room. "Now go get your daughter."

Four Percent

June 2, 2043

"Man, it stinks." Julio Ortega smiled at his six-month old niece in the car seat. "Was that you, Vanessa?"

Maria took her eyes off the road to glance at her brother in the rearview mirror. "It's all the meat processors." She pointed. "That's Farmer John's over there. And up here on the right is Bristol Farms. The whole area smells."

"So why'd they bury the DMV all the way back here?" Julio asked.

Enrique, Maria's husband, said, "I'm sure part of it was the cheap cost of land. The other…"

"We're here," Maria interrupted. She pulled their beat-up Buick into the parking lot and said, "I'm just glad they only handle licenses. Enrique, do you remember how long you'd have to wait at the old DMV's? It took hours just to register this thing."

Julio said, "How would he know?"

Enrique turned in his seat and glared at Julio. "I've been to the DMV before."

Maria shot Julio a look in the mirror. "Drop it."

Julio kept quiet because he lived in their house. If he ever got his own place, he'd tell Enrique what he thought of him.

Maria shut off the car.

Julio glanced out the back window, amazed at how large and intimidating the building was. "It's awful big for a DMV." He unbuckled his niece and took her out of the car seat. Maria wouldn't allow him to carry her today. He understood.

Outside, Julio gagged on the stench. They all gagged. "Jesus, that shit's terrible," Julio said.

"Language, Julio." Maria acted as if the smell didn't bother her while covering Vanessa's nose and mouth with her blanket.

Julio hurried to the entrance and held the door open. A steel wall separated the employees from the public. Maria and Enrique moved past him without a thank you and stood in line at the second of three dark-tinted windows. Figuring they wanted to be alone, Julio found a group of empty seats and took it all in so he'd know what to expect when he came back on his own.

Three lines were a lot fewer than he'd imagined, nothing like the stories. The longest line, labeled Forfeitures, was closest to the employee entrance. Four couples were in front of Maria and Enrique in the Renewal line. The last line, which only had two guys in it, was for new licenses. Both boys looked about eighteen, the magical number Julio had to wait one more month for. These guys were nervous, moving their jaws back and forth, one of them chewing on his lip.

On the other side of the wall, Julio noticed one last window. This one had no glass and it was waist level, much smaller, roughly the size of the TV they had at home. He didn't see how anyone could possibly have a conversation with the clerk on the other side of the wall.

There wasn't anyone in that line. An electronic display with the number twenty-seven hung above the window. Another display loomed above the door he had thought was for employees.

Enrique and Maria were next. Julio glanced around the hushed lobby. Over a hundred people, yet it was quieter than church at communion, only the occasional sighs and stifled sobs breaking the silence.

The light above the steel door blinked the number seventy-two and blinged three times. An older man at the end of Julio's row stared down at the wrinkled piece of paper in his hand and then back at the light. The man took hold of his wedding ring and spun it round his finger. The light blinged again and the man struggled to his feet. Julio wished him good luck as he limped by.

Enrique sat in the chair two feet away from Julio so Maria and Vanessa could sit in the middle. "Who's he?"

"Some old dude."

"You hope he gets his renewal?"

"I hope everyone gets theirs."

"Well, not everyone can."

Julio was about to say something. Maria jumped in. "Look, mi amor." She handed a piece of paper to Enrique. "Seventy-seven."

"Is that good?"

Maria rocked Vanessa and tried to smile. "Seven's my favorite number."

"Good," Enrique said. He placed a kiss on Maria's cheek. "Everything is going to be okay. You're gonna get it."

Maria held her baby close to her chest. "Of course I will. Won't I, Vanessa?"

Julio looked at the ticket Enrique held. "Why are there two numbers on it?"

"I keep one half and Enrique takes the other. Here."

"I won't need it," Enrique said.

Keeping her voice low, she told him to take it.

Enrique ripped off his half and gave back hers. The display blinged again and number seventy-three appeared above the steel door. A teenage girl wept in the front row. "I changed my mind," she told the bald man beside her. "I don't want to drive anymore."

The man hugged her and whispered something in her ear. She continued to cry.

The steel door opened and two armed guards stepped into the lobby. The bald man helped the girl to her feet and walked her to the door. Her trembling legs buckled when the man passed her on to the guards.

"I suppose you want her to get hers, too," Enrique said.

"At least she has a license to renew."

"Stop it," Maria said. "I love both of you, but you need to stop fighting."

"Well, how can he talk, he's never gotten one?"

"Neither have you," Enrique said.

Julio was tempted to tell them how he'd been practicing out in the desert, and already knew how to drive. "I'm going to."

Maria looked ready to slap him. "Why would you do that? What's wrong with the bus? You don't even have money for a car."

"I start at State this fall and I'm not even trying to take the bus down there. It'll take me forever and make it so I can't work enough."

Enrique asked about Julio's bike.

"It's over thirty miles to Long Beach."

"So?" Enrique said. "It'd be good for you."

"Yeah, just like not having my license in high school has been good for me. You ever try picking up a girl on a ten-speed?"

Maria pulled Vanessa closer. "Well, some things are more important than others."

"Like family?" Julio asked.

She bent down and kissed Vanessa's forehead. "Exactly."

"That's why I'm getting a license. So when I get married, my wife won't have to."

"Damn it, Julio. Don't make me ask you to wait in the car," Maria said. "Why can't you understand? I need a license for my job. If I can't drive, I'll have to take a job where I work twice the hours for half the pay. We can't make it on that. Plus, it only takes Enrique ten minutes to ride to work."

Julio shrugged as number seventy-four blinked on the display. An elderly lady with a cane hobbled over to the steel door, stood in front of it as tall as she could.

"You know Enrique can't drive, so stop acting like he can. It's not his fault."

"He doesn't care," Enrique said.

"When I married him, everyone could get a license. They didn't have all these stupid rules." Maria shook her head. "Dyslexia? Come on."

Julio kept staring at Enrique, thinking what a coward he was.

Maria looked at Vanessa, then Enrique. "Even if they let him, I wouldn't. We're fine the way we are."

"Are you serious?"

Enrique's eyes were on the door. His fingers played with the beads of his rosary necklace. "Drop it, Julio. This isn't the time."

"Whatever." Julio looked at Maria. "I'm just saying if I can't get my license, I'm driving without one."

"Are you crazy?" Her shout woke Vanessa, but Maria kept going. "Do you have any idea what happens to unlicensed drivers? If you get pulled over?" She stopped herself and made the sign of the cross.

A guy who looked a few years older than Julio rose from his chair when seventy-five blinged on the display. He defiantly waited in front of the steel door before the guards fully opened it. That was how Julio would do it. Like a man. Everyone was so worried about being in the four percent that got their renewals denied. What they didn't see was the ninety-six percent chance they wouldn't.

"Is that your renewal?" Julio pointed at the wrinkled paper in Maria's hand. "Can I see it?"

She handed him the sweaty slip. He pointed at the bar code. "This is what they scan to see if you get the renewal. There's gotta be a way to change it. I've got some friends that are really good with computers."

Enrique said, "It's a little late for that."

"We'll come back."

"They give it to you the day before your renewal date," Maria said. "You can't change it."

Enrique said, "You think you have the answer to everything. You think I haven't researched it? You think I don't care?"

Julio shrugged. He handed the slip back to his sister as the display chimed. A middle-aged man headed for the door. Maria was next.

"It's only four percent," she said. "I'll get renewed."

Julio agreed. "Only one out of twenty-five don't. I wish Vegas had those kinds of odds. I'd move there tomorrow."

Maria chuckled. It sounded all wrong, not like her at all.

"You've done this a bunch of times already. No big deal." Julio tried to preoccupy her mind, asked her how many times it was for her.

"I started driving when I was sixteen. Back then you only had to get renewed once every four years. They changed the law when I turned nineteen so this is my ninth, I think."

"See," Julio said, "those are great odds."

Enrique wrapped his arms around Maria and Vanessa.

All three sat in silence until Maria's number appeared on the screen. Julio gave her a hug and wished her good luck. Enrique walked her to the door and came back with Vanessa in his arms.

"She'll be okay," Julio said.

"Thanks."

Two more people went in for their renewals before Enrique spoke again. "So why do you want to go to college anyway?"

"Are you saying I'm not smart enough?"

"No, no, not at all. I just didn't know if you know what you want to do with your life yet. College isn't for everyone, especially with no jobs out there."

"Shit, maybe I'll go into politics. I'll change this stupid law."

"Do you even know why they came up with the Four Percent regulation?"

"Yeah. Sort of."

"How are you going to fight to change it if you don't know why it exists?"

"There should be exceptions. I know that much. I don't care what the reasons are, but moms and old people and teenagers should be exempt."

"Pretty much everyone."

"Well, at least mothers."

"What about single fathers? What about grandparents who take care of an orphaned grandchild? There would be too many loopholes. Everyone would fight it."

"They'd all have good reasons."

"Oh, I agree," Enrique said, "but that's not what they would say. They'd say if we got rid of the law we'd be in the same spot we were back ten years ago. Freeway shootings every day, riots."

"Was it really like that?"

"I don't remember it being as bad as they say, but I know there was a time when it took three hours to drive from here to Pomona."

"That's only twenty miles."

"Exactly."

"Just four percent couldn't fix all that."

"Think of all those people who opted out. The ones who have never set foot in this place. Plus those who don't qualify, like me."

"It's still stupid."

"It is what it is. All we can do is pray."

Julio heard the chime and glanced to see what number they were on. It was the display above the tiny window. Number fifty-two blinked three times. A man in the second row moaned.

"Ah, Jesus. We don't need to see this," Enrique said quietly.

Enrique took off his rosary and looked away. Julio couldn't. The man stumbled to the window, holding a hand over his heart, saying over and over again there had been a mistake.

The man put his mouth to the window and shouted, "You're wrong. It's not fifty-two. My wife is fifty-two."

Two small bags were pushed into the opening. The man's hands fumbled as he undid the string around the top of the black bag. He pulled out a silver watch and read the inscription. His voice cracked gently into the opening, "Give her back. Give me back my wife."

The man grabbed the yellow bag and threw it against the wall. The bag burst, a cloud of fine, gray dust floating down upon him as he fell to his knees.

The steel door opened and the two armed guards rushed to the man's side. They took him by his shoulders and helped him to his feet. Before they took him outside, one of the men grabbed the black bag and brought it with them. As soon as they were out of the way, a little man with a broom rushed over to the window and swept up the ashes.

Julio told Enrique it was over once the janitor was finished.

Enrique's voice wavered when he said, "Thank God." He wouldn't look away from the beads of the rosary running under his thumb. "Poor guy."

The more Julio thought about it, four percent was a low number, but it was a real possibility. He had to remain optimistic. Maria would make it.

"No, mija," Enrique said softly. "No, Vanessa, let go."

Vanessa had both her little hands wrapped around the necklace. Instead of brushing them off, Enrique put his hands over hers and whispered it was okay.

Julio watched as the smile crept across Vanessa's face. It would be good to see her grow up. He'd even consider finding a closer college he could bike to.

Enrique said something Julio didn't hear.

"I asked what was the number up there before."

"On which one?"

"Above the window."

Julio looked at the fifty-two blinking on the display. "I'm pretty sure it was twenty-seven. Why?"

The beads crashed to the floor, scattering everywhere. Vanessa shrieked in approval, but Enrique didn't seem to notice. "Maria's seventy-seven."

"So? It's random, right?"

"I thought so." Enrique held up the number. "But what are the odds?"

"Of what?"

Enrique moaned, rocking back and forth with Vanessa. "Oh, man, it can't be."

"I don't get it. What's wrong? She'll be fine."

"Seventy-seven, fifty-two, and twenty-seven. Increments of twenty-five. It can't be totally random."

Julio told him to relax.

"They're taking every twenty-fifth person in line."

Enrique handed Vanessa to Julio and ran to the steel door. Julio headed with Vanessa toward the exit. She was too young to remember any of this, but there was no reason for her to listen to her dad pounding on the door, screaming and crying like a baby. As he headed outside, Julio wondered how they were going to get home.

Twenty-One Seats

June 20, 2044

The tall woman wiped her tears and stepped back from the podium, signaling she was done wasting their time. Longley got up from behind his desk and shook her hand.

"How about a round of applause for Mrs. Edgefield."

While the rest of the class clapped like the mindless puppets they'd spent the entire year proving they were, Todd raised his hand. Longley saw him and looked away.

Todd wasn't about to be ignored by some asshole pretending he wanted to make the world a better place. "I have a question."

Longley guided the woman into the hallway and closed the door behind her. He returned to his desk and said, "Of course you do, Mr. Jaworski. What might that be?"

"Why should we clap for her?"

"Where do you want me to start?"

"She's a nurse. Big deal. She doesn't even like her job."

"For one, it's polite to clap for someone after they give a presentation. Robert's mother took the time out of her day to come down here and talk to you, and it obviously wasn't easy for her. It's also proper etiquette to clap for someone who gives a good speech, which you would have noticed she did if you had been paying attention."

Todd's hand crept to his waistband where he'd tucked the particle pistol he'd borrowed from his brother, Brian. "Just because it's the last day of school doesn't mean you can talk to me like I'm an idiot."

Longley slipped a stack of papers into his briefcase. "I apologize if that's how you took it."

"I'm just saying, I don't think it's right to honor someone for having a job they can't stand. And how about Jen's dad? A janitor at the police station? Why would I clap for a guy that spends his whole day scraping criminals off the floors? Both of them made bad choices in their life and I won't clap for them just because you tell me to."

"That's fine," Longley said. "You have the right to clap or not clap for anyone you please. But you obviously missed the point of today."

Todd hoped Longley realized how stupid he sounded, standing up there thinking he was better than the rest of them. "Obviously."

Longley said something under his breath that scored a couple chuckles from Tammy Wells and the other kiss asses in the front row.

Speaking loud enough for everyone to hear, Todd said, "What'd you say?"

Longley stopped what he was doing. "I'm not doing this today, Jaworski. It's my last day at this school and I'm not going to spend it locked in yet another senseless debate with you."

Todd was unable to think of anything clever to say. He was tired of this homo staring into his eyes, so he turned away. A few of the kids glared at him. One of them was the six-foot-five Robert Edgefield who sat two seats over. Todd asked him, "What the hell's your problem?"

"You shouldn't talk about my mom like that," Robert said.

"Or what? Are you going to cry like your mommy?"

Longley told Todd to knock it off. "Listen up, class. Before I call in the next speaker, I want to go over a couple of things."

Of course Longley wanted to go over something. He loved to hear himself talk.

"First, I want you all to take a moment to look around yourselves."

Only the morons in the front turned around.

"Go ahead," Longley said. "I can wait."

Everyone except Todd looked about. Longley locked eyes with Todd and instead of making a big deal of it, Todd looked left then right.

Longley told the class, "Tell me what you see?"

Before anyone else could answer, Todd blurted out, "You sure you want to know?" He had access to Controller documents and knew everything about all his classmates and Longley.

"If you're not going to say something nice, then don't say it." Longley pointed at Paul, the pencil-neck pussy, not even giving Todd the chance to answer.

"Fear," Paul said. "Uncertainty."

"Good, very good," Longley said.

"That's bullshit," Todd said. "Maybe you guys are scared. I'm not."

"Well, not everyone has family members in the Controllers' main office."

"What's that supposed to mean?"

"What do you think it means, Jaworski?"

"I think you're saying something bad about the Controllers."

"I'm simply saying I understand why certain students are afraid of the future and certain students aren't."

If Todd was going to report any insubordination to his father, he would need something more concrete. Instead of trying to drag Longley into a discussion, Todd sat back and relaxed. Longley was a prick through and through. He'd say something to get himself killed. Todd just hoped he'd do it in the next fifteen minutes, before the bell rang.

"What else do you guys see? What else is there to notice?"

Tammy raised her hand real slow. When Longley called on her, she said, "I see courage. There are a lot of empty seats in here. The fact that not all of them are empty says something."

"Very good, Tammy." Longley motioned about the room. "We started out the semester with forty-four students. Now here we are at the end of the year, twenty-one empty seats."

"Less bullshit to put up with," Todd said.

"That's one way of looking at it," Longley said. "Or you could see it as a sad sign of the times. This is arguably the best and most expensive high school in San Angeles and our attendance is below forty percent. So many moved to the Inner Blocks, or dropped out to work. Half the girls are pregnant."

"What's your point?" Todd asked.

Acting like he didn't hear, Longley said, "Tammy's right about seeing courage. Instead of empty seats, she saw each of you. She saw that you stuck out the year despite all the hardships and reasons to stop attending."

Todd said, "The only reason I stayed is because I won't get any money from my dad if I don't graduate."

"Well, you're still here so it's a good thing. Be sure to thank him for me," Longley said. His stupid smile earned him a couple laughs.

The chickenshits held their hands to their faces so Todd couldn't see who was laughing. "Yeah, that's pretty funny. Know what else is funny? I know where each of you live. Maybe this summer me and my family will stop by and say hi."

The class went silent. Then Longley said, "Just be sure to call ahead. And bring ice cream. We'll make a party of it."

It took all of Todd's restraint not to pull out the pistol and erase Longley's smartass face. He was trying to think of what to tell him when Longley walked over and opened the classroom door.

"We still have two speakers. Please save the questions and comments." Longley shook hands with a small man who looked about as old as Todd's father, but with ash-white hair.

Longley introduced the man as Mr. Dobbs and showed him to the podium. Even though Todd was at the back of the room, he caught a whiff of something so fierce his eyes watered. It smelled as if the guy had spent the last ten minutes in the hallway singeing off his body hair.

"Some of you know me," Dobbs said. "For those that don't, I'm Stacy's father."

Stacy cringed in her seat. Todd couldn't help thinking how much he'd like to give her and her very developed freshman sister, Stephanie, something to cry about. While he dreamt of simultaneously slamming the sisters, he remembered they had both been voluntarily sterilized, probably to help the sniveling man up front pay the bills. Todd could screw both of them all day long and never worry about them popping out pups.

"I graduated from high school and worked for the school district until the disaster hit," Dobbs said. "Then I saw a chance to make some extra money and took a job at the scale house."

Todd's eyes moved away from Stacy's long creamy legs. Her father was suddenly interesting.

"I never should've done it, but as I'm sure you've heard your parents say, jobs are hard to come by. That's why you should stay in school. You can all do better than I did."

Dobbs licked his lips. "I didn't have someone to tell me that. I didn't have anyone warn me that if I didn't stay in school, I might end up cleaning out furnaces. I'm there every day, right below all the action. I get to hear all the pleading, all the cries, all the screams, all the burning. Now I'm nothing more than an embarrassment to my daughters. I can't get the horrible smell out of my clothes, my hair, my dreams."

Stacy told her dad what he'd said wasn't true. Dobbs got choked up. He took a second then continued. "Stay in school and watch what you eat. Start dieting now. Most of you will be eighteen sooner than you know it. The last thing I want to hear is you up there crying that you didn't know what weight you had to be under. I can't tell you the number of kids who think they should be given another chance. Everyone has to make weight. The Controllers don't care who you are. And mark my words, it won't always be random."

Dobbs rushed out of the room before Longley could ask them to clap. While Longley waved in the next guest, Todd said, "I hope you know he's wrong."

Longley showed a large man in an all black uniform to the podium. "Wrong about what?"

"Not everyone has to make weight. Controlling Force Agents don't."

"Neither do those with money for a waiver, but that's not the point," Longley said. "So how many of you would want the job Mr. Dobbs has?"

No one raised their hand.

"Well, those are the kinds of jobs out there for people who only finish high school. Hopefully these talks will give you something to think about over summer. I want you all to not only come back and finish next year, but with grades high enough for college. I want you to discover ways to fix our farm lands, solve the energy crisis, decontaminate the water. Fight to improve civil rights."

Todd had heard enough. "If you have some negative thoughts about the Controllers then I think you should say them."

Longley's jaw tightened. "Of course I don't have a problem with the Controllers. No one ever does. No one ever should. They've done such a great job with everything." Longley introduced the man in the uniform as Sergeant Williams then sat behind his desk.

Williams looked at Todd and said, "You're right, by the way. Military and law enforcement agents don't need to make weight."

Todd nodded with a smirk and waited for the sergeant to continue. Finally, someone with something to say.

"As you can probably tell, I'm well over the cut-off for males. It's a nice benefit, but what happens if I get injured and lose my job? What if there are budget cutbacks, which there always are? Those are some things to think about if you are interested in my line of work."

Todd didn't recognize the uniform and wondered what organization Williams was with.

Williams asked, "How many of you have your driver's license?"

Only Todd and Joanne, whose dad was high up in the Church of the American Way, raised their hands.

"I'm stationed at the DMV with a job I never would've considered eight years ago when I was your age. I run the denials."

Since the so-called sergeant wasn't the biological father of any of the kids in this classroom, Todd figured Williams was a friend of Longley's. "You're not even really law enforcement. No wonder you don't carry."

"I'm not carrying because I'm off-duty and in a classroom. It's called showing respect. You should look into it."

The thought that this asshole put himself in the same class as an actual Controlling Force Agent made Todd sick. His classmates' last image of Todd wasn't going to be him getting punked. "You should be careful who you talk to like that."

Williams smiled. "And why should I do that?

Longley got up from his desk and told Todd to be quiet.

Williams said, "No, I'd like to hear your answer."

Feeling everyone's eyes on him, Todd said, "I don't need your permission to talk."

"You're right. I can tell you're a big man. I was in the hallway listening. You're not scared to speak your mind."

"Fuck you."

Longley waved his arms. "All right, that's enough."

Williams' eyes never left Todd. "I've got this, John."

"Yeah, John. Listen to your butt-buddy. Mr. DMV has everything in control."

Longley said class was dismissed, grabbed his briefcase, and left the room. No one else moved.

Williams gripped the front edge of the podium with his massive hands and stared at Todd in a sad attempt at intimidation. "What were you saying, Mr. Jaworski? Were you saying that you would like to discuss this somewhere else? That you were such a big man you could disrespect all of your classmates and their families and anyone else you pleased?"

Trying to sound confident as he looked at the idiots surrounding him, Todd said "Yeah, that pretty much sums it up."

The bell rang, announcing the start of summer. Outside, students ran through the halls, screaming, throwing paper everywhere. Inside the classroom, everyone remained.

"Fair enough," Williams said. "I guess everyone's entitled to their opinion, right?"

"That's right."

"Good, because there are probably a few things your classmates would be saying if you hadn't convinced them all that your brother's a big bad Controlling Force Agent and your daddy's oh-so powerful. I bet they'd say what an arrogant little shit you were. I bet they'd say your pockmarked face has more craters than the moon. That your eyes are a little too close together and maybe your mommy and daddy are related."

Todd sat up in his seat, slid his hand under his shirt and gripped the gun. "Fuck you."

"Two fuck-you's in under two minutes. Let me guess, you're top of your class."

"You should shut your mouth."

Williams stepped away from the podium. "Look here, little boy. I don't care who your family is."

"You'd better."

"Or what?"

"You'll see."

"You're all talk. Nothing but a coward." Speaking to the others, Williams said, "Whatever you do in life, don't bow down to anyone, especially people like him."

Todd jumped out of his chair and pulled the particle pistol from his waistband, aimed at Williams' chest. "Oh yeah? I'll make you bow down. I'll show everyone who the coward is."

"The coward is the one aiming a gun at an unarmed civil servant," Williams said. He stepped into Todd's aisle, waved the other kids to move out of the way.

As his classmates slipped out of their chairs and ran to the far wall, Todd told Williams, "I'll shoot you. Stay back."

"Nice piece." Williams moved toward Todd. "That's government issue. Your brother really let you borrow that?"

"It's none of your business. All you got to worry about is the hole it's going to leave in you."

"If that's how you want to handle this, go right ahead and shoot me." He took another step, leaving a few feet between them. "Just know that if you do, you and your brother will burn. He'll be kicked off the force just for you having possession of his firearm."

"No one will ever know."

"Are you going to shoot all of us? There's not enough juice in that pack. Look at how low the proton level is."

Todd tilted his head to glance at the grip. The proton pack was full. "There's plenty…"

Williams tore the pistol out of Todd's hand and pushed him down in the chair. "Now what?"

"Give it back."

"Gladly." Williams slammed the gun onto the desk, the barrel breaking free and falling to the ground. "Here you go."

"What the hell am I gonna tell my brother?"

Williams turned his back on him and headed for the exit. "To be more responsible with his weapon."

"You have to give me a new one!"

Williams stood next to the door, ushering out all of the students. "No, the only thing I need to do is head on over to work." Williams disappeared out the door and said, "You have yourself a nice summer, Todd."

Todd gazed at the broken pistol in his trembling hands. There was no way to fix it.

He was dead.

Fifteen

May 20, 2045

The driver of the white Cadillac stepped out of the car. He was mixed, several shades darker than Claire's fair skin. His tailored suit made him seem at least eighteen. "Miss Wells?"

Claire nodded, afraid she'd blow the whole thing the first time she opened her mouth.

He said his name was Darius and opened the rear door, placed his hand on Claire's elbow to help her inside.

The car's leather was soft and smelled of violets. Nothing like the Sentra her family sold when they ran out of motel money, or the Camry that had been their home until they couldn't afford food.

Darius went up front and gazed at Claire in the rearview, his light brown eyes as warm as his smile. "Get comfortable," he said. "It's going to be a while."

Claire didn't want to sound cheap, but she only had the five-dollar bill her dad forced on her. "If things don't work out, will someone bring me back?"

Darius pulled away from the curb, eyes on the road, and followed the security fence that circled the Block. "I'm afraid I'm not allowed to have discussions while driving."

They drove out the front gate and into the chaos of the city. People and cars were everywhere, move-alongs and canine patrols every couple blocks.

Claire sank into the seat and closed her eyes.

Her older sister, Tammy, had been in a car like this. She'd gone to the prom as a sophomore and said it was the best time of her life. She told Claire and Becky all about the limo, the flowers, the music. Tammy whispered all the other details to Becky because Claire would've made a face and said ewww.

Back then, Claire still thought she'd go to prom one day. Unfortunately, no house meant no school, and every city was the same. No work, keep moving. Their family had been begging for the last few months and they slept in shifts.

Claire had been running on adrenaline since she'd received the news three days before. She was still shocked she'd been selected. The hum of the engine lulled her to sleep. Dreams of life in a dress.

Claire awoke when they turned off the freeway. The Hollywood Hills lay straight ahead. They drove to the security gates blocking the street at the bottom of Mulholland.

Darius stopped at the gatehouse and rolled down his window. "Hey, Johnnie. Bringing in Claire Wells."

Johnnie looked about Darius's age, his blue blazer doing little to hide his muscular build and the gun at his waist. He stuck his head in the window and nodded at Claire. "Put her down as permanent?"

"Yeah, man, of course."

The view was amazing with the sunset she'd seen in so many movies. The city wasn't so smothering at this elevation.

After a few minutes on Mulholland, Darius made a right, then a left, and drove up to the gate at the end of a cobblestone driveway. He put his palm on the scanner and waited for the beep.

The gate peeled back, revealing a circular driveway with a marble fountain, a giant house stretched behind it. Three young men in green jumpsuits trimmed the dense foliage. Darius waved to them as he swung the car around and parked next to the front door.

Claire breathed deeply and said a short prayer. She mumbled a thank you as Darius escorted her from the car to the door, his hand on the flat of her back.

A middle-eastern girl stood in the doorway. Her pink sweat suit showed a body men desired. She said her name was Amira and told Claire to come in.

Claire stepped into the foyer. Her boots echoed off the black slate. Amira was barefoot. Her perfect pink toenails matched her pants. "Should I take off my shoes?" Claire asked.

Amira said, "Please. But leave on your socks for now. Just until you bathe." She walked to the red curtain draped along the side of the stairs and whispered, "House rules."

Behind the curtain were forty small cubbies built into the wall, a name under each. Less than a dozen had shoes inside.

After Claire stuffed the boots inside the space with her name on it, Amira closed the curtain and said, "Mrs. D is waiting." As she was speaking, Darius came in with Claire's backpack.

"Just leave it there," Amira said. "I'll send it to her room."

Darius set it by the stairs. He spoke so low, Claire had to listen. "How's she seem? You heard anything?"

Amira shook her head. "Later."

Darius closed the front door on his way out.

Claire couldn't shake the feeling she was being watched. When she glanced up, a flash of blond hair ducked away from the upstairs railing.

Amira glided along the hallway as if being beautiful were no big deal. The white shag carpet soothed Claire's feet. Lush green plants lined both sides of the hall. A ponytailed brunette in tight jeans and a blouse lowered her watering can long enough to say hello.

Amira kept going and said the girl was Tiffany, their masseuse. "And that's Jayden," Amira said as they passed a doorway.

A strawberry blond dusted the top of a dresser crammed into a room not much bigger than the bed. Claire waved at the girl and hurried after Amira, the scent from the kitchen reminding her how long it had been since she'd eaten properly.

The kitchen was glass doors and stainless steel, same slate as the foyer. An older Hispanic teenager in an apron was placing bowls in the first fridge while a simple-looking boy, with skin the same shade as Amira's, waved and said her name like it was three words.

"Not now, Yusef," Amira said. She faced the middle-aged woman who sat on the other side of the center island, her short blond hair so yellow against her purple blouse. "Mrs. D, this is Claire."

The woman's blue eyes lit up and she clasped her hands. "Oh honey, welcome, welcome, welcome!"

"It's a real pleasure to meet you, ma'am."

The woman shook her head. "Oh no, child. First off, Suzie or Mrs. D are the only names I'll answer to. Second, how could it be such a pleasure if that's how you say hello?"

Claire shifted. The others were watching her make a fool of herself.

Mrs. D spoke to the boys without looking away from Claire. "How's anyone supposed to have a decent conversation with that racket? You two can finish up when we're done."

Both boys said sorry and left through the back hallway. Mrs. D smiled at Claire and said she was only joking. "Come over here and give me a hug."

The contract had been signed, but the audition was just starting. It would continue for three years if Claire didn't blow it. She stepped around the island, ignored the wheelchair, and put her arms around Mrs. D.

Mrs. D's hug was suffocating. Claire squeezed back just as hard and the hug warmed into something else, a sense of safety Claire hadn't felt in a long while. When they let go, Mrs. D wore a huge grin. "Oh, I knew you weren't lying. Your hugs are wonderful."

Claire barely remembered the application video and what she'd listed as her strengths. She told Mrs. D, "You're not so bad yourself."

Mrs. D squealed. "Oh, that's good!" She smiled at Amira. "We've got ourselves a keeper. Now be a dear and fetch Brianna."

Amira excused herself. She said hi to the long-legged redhead she passed in the doorway.

The redhead looked more woman than girl in her tight black skirt, thin-framed glasses and hair in a bun. She reached across the counter, the top three buttons of her white blouse undone, her breasts pushing on the fabric. Her hand was as soft as her voice when she said her name was Kristine.

Mrs. D asked if her husband was in his office.

Kristine released Claire's hand and stood back. "No. Mr. D has yoga Monday, Wednesday, and Friday." She waved her fingers at Claire and said, "Got to run. Just wanted to say hi."

Mrs. D waited until Kristine left. "Would you call that attitude?"

There might have been a little, but Claire said, "She seemed nice."

Mrs. D shrugged it off and rubbed her temples. "She's nice all right. All our girls are."

"Are you okay? Can I get you something?"

"What a sweetheart." Mrs. D patted Claire's hand. "Some days are rougher than others. I need my pills, but I want to go over a few rules first.

"One: we're a family, so we always act like it. Treat one another with respect and kindness. Two: Mr. D and I are the only people who give orders. God gave us a mouth for more than one reason. If something doesn't sound right, you come tell me."

"I will."

"Three: this isn't like other families. The door is always open. You let us know if you want to go your separate way. We don't want anyone here that doesn't want to be."

Claire said she understood. She didn't know how she'd gotten so lucky.

"Last thing to remember is, do not talk to Ian. He has no authority."

A homely blond girl, too old for her pigtails and red gingham dress entered the kitchen with a wide smile. "Do I?"

Mrs. D said no way, but it sounded like a joke. "Don't listen to this one, Claire."

The girl came around the island and kissed Mrs. D on the cheek. "Mother, why would you say that? She might believe you."

"And be the better for it." Mrs. D turned back to Claire and said, "But like I was saying, stay away from Ian. You're not to speak to that boy."

Claire asked if he was a servant.

Mrs. D shook her head, the light flashing off her diamond earrings. "My own flesh and blood. He turned on us, got himself arrested. We didn't raise him like that."

The girl's baby blue eyes tried to sparkle when she introduced herself as Brianna. "So what do you do? Please tell me you're not another tutor."

"You girls will have all day to talk," Mrs. D said. "Let's get Claire settled in."

Brianna wheeled her mother out from the counter and Claire moved next to the stove. Green beans with bacon in one pan, grilled chicken and pasta in the skillet.

"Oh, honey, how rude of me. Have you eaten dinner?"

Claire hated to impose and was used to sleeping on an empty stomach. "I'm okay."

"Don't be silly." Mrs. D pressed a button on the keypad at the end of her armrest and the intercom by the doorway buzzed. "Cesar, warm up a plate and send it to Claire's room."

"I don't want to be a bother," Claire said.

"Nonsense. That took all of five seconds," Mrs. D said. "Let's go."

Brianna rolled her mother down the rear hallway. Claire remained a few steps behind. Mrs. D pointed at a set of closed double doors and said, "That's the living room where dessert is served. And up here's the library."

All three of them stopped so Claire could see inside the room, books lining the shelves on every wall, fifteen desks in the middle.

"School's from nine to three," Mrs. D said. "Your teacher's great. She got pink-slipped by the university."

They came to an elevator at the back of the house. Mrs. D used her remote so the doors opened the moment she rolled up to them.

The elevator's walls were tinted glass with the view of a kidney-shaped pool on the other side. A dozen boys were swimming, and at least that many lounged around. A handsome blond with six-pack abs bounced on the diving board.

Mrs. D pushed a button on her keypad and lit the number two on the elevator's display. "Girls get the pool from three to five, and all day on Saturday."

From the second floor, Claire could see their land stretching down the hill. Two girls were rallying on the tennis court, and boys in green were hanging out by the horse stables.

"I've never even seen a horse," Claire said.

"I'm afraid we moved ours to our ranch in Utah. This air's not good for them."

Brianna pointed out the stocky boy walking two German Shepherds. "That's Corey. You'll want him to introduce you to Max and Milo. They can have a temper."

"That's true," Mrs. D said, "but no need to worry. You'll meet him tonight at dessert."

"Did Father already finish the cards?"

Mrs. D used her remote to spin around. "Since when do you care about that?"

"Just curious, Mother."

"Funny. I was about to tell you to join him tonight."

"I have quite a bit of homework."

"I want you to make sure Claire is comfortable. It's intimidating meeting new people."

Brianna studied her stubby toes. "Yes, Mother."

"See Claire to her room so she can change and eat dinner."

Brianna took Claire's hand. "It's this way." A few doors down, Brianna pointed to the three circles above the handle. "There's no lock on the bathroom so pay attention to the lights. Blue means a boy's inside. Yellow means a girl." She pushed open the door and stepped inside. There were glass-enclosed showers in each of the four corners, a sink and mirror on two walls, a toilet stall on the third.

Mrs. D shouted Brianna's name. She sat still in the elevator, eyebrows in a V. "You can finish the tour tomorrow. If Claire wants to take a shower tonight, she can use yours."

Brianna mumbled an apology and pulled Claire behind her. When they got to the next hallway, she said, "My room's second on the left. Father's is at the end." She nodded to the right. "Ian's is that way."

They came to the office at the top of the front stairs. Kristine sat behind the mahogany desk. Blank monitors covered the wall beside her. She waved at Claire and pressed a button. The office blinds closed at once.

Claire followed Brianna around the corner and into a tiny room identical to the one she'd seen Jayden cleaning. Except on her dresser sat a steaming plate of food and a glass of ice water.

"Lights out is at eight o'clock so you might as well get comfy now. PJ's are in the top drawer." Brianna tapped the intercom next to the door. "Press four if you need me for anything. Two if you want Mother."

An older boy with a dingy white robe and patchy brown beard stepped into the doorway. "Or three if you get lonely."

Brianna told Ian to go to his room. Claire backed up until her legs touched the bed.

"What's wrong, little sis?" he said with a slur. "Just want to say hi to the new girl."

Brianna hit the bottom button on the intercom. "Robert! Room One."

Ian held out his hand. It was shaking. He told Claire, "Remember, keep smiling and be a good girl."

Footsteps pounded the hall. A boy shouted, "Get away from there."

"Just chatting with my sister."

The boy had a shaved head and a tank top, muscles popping out everywhere. He grabbed Ian's arm and jerked him. "Come on."

Ian yanked his arm away and smiled tauntingly.

Robert's cheek flushed red and he narrowed his eyes. "Move it."

Ian gazed at Claire. "Give someone an inch of…" His face scrunched up as his left leg jerked off the ground, the bracelet around his ankle red and sizzling. "You fuck!"

Robert remained calm. "Move it. I won't tell you again."

"You're such…" Ian's scream lasted longer. He limped away and said, "And I'm the crazy one." He screamed again.

Claire sat on the bed. Brianna said not to worry. "I'll make sure they keep a better eye on him."

"What did he do?"

"Something he shouldn't have." Brianna closed the door behind her.

Claire took the plate from the dresser. The food tasted delicious. Each bite was a guilty wonder. After she finished, she opened the top drawer and found three neatly stacked piles. Silk, flannel, and cotton. All colors. She slipped on light blue cotton pajamas and lay on the bed, staring at her reflection in the black dome above.

The crackle of the intercom woke her. A man said dessert would be served in five minutes. Claire got up, opened the closet and dug a scrunchie from her backpack. She put her hair up in a ponytail, amazed at all the wonderful clothes. The price tags made her wince.

Dessert sounded awful, but Claire wasn't going to make waves. She grabbed the china and fork from the dresser and left the room. In the hall, she heard boys talking. Claire went to the stairs and peeked over the railing.

White T-shirts and tank tops filled the foyer. The boys were checking their cubbies, cracking jokes and name calling. Several stood in the back eating bowls of chocolate pudding, stacking the empties by the door on their way out.

Claire recognized Johnnie from the gate and watched as he pulled a bowl from a top cubby. "That's some bullshit. This is my third day in a row."

Mrs. D came on the intercom. "I heard that."

Johnnie shoveled down the pudding and headed out the front door. "Guess that makes it four."

A skinny boy Claire hadn't seen showed a white envelope to the boy beside him. The kid socked his shoulder and called him a lucky bastard. "Look what Timmy got."

Some said good for him. A couple clapped. The others walked away.

A large hand touched Claire's shoulder and she jumped. The plate flew from her hand and shattered on the hardwood. The man was in his fifties with hair as jet black as his pajamas. "You didn't get hurt, did you?"

The plate lay in a thousand pieces. Claire wanted to cry.

The man leaned over the railing. "You all need to hurry. Timothy, come clean this."

"Sure thing, Mr. D."

The man told Claire to call him Bradley and led her down the stairs. "We don't want to keep everyone waiting."

The foyer was empty, the cubby curtain closed. When they got to the living room doors, Bradley said, "See Kristine in the kitchen for your dessert. Tell her I'm ready for my usual."

Kristine stood at the counter in silver silk pajamas, a bright red bow tied around her ponytail. She pointed at the three plates of lemon meringue on the counter. "Pick one."

Claire chose the smallest piece of pie and told Kristine what Bradley had said.

Kristine put some ice in a glass and filled it to the top with Johnny Walker. She handed it over and said, "His coffee is just as simple. Straight black."

Claire thanked her and went into the living room. A brown couch wrapped around two walls where eight girls in pajamas and five boys were chatting quietly. Empty dessert plates cluttered the giant ottoman.

"Over here." Bradley sat in a brown recliner, newspaper in hand. He took the glass and gazed at the digital TV hanging five feet in front of him so the rest of the room only saw the back. "You watch much?"

It was a football game, but that was the extent of Claire's knowledge. "Afraid not, sir."

"Bradley," he corrected. He motioned her closer and lowered his voice. "Forget about everyone else for a moment. You need to lighten up, Claire. Be happy. This is a good thing. You have a home. Your family has a home."

"Thank you, Bradley."

"Of course, sweetheart. And remember, you're an adult. You make your own decisions. Got it?"

Claire nodded. Brianna sat where the couches came together and patted the empty corner cushion beside her. Claire squeezed past Corey, the dog handler, who was cuddling with Amira, his hand caressing her pink silk pajamas. Jayden, the slow-moving maid, had on a dark blue sleepover. She talked to Tiffany, the plant girl in red flannel with a red ribbon tied around her ponytail. Claire moved past Robert, who sat by himself.

Claire sank into the couch and mumbled hello to the diving board boy. He said his name was Austin and introduced the blond in yellow silk who had her arm around his waist as Hailey.

Brianna said Hailey taught yoga then pointed out the others. Loralei, the tiny tutor, sat crossed-legged in a forest green flannel. Madison sat next to her, her braided black hair hanging down the front of her white silk button-down. Talking to the two girls was Taylor, the tennis pro, in gray cotton. The girl had the same chin and upturned nose as Robert. Claire wasn't surprised when Brianna said they were twins. "You know Darius, and the guy at the end is Alex."

Claire said, "That's an awful lot of names."

Brianna laughed. "You won't be tested." She nodded at the pie and said, "Dig in. It's delicious."

The meringue melted in Claire's mouth and the lemon burst on her tongue. Four bites and it disappeared.

Kristine and Timothy came through the double doors and sat on the ottoman facing away from Claire.

Brianna leaned in, her breath warm on Claire's ear. "So who do you think's cute?"

Claire didn't know what to say. She surprised herself with the truth. "All of them."

"Which one's the hottest?"

Claire glanced around until she locked eyes with Darius. She liked the way his shorts hugged his legs, the way his full lips moved.

Brianna's breath came back. "Anyone you'd want to do?"

"Do?"

The double doors opened and Yusef shuffled into the room, gathered all the plates and forks, and piled them onto his tray. He finished in front of Amira and whispered to her. She shushed him. "Not now, Yusef. Please go."

Claire felt a little light-headed and figured maybe she'd eaten too much or was on some kind of sugar kick. She gazed at her wrist, the red circle where they injected the chip. Surprisingly, it didn't hurt to touch. To poke. To pinch. No pain. Nothing.

Austin shook her shoulder, his hand gentle yet strong. "Don't do that," he said. His voice gave her goose bumps.

"It's trippy, but you'll still bruise," Hailey said. "Got to be careful."

Mrs. D wheeled in, wearing a long lavender nightgown, matching robe and slippers. She snapped, "Amira!"

Everyone went silent and Amira sat up, pulled her hand off Corey's thigh and placed it on her lap.

Mrs. D set one foot on the carpet, then the other, pushed herself upright and headed their way. Brianna scooted closer to Claire and patted the cushion beside her.

Mrs. D ignored Brianna and sat next to Claire. "Did we get your size right?"

Claire felt her sleeve, so soft and fuzzy up and down her arm. "It's perfect."

"We'll hit the stores tomorrow to accessorize. For now, how about we get rid of this." Mrs. D tugged Claire's scrunchie and tossed the ponytail loose. "We'll get you all fixed up tomorrow. My guy can work wonders."

"He's great," Brianna said.

"Was I speaking to you?"

Brianna said, "No, but..."

Mrs. D hugged Claire tight, surrounded her with lilacs. "I just wanted to let you know my door's always open. Come up whenever you like." Mrs. D whispered the code in Claire's ear, laid a kiss on her cheek. She stood and faced the room. "I want all of you to welcome Claire with open arms."

Everyone sounded sincere when they promised they would. No one spoke until Mrs. D wheeled away.

"Well, that was fun," Bradley said. He finished his drink and set the empty glass on the floor. "I'm about ready for bed. What do you say we get started?"

Kristine and Tiffany left the room without a word, their red bows shining bright. Madison tried to stand and fell back onto the couch. Robert called her a lightweight while Taylor helped Madison to her feet.

Claire saw Timothy's foot pumping up and down. Then a rustling as Loralei crawled across the ottoman, scooted behind Timothy and told him to relax.

Austin held up his envelope, the number one marked on the front. He peeled open the back and slid out the card. He squeezed Hailey's leg then crossed over to Jayden and led her out of the room.

Corey said, "I'm two." He tore open his envelope, barely glanced at the card. Both he and Amira got up at the same time, said good night to everyone as bathwater began to run upstairs.

Alex had number three. He took out his card, smiled at Taylor, met her at the door.

Under his breath, Robert said, "A goddamn gardener."

Claire's mind moved in slow motion. There were three boys and four girls and Brianna never played. Claire put her hand on her heart. Her other hand squeezed Brianna's.

Robert had the fourth envelope. He leaned over and stroked Loralei's calf. She patted Timothy on the back and walked away with Robert, the top of her head barely reaching his shoulder.

From the recliner, Bradley said, "Go ahead, Timothy. You've done a good job. You deserve it."

Timothy cleared his throat and read his card, stammered Hailey's name. She met him at the door.

The bathwater stopped. Bradley dropped his newspaper next to his glass and lowered the recliner.

Brianna begged Darius, "Just say her name."

Darius glared at Brianna then pulled out his card. Without checking it, he said, "Claire." He offered his hand. "You ready?"

Claire could barely breathe.

Brianna took her by the elbow and helped her stand. She sounded like she was about to cry. "Claire hasn't had a chance to clean up."

"That's fine," Bradley said on his way out. "Darius, go wait in her room."

Claire had nothing to say, no way of saying it if she did. Brianna pulled her down the hallway. Outside was dark, except for the stables, seven, eight, nine boys passed out on the ground, a couple more crawling.

"That's just the pudding. Helps them sleep." Brianna held open the elevator door. "You're coming, right?"

The elevator's keypad was right in front of Claire. The code sang in her head. But Mrs. D wouldn't have sent her to dessert if she didn't want her to participate. Claire grasped Brianna's hand. They hurried to her room. They sat Indian style on the bed with the sheet draped over their heads.

Brianna's lips were inches away. "Have you ever been with a boy?"

Claire shook her head.

"And there's nothing you're good at?"

Claire wished it wasn't true.

"You need to go to Darius. He'll be gentle." Brianna put her hands on top of Claire's, her lips brushing Claire's ear. "Tell him I'm sorry."

"For what?"

"He'll know."

The lights flashed three times and the intercom buzzed. "Lights out in one minute," Mrs. D said. "Get to your rooms."

"I'd better go," Claire said.

Brianna didn't move her hands. "You'll go to him?"

Claire nodded and slipped out of the cave. She heard Brianna say her daddy was dead, that she had three little brothers. It made no sense, but not much did. Claire stumbled into the hallway and steadied herself on the wall. The bright white of the fluorescents flipped off and red floor lights switched on.

A splash came from the end of the hallway. A soft giggle. A firm smack. A delighted sigh.

Claire went the other way. The thought that Bradley and Brianna looked nothing alike trickled through her fuzzy mind. And Brianna looked nothing like Mrs. D or Ian who was lying flat on his back down the hall, his brown eyes rolled back in his head.

Claire forgot how to get to her room, figured she might feel better if she threw up. She entered the bathroom, which had the same red tint as the hallway. Except the third shower: lights on, black dome overhead, Hailey holding a washcloth, Timothy's eyes closed.

Claire backed out of the bathroom and bumped the wall.

Ian sat up, slumped against the wall. "Go make us some money."

Claire ran for the elevator. She punched in the numbers.

The elevator opened, the hallway long and dark, the eerie red lighting the way. Claire kept one hand on the wall for balance and nearly fell when she reached the first alcove. Her hand brushed a young girl's cold face. Claire jumped back and said sorry, her heart thudding.

The pigtailed blond stood silently on the stone in her red-checkered dress.

Claire stumbled down the hall and passed another petrified girl, same pigtails as the first, her face a little fatter.

The next girl was dressed the same. Her shiny blue eyes stared off into nowhere. Claire reached forward to feel the wax and jerked her hand away from the leathery flesh.

The door opened and Mrs. D stepped out. "I'm afraid they're not for touching."

Claire put her hands by her side.

Mrs. D came up to her and said, "There, there, don't cry." She pulled Claire close. "I knew you'd do the right thing. That's all you have to do, baby. Be my good girl."

Nineteen in a Row

April 24, 2046

Emily Jaworski stopped at the front door and hovered her hand above the reader. Try as she might, she couldn't bring herself to go inside. She was at the wrong house. Unlike Justin, the man she should've been with, Brian didn't understand what she was going through. And he never would.

After wiping her eyes with her sleeve and fixing her hair, Emily placed her palm against the reader. There was a soft click and the door slid open. A cold blast of air greeted her when she entered the house. The place that would never be a home.

Emily crossed the living room, leaning her briefcase against the wine cabinet, no one asking how her day went, whether a decision had been reached. She didn't know if the house was quiet because Brian already knew the answers to those questions, thought he knew them, or did not care.

Uncaring. That's what she was becoming. Not about her work, she would never give up on that, but about the important things, the things she'd dreamt about as a child.

Emily no longer cared about her husband, what he thought of her, or how he didn't appreciate her. She was ashamed how much she disliked him. This wasn't the relationship she had been promised. It wasn't the type of relationship that Justin proved possible.

Brian broke the silence, calling out from the kitchen. "I want to talk to you."

Emily took a deep breath and blew it out. She moved down the hallway, past the mirror she'd repeatedly asked to have removed. It was fine if Brian wanted to talk. This time she was ready.

There was her Prince Charming, the stud she should be forever grateful for. He sat at the table in his too-tight tank top, a half-finished drink in his hand, even though it was still light outside. Flexing his arms so it'd look like he wasn't trying, Brian downed the rest of his drink and poured another from the bottle of whiskey beside him.

He waved Emily over. "Have a seat."

Emily was halfway across the kitchen before she realized she was moving, responding to his commands. To prove she had a mind of her own, Emily opened the refrigerator and got a bottle of water. While she unscrewed the cap, she watched him watch her, knowing her little detour made him that much angrier.

Brian gulped half his glass, cleared his throat and waited, the tattoos on his upper arms rising and falling as the muscles twitched. The Controllers' clenched fist covered his right arm. The Way's path of fire cutting through the clouds decorated his left. Emily thought it fitting that the only thing separating Church from State was Brian's broad chest. Too bad even less separated it in the real world.

When Emily made no move to join him at the table, Brian rose from his seat, his particle pistol holstered on his hip. "I asked you to sit."

Emily took her time walking to the table and pulling out her chair. "Do you have to wear that in here?"

Brian's eyes narrowed and he took his seat. "Unlike lawyers, Controlling Force Agents are always on duty. I need to wear it and I will wear it."

"Well, I'd feel better if you left it off when you got home."

"Yeah, well, I'd feel better if I had your job and could stop working the second I left the courtroom."

His daddy could have bribed Brian's way into a law school, but not rig it so he passed. She was tired of fighting, of making the day worse than it already was. That's why

Emily kept quiet.

"And you know what else I'd feel better about?" Without giving her a chance to guess, he said, "Moving out of this goddamn place. How long are we going to live here?"

"Sorry it's not as nice as your Aunt Suzie's." She'd only been to the house, but vowed never to return, not about to believe anyone related to Brian would act out of self-sacrifice. "Afraid we'll never make enough to live in the Hills."

"It doesn't have to be the Hills but it has to be better than here. How long before you stop wasting your time and start making some money?"

"I'm not wasting my time."

"What else would you call nineteen consecutive losses?"

"I told you what was important to me when you asked me to marry you. I told you what I wanted to do with my life."

Brian couldn't say a word about that, having lied to her about everything, tricking her into marrying a man he was not and had no intention of becoming. So as always, he raised his voice, the only way he knew how to win a debate.

"Look at this shithole. It's an embarrassment. We could live wherever we wanted if you'd just stop fighting the goddamn losing battle." Brian took a drink. "I hope you're smart enough to accept you're never going to win. You can't go against the government."

Emily sipped from her bottle, hid the rage inside. "Until they change the law, I'm not stopping anything. I'm not asking for much. Just one change."

"Things are fine the way they are and they're not going to change."

"Things aren't fine," she snapped. "They killed my father!"

"Lower your voice."

Afraid what could happen if she didn't, Emily regained her composure. "He didn't even have a trial. The Five Minute rule is bad enough, but without a trial, allowing it is unthinkable. I'm not trying to change the world. I just want to amend one law."

"And it's not going to happen. How many more times do you need to lose before you realize this?"

"As many times as it takes."

"I don't mean to get upset," he said as if talking to the child they would never have, "but I worry about you. It's bad enough that you don't go to services with me, then you wear that thing and go blaspheming the government."

Emily fingered the silver St. Michael medallion lying against her chest. Her uncle Terrance had given it to her as a constant reminder of her father, not that she needed one. "I'll wear what I want and believe what I want. Remember that's what people did when this was a free country."

"It still is."

Emily laughed.

Brian kept talking. "You can't expect to say and do whatever you want. I don't know how long they'll leave you alone. Thanks to that bullshit stunt Todd pulled, I'm only an agent and until my dad gets his grandchild, he's not going out of his way to help us out."

"I'll take my chances. What's the worst that can happen? They arrest me for a crime I didn't commit then let someone beat me to death that same day. No big deal, right?"

Brian stared at her in a way that Justin never would, the hatred undeniable. "Give it a rest, will you?"

"No."

"And in the meantime, I can be the laughing stock of the entire force and just suck it up. You got any idea how this makes me look?"

"It shouldn't matter."

Brian's fists clenched, his eyes on her throat. "You know what they call me? You know my fucking nickname? O-fer." He pounded the rest of his drink then slammed the glass on the table. "How's that for a fucking name?"

"Loafer?"

"O-fer. As in zero for seventeen, eighteen, nineteen. As in you won't stop beating this goddamned dead horse. As in I can't get my own wife to see reason."

Emily kept quiet and took another sip of water.

"O-fer," he repeated, his face bright red. "As in zero for however many times we've had sex."

"It's not my fault you told them I wasn't sterilized."

"I didn't."

Emily's anger swelled and she didn't know how much longer she could hold it. "Then how would they know? What, did your dad show them his little list?"

"What list?"

Brian's dad had used his power to obtain a list of the unsterilized women in San Angeles. She had found it in Brian's drawer when cleaning. Nearly every other woman had been crossed off, rude comments next to their names. Fat. Hideous. Hispanic. Boring. Low H.I.S. So on and so on, until he finally got to Emily's name, her Health Index Score, hobbies and interests scrawled beside it.

Emily decided it couldn't go left unsaid. She no longer cared if he slapped her, or punched her, or even pulled out his gun and shot her in the face. "You didn't just bump into me at the library."

"Drop it," he warned.

"You haven't read a book since we started dating. You've never once taken me to a museum. You're nothing you pretended to be."

"I am who I am."

"Why'd you pick me? That's all I want to know." Emily used the voice she saved for the courtroom, the one she never used with him. "Were you tired of looking, so you just gave up on the list? Was your daddy pushing you too hard for a grandson?"

Brian pressed his fist to his lips, rocked back and forth, and watched her.

"That's why your friends make fun of you. Because you married an ugly girl just to make a kid and after five years you still don't have one." Emily drew a breath. Before Brian could speak, she said, "And don't you dare say I'm not ugly. I am what I am too. I know why we only have sex with the lights off, why we never kiss in public, why you won't hold my hand and always walk ahead of me. So don't give me that shit."

"Are you done? Any more questions?" A sick smile twisted into place. "No? Good, because I've got some of my own."

Emily's stomach dropped. Brian knew something and the only thing she could think of was he'd finally discovered what she'd been doing. And if he knew that, nothing else mattered.

"You know the law, right? You're so fucking smart, you know all the little laws."

Emily nodded, afraid of where he was headed.

"So you know what would happen if I uploaded certain photographs of you and your little faggot boyfriend to the Controllers? You know what would happen to the both of you?"

Emily placed both hands on the table to keep them from trembling. He had known all along and let it continue, probably just so he could get proof.

"I'm guessing you don't want that to happen. I'm guessing you'd be crushed if anything were to happen to that fucking pansy. You also know you won't be granted a divorce unless I ask for one, so you've got a decision to make."

"What?"

"Stop taking the birth control pills you've been hiding and give me a damn son."

"So you and your dad can corrupt his mind to follow the Way?"

"Or I send those photos. Two choices, one decision, yours to make."

"You don't even care that I've been with another man."

Brian shook his head. "I don't care about you. I might've once, but that's over. You're a slut and for that you'll burn." He took a drink. "Give me a son and I'll divorce your sorry ass. You and your little boyfriend can fight the good fight and fix the world."

"I hate you," Emily said as her eyes began to water.

"Think of your wonderful Mr. Adams," Brian said. "I really don't think you want me to visit him."

"If anything happens to him…"

"What? You can't touch me."

"And I won't," Emily said. "You hurt Justin and you'll never get a child."

"So I leave him alone."

"Forever."

"Fine. I don't care about him. He's nothing. He can have you."

For the first time in their marriage, Emily realized her power. "And I'll still see him."

It took Brian a moment to answer. "You better be pregnant in six months and if it's not mine, you both die."

The tears slipped down her cheeks.

"So what's it going to be?" Brian asked. "Are you going to give me my son?"

Emily cried too hard to speak.

"That's not an answer," he said.

She wanted to tell him he was too stupid to realize the tears were exactly that.

Ten Drops of Bleach

May 30, 2047

Brian Jaworski pointed to the curb in front of the crumbling project that looked like it had been built back in the nineties. "Pull over here."

San Angeles Controlling Force Agent Miguel Guerrero did as he was instructed even though the monitor placed the subject two blocks inside the once-gated community. Before he turned off the hovercar, he said, "The prompter said it was a bad accident. Maybe we should hurry and drive in."

Jaworski laughed his asshole laugh. "Yeah, right. You want to explain to the LT why we risked a half-million-dollar vehicle to status check some unlucky fucker? I bet five to one this guy doesn't even have insurance."

"All the more reason to get to him. The State'll take forever to pick him up."

Jaworski released the particle rifle from the dashboard and got out of the vehicle. "Can't say I blame them."

Guerrero lowered the landing gear and turned off the cruiser. Before he had both feet on the ground, Jaworski reminded him to lock the car.

Guerrero wrapped his hand around the handle, the locks engaging after his vitals were confirmed. "Think I should?"

"Are you crazy? Hell, yes, lock it. These bastards will reduce this baby to a shell in five minutes. You know how quick your kind is with a screwdriver."

Tired of Jaworski's constant abuse, Guerrero asked, "Ever heard of sarcasm?"

Jaworski switched the rifle's safety off and waved Guerrero forward. "Take the lead, rookie."

Guerrero put on his helmet and entered the project, which had probably once been a nice apartment complex. He ignored the graffiti on the abandoned guard shack.

Jaworski didn't. "Fuck The SACF, No Pigs Allowed. See this shit? I don't know why we even bother. My dad always said we should just let them all kill each other. The world would be a much better place."

Since his shock suit couldn't deflect bullets, Guerrero crossed to the left side of the street and kept his back to the wall.

Jaworski stuck to the middle of the street, his chest puffed out, holding the particle rifle so everyone could see he was anxious to use it.

They turned the corner. Down the block, a bloody lump lay crumpled on the sidewalk. Guerrero jogged toward the man, ignored Jaworski's warning that it could be a trap.

When Guerrero knelt down and felt for a pulse, the injured young man turned his head toward him. Guerrero nearly gagged. The skin on the left side of the man's face was bubbling in sections, eaten through in others. The left eye had completely dissolved, the gooey remains puddled below the empty socket. Guerrero read reports, but it was his first time seeing an acid attack victim.

"Can you speak?" Guerrero placed his hand on the man's trembling shoulder. "Can you hear me?"

He looked about Guerrero's age. The man coughed up a wad of bloody phlegm. He opened his eye to look at Guerrero. "My bike. Where's my bike?"

The mangled hunk of metal rested across the street in the gutter. "It's here. What's your name?"

The injured man's teeth were visible through the hole in his cheek. "Julio Ortega."

"I'm going to get you help, Julio. Do you have insurance?"

Tears streamed down the right side of the injured man's face and he tried to speak. No words came out.

Jaworski walked next to Guerrero. "The man asked if you had insurance. Habla English?"

"He speaks English." Guerrero glared up at his partner. "I got this. You want to check for witnesses?"

"We need to know if he has insurance." Jaworski grabbed the collar of Guerrero's shock suit and hauled him to his feet. He dug a hand into Julio's pocket. "Watch my back."

"You're going to hurt him," Guerrero said.

"Worse than he already is? I'm afraid your amigo's pretty fucked up."

A worn black wallet lay on the grass a few yards away. Guerrero retrieved it while Jaworski searched the injured man. Guerrero flipped through the wallet and confirmed it was Julio's by the sole piece of paper left inside.

"Can't believe I got hit riding my bike." Between sobs, Julio said, "My sister always said I'd get killed if I got my license. 'Ride your bike, Julio. It's safer.'"

"You can stop searching him," Guerrero said. "Here's his wallet. Someone cleaned it out."

"That's a surprise."

"My brother's not going to believe this." Julio clenched his fist. "I have to be okay. I have to be okay for Vanessa."

"Well, I hate to tell you this, but you're not going to be." Jaworksi pulled the vitalic meter from his utility belt, pressed it against Julio's neck and read the results. "Paralyzed from the waist down with six, no, make that five, percent chance of walking again if you get immediate medical treatment. So what's it going to be? Do you have insurance or not?"

"I ride a bike. What the hell do you think?"

Jaworski snapped his meter shut and stuffed it back into his pocket. "Call the Turtle, Guerrero. Let 'em know they got a smart ass on their hands."

After Guerrero radioed the State and told them to dispatch an ambulance to his location, he asked Julio if his brother lived in the complex.

Julio shook his head. "We live together."

Jaworski grabbed the wallet out of Guerrero's hand and pulled out the ID. "He lives in El Monte. Why the hell were you over here?"

"I came to see a friend."

"Sure you did. Your friend do this to you?"

"No."

"Who did it then? Why'd they do it?"

"I don't know."

"You don't know or you don't want to tell me?"

Guerrero searched the windows of the nearby apartments. A face disappeared behind a curtain on the second floor overlooking their location. Guerrero was about to point it out, but saw Jaworski kneeling on Julio's stomach, and yelled, "What are you doing?"

"Trying to get some answers," Jaworski growled over his shoulder. "So what'd you come here to buy? Sterlins? Super X? Bleach? What was it?"

"Get off me. Please."

"I will arrest you if you don't cooperate. I don't care how fucked up you are."

"I didn't do anything wrong."

"Then tell me why you're here."

"To see my friend. I already told you."

"Where's he live? I want to talk to him."

"I can't remember. This hurts like hell. Look at me!"

"Relax or I'll cuff you right now."

"For what?"

"For soliciting. I'm guessing bleach."

"I need it for Vanessa."

Jaworski pumped his fist and grinned at Guerrero. "Told you this shithead was trying to buy. Dumbass just confessed."

"He'd probably admit to killing his own mother right now. Get off him."

The officer jumped to his feet and went over to Guerrero, his face inches from Guerrero's neck. "My dad always…"

"I know, I know," Guerrero said. "Your dad's the smartest man on earth, but right now it's just you and me, and I don't give a shit what either of you has to say."

"Let's get one thing straight, you son of a bitch. I don't like you and I never have. Back off or you'll be sorry."

Guerrero stared at Jaworski, proud of himself for not knocking the man out cold. Keeping calm, he said, "Right now you have nothing on this guy but some bullshit confession on an even more bullshit charge. I know you hate Hispanics, that's no secret, but wouldn't you rather let this guy go in exchange for some real info, something you can take back to the LT?"

"Like what?"

Guerrero lowered his voice, leaned in, and said, "I'll find out who his connect is."

"He won't tell you shit."

"Give me two minutes." Guerrero brushed past Jaworski and knelt next to Julio. "And do me a favor and watch that window up there. I got a feeling those could be our guys."

Guerrero laid a hand on the uneaten side of Julio's face and assured him the paramedics were on their way and that he'd be fine. "I don't want to see you arrested and I'm sure you don't want that either so what I need right now is for you to tell me what happened."

"I told him already. I came to score bleach."

Guerrero didn't bother asking why Julio would risk arrest to buy something proven to cause as much harm as it did good. Julio was just another number, a meaningless face in the ever-increasing population that couldn't afford the Controllers' approved alternative to decontaminate the water. But Guerrero did need details.

"Have you bought bleach here before?"

"Twice."

"Same guy?"

"Yeah."

"You call him first?"

Julio mumbled something unintelligible.

"I know you're in a lot of pain, but I need you to concentrate. Did you call this guy before today? Did he do this to you?"

"I called him, but he wasn't here. Another guy. The picture on my phone was fuzzy, but it looked like him. Younger."

"Why would he do this to you?"

When Julio finally spoke, he talked so low Guerrero could barely hear. "I was stupid, told them I needed three bottles. I didn't think they'd check to make sure it was all there."

Guerrero didn't need to say a word to make the kid feel any worse.

"One of them knocked me down, snatched the bottles back. Other guy splashed my face."

"Who hit you?"

"I got on my bike and tried to ride, but I couldn't see. A hover hit me. Never even heard it."

"Time's up, amigos," Jaworski said.

Guerrero ignored him. "What's your connect's name? What's he look like?"

"He's big time. I rat and he'll kill me."

"He almost did already. Give me his name, Julio, or Agent Jaworski will arrest you."

Julio was silent for a moment. "Danny. Spider. Mexican. Shaved head. Goatee."

"You sure?"

When Julio said he was positive, Guerrero told Jaworski he'd be right back and sprinted to the entrance. The resident roster was black, but after banging on it several times, it flickered to life, the names of each occupant at his fingertips. It took three touches to find his suspect.

Guerrero jogged back to Jaworski. "Daniel Lopez, unit nineteen. Don't look now, but it's the building right behind you. Got one in the window."

Jaworski checked his rifle's proton powerpack. "We'll pretend to leave and walk back along the walls so they can't see us approach."

"We won't do anything."

"What are you talking about?"

"We're not blindly storming a unit inside a crowded complex without support. No way."

"Are you serious? Are you that much of a pussy?"

"I'm not raiding some drug dealer's lair, especially when he knows we're coming. Call it in for backup."

"We're going or your buddy's under arrest."

"I got the info like I promised. He cooperated. You're not arresting him."

"You don't tell me what to do, hombre."

"Today I do." Guerrero tried to control his trembling. Before he lost his nerve, he pressed his mic and said, "HQ, Charlie-12B. We have info on a 78-11. Requesting backup."

"You asshole." Jaworski slapped Guerrero's hand off his mic. "You want those guys up there to flush all the evidence."

Headquarters radioed back that agents were being dispatched.

"It'll still take it off the streets and no one's hurt."

"I'm going in and if you don't have my back, you'll be out of a job."

Guerrero took a step back, placed one hand on the butt of his pistol and the other on his mic. "HQ, Charlie-12B. 12A wants to approach the 78-11 unaided."

"You rat son of a bitch. You'll never work in this state again."

The radio squawk cut Jaworski off. "Charlie-12A, HQ. Stand down. Repeat, stand down and wait for assistance."

Jaworski turned for the apartment building behind him. Guerrero hit his mic and reported that Jaworski was not standing down. As Guerrero repeated his call, he noticed the face at the window disappeared.

"Charlie-12A, HQ. Stand down and respond. If you do not, you will be terminated immediately. Stand down this instant and respond."

Jaworski ripped something from his suit and threw it back at Guerrero. The Controlling Force patch floated to his feet.

Relieved he'd never have to work with the man again, Guerrero radioed in Jaworski's resignation. He kept an eye on apartment nineteen's curtained window as he knelt next to Julio and tried to comfort him.

"The ambulance will be here soon." Guerrero watched Jaworski disappear up the stairs. "You're going to be all right."

Julio brought his bloodied hand up to Guerrero's and squeezed it tight. He cried when he thanked Guerrero for staying with him.

In an attempt to cheer up Julio, Guerrero asked, "So who's Vanessa? Your wife? Girlfriend?"

"My little niece."

"How old is she?"

There was a loud crash and a man exploded out apartment nineteen's window. Struck by a fully charged particle beam, the body vanished in midair, the sound of smashing glass and a barrage of gunfire covering the soft thud of the man's boots and jeans slapping the concrete.

Guerrero radioed it in and ran for the stairs. He was halfway up, his pistol drawn, when Jaworski came reeling out of the apartment's front door and bounced off the hallway, falling face first on the landing. There were at least a dozen holes in his shock suit, all of them leaking blood.

Guerrero grabbed hold of Jaworski's arm and pulled him down the stairs as bullets poured out the open doorway. He was starting back up when Jaworski said, "Ambulance. Call it. Agent down."

"Ex-agent," Guerrero reminded him. "When I get done, I'll call you a Turtle."

The gunfire ceased. Guerrero knelt halfway up the stairs and pressed himself against the wall, his pistol aimed at the door.

Someone yelled, "Grab the suitcases and as much shit as you can carry."

Someone else shouted back, "There's another one out there."

"He was out by the cripple. Check to see if he's still there."

A third, deeper voice said, "To hell with him. I'm out. Cover me from the window."

The man poked his head out the doorway and Guerrero fired, the beam vaporizing an inch-wide hole through his forehead. As the man fell to his knees, his eyes blank, the hole slowly widened as nearby cells began to dissipate. The powerpack reading was full, but the gun obviously had a very weak charge.

Unsure how many more shots he had left, Guerrero lowered his visor and pulled a freeze grenade from his belt. He depressed the activator and tossed the grenade through the doorway. When the blast of pure white blew out of the apartment, Guerrero sprinted up the stairs and dove over the headless body lying across the threshold.

Guerrero rolled inside, sensitive to the quickly warming room. Freeze grenades seldom worked on the muscles more than a few seconds and the victims' minds were unfrozen shortly after. Outnumbered, with no time for hesitation, Guerrero fired a shot at the man crouched behind the couch and then spun to his right and fired two more shots, both hitting the teenager over by the blown out window.

Even though he'd been hit, the guy from the couch leapt forward and knocked Guerrero down. Guerrero struggled to keep hold of his pistol as they rolled on the ground. He spotted the small hole slowly burning away in the man's chest.

The muscle-bound behemoth stopped fighting for the pistol and grabbed Guerrero by his throat. When he cocked back his free arm, Guerrero brought up the pistol, shoved it deep into the hole caused by the first beam and pulled the trigger. A loud gasp escaped the man as he collapsed onto Guerrero, the point-blank beam sufficient to erase his heart.

Guerrero rolled the man off and got to his feet. He tossed his spent pistol onto the couch and grabbed the metal revolver lying next to it. It had been five years since he'd fired one of the outlawed weapons in the academy, but the technology was simple. A child could use it.

Daniel Lopez wasn't among the three men he'd just killed and the door to the bedroom was closed. After a quick glance to make sure the gun was loaded, Guerrero radioed in the developing situation and approached the bedroom.

Guerrero put his back to the wall and pounded on the door. "Come out now and you won't be killed."

No response.

"You want to end up like your homies? If you come out now, you might be able to catch a last glimpse of them before they completely disappear."

Gunfire exploded and bullets tore through the wooden door, splinters bouncing off Guerrero's visor. He pretended to call headquarters as he yelled, "Agent down. Agent down. He shot me. Hurry."

Footsteps approached. When the door moved backward, Guerrero kicked it hard and rushed inside the room.

Spider, who couldn't have been much older than Guerrero, backpedaled, spinning his arms as he tried to regain his balance. Before he had the chance to recover and bring up the submachine gun, Guerrero fired two bullets into his shoulder. The man went down fast, dropping the gun as he crashed into the mountain of bleach bottles filling half the room.

Guerrero kicked the gun out of Spider's reach and told him he was under arrest. "And whether or not you were the piece of shit that threw the acid on that young man outside, you're going to pay for it."

Spider rolled on the ground, holding his shoulder. "You killed my brother."

"You killed a Controller."

30-Day Program

March 23, 2048

The bell rang and Gabe got up from his desk. He pretended to look for something in his bag, waited until everyone had left the room. He threw two pills in his mouth, swallowed them dry.

Gabe's locker was ten feet from the door, but in the wrong direction. Only left turns when leaving classrooms, another stupid rule. It took him almost two minutes to circle back around each time.

He took the left, and someone kicked the bottom of Gabe's shoe. Fucking Frankie, been doing this shit since they were five. Through his nasally laugh, Frankie said, "Hold up, man."

Gabe kept going, made a right at the first hallway.

Frankie popped up beside him. "Gotta hit your locker?"

"No, I'm just taking a tour, dumbass."

"You don't have to be a dick."

Gabe switched his focus to Derrick, the new kid, his blond hair bouncing off his shoulders. A couple of days ago they got partnered up in chemistry. Derrick wasn't like most of the others transferred here. He didn't seem to care if he fit in or not, hardly spoke at all. Until this morning. Derrick had asked Gabe if he shot hoops. Gabe thought it might be some new drug, but Derrick was just talking about basketball. At the end of class, Gabe agreed to play him one-on-one after school.

A line of students filed through the archway toward everyone waiting for Transport, but Derrick swerved right, snuck through the fence. Not asking permission to opt out of Transport was cause for expulsion, but Derrick walked like a man without a care.

Gabe turned the corner, and Frankie asked, "So, would you do it?"

Gabe moved onto the walkway closest to the window, split his attention between the dumpy girl in front of him and the idiots attached to their screens, oblivious to everyone around them. No one more oblivious than Bryce, standing there, drool glistening in the corner of his mouth, a different dude after The Program.

Frankie repeated, "Would you?"

"Huh?"

"Get Connected?"

"That's just for the Controllers."

"Didn't you hear anything Torres said? This summer it's open to anyone."

Gabe had been daydreaming in class, thinking about what Derrick had said in chemistry the first day they'd been paired up, that he recognized him. Gabe had never seen him before last month when Derrick transferred.

"I could never afford it," Gabe said.

"But if you could?"

They made their final right, stopped at Gabe's locker, ten feet from where he'd started. Gabe pressed his thumb to the lock to open it. He said, "We're already too connected as it is."

"Well, I'm definitely asking my uncle." Frankie's uncle raked in the big bucks as an anchorman, but Frankie never saw a dime. His parents were in the same position as Gabe's.

"You need to lighten up," Frankie said. He dug in his back pocket and pulled out a pink envelope. "Trisha asked me to give this to you."

Gabe looked past the note at Rocky's locker. It'd been over 3 months since they put him in The Program. No one had heard a thing. No one was asking.

"Here, man," Frankie said.

Gabe grabbed the card, "Gabriel" in cursive flowing across it. He shoved the envelope in his bag, merged back into the herd.

"Well, what should I tell her?"

"I don't know."

"She digs you, man. You can't keep ignoring her."

They headed for the archway. Landon, a chunky senior training to become a True Resident for Peace, stood near the loading area in his silver sash, scrutinizing everyone.

"Man, I'm telling you," Frankie said, "if Trish even looked at me like that, we'd have fifty fucking babies by now."

"You're a moron." Gabe didn't just mean about girls. Just like all their classmates, Frankie believed the lies his uncle spread on the news.

Gabe didn't. His dad had explained how everything worked the last time they'd gone hiking, left their electronics behind. His dad had stood up to the Reverend and turned his back on The Way, lived to whisper about it. They hadn't talked about it since Gabe got chipped for school, but Gabe remembered every word.

Through the six-inch slit in the wall, Gabe saw a couple of kids out on the sidewalk, only those that lived within three blocks were given free passes to be on foot. Then there was Derrick, across the street slipping through the trees.

Gabe said, "You know what? I'm not taking TP today. I'll see you in the morning."

Frankie chuckled. "You serious? We have to take it."

They only lived five blocks from campus, but Transport was the rule unless they personally opted out. The glorified hall monitors rarely granted passes. The Way got paid for each body on board.

"Yeah, I'm just going to walk."

"Dude," Frankie said, "that's not a good idea."

Gabe didn't care. He told Frankie, "I'll be fine."

Frankie shook his head, continued down the fenced walkway, joined the students standing four across waiting for Transport.

Gabe straightened his back the way his dad used to, tough and strong, not a scared little coward, and headed straight for Landon checking off names on his electronic clipboard. Gabe ignored the recog glasses, focused on the acne covering the senior's face. Gabe held out his wrist. "I'm opting out of TP."

Landon pushed out his chest so it almost matched his belly. "You have a note from your mommy?"

There was no chance of lying with Landon wearing the glasses so Gabe recited p. 53 of the school manual. "Students can be granted permission if they are fifteen years of age and request to opt out."

Landon studied Gabe's face, the recog glasses checking his vitals. Gabe slowed his breath until Landon scanned his wrist. "Don't get bleached, weirdo."

Landon wasn't a True Resident for Peace or a Controller, but he was the kind of guy who'd track Gabe down the moment he became one. With no reason to upset Landon anymore, Gabe asked, "May I go?"

Landon flicked him in the head, and Gabe bit his tongue, walked off. The sun was brilliant, Gabe cut through the trees, stopped for a second, heard the slap of the basketball on cement. Derrick was directly across the street bouncing the ball, his button-down shirt off, now tucked in his back pocket, tight white tank top hugging his chest. At six feet, with all those muscles, he had to be close to the cutoff weight.

Derrick kept bouncing the ball. "There he is. I knew you'd follow me. You ready to get your ass handed to you?"

Gabe acted like it was no big deal. "Not today." He lunged to steal the ball.

Derrick spun and laughed when Gabe slammed into his back. "With those moves, this is going to get ugly."

"Yeah, we'll see. I told you, it's been a long time since I played."

"Oh, I believe you." Derrick dribbled the ball a foot in front of Gabe. "You ready?"

"I have to stop by my house first to check in." A giant silver and black Transport rumbled down the street. The sidewalks were practically empty. There were no signs of the local gangs, no threat of having bleach thrown on his face. "Plus, I need to change."

"Lead the way," Derrick said.

"Nah, I'm all right."

Derrick followed anyway. "You better not be thinking of chickening out."

Walking with Derrick behind him let Gabe breathe a little easier. He hadn't been out on the streets by himself since his uncle Julio's accident left the man in a wheelchair.

Derrick bounced the basketball off Gabe, went back to dribbling. "You've never opted out, have you?"

Gabe shook his head, counted the houses that'd been torn down, the others with "Reverend's Real Estate – Sold" signs marking their destruction. Gabe's dad had explained how all the empty lots were the work of the Controllers. They paid beyond top dollar so The Way made an easy profit.

Derrick stepped into the street so they were side by side. "Love what they've done with the neighborhood."

Gabe turned to him. "I thought you just moved here."

Derrick shook his head, his fine blond hair brushing his shoulders. "Grandparents. Mom and Dad used to bring me down every Sunday. Now it's just me and my Gram. She's happy to have company."

Gabe didn't ask what happened to Derrick's parents, wasn't in the mood to hear a story like his aunt Maria's. But he finally understood why Derrick said he recognized him.

The next block down, they came to where the library had been before the Controllers converted it into a parking lot for their heavy equipment. Gabe's house was just around the corner. He said, "Hey, man, you mind waiting here?"

Derrick took a whiff of his armpit. "Come on, I want to meet your mom. Older women love me."

"Very funny. No, she's already going to freak over the whole Transport deal."

"Whatever. But if she doesn't want to let you out, just tell her I'll protect you." Derrick flexed his bicep.

Gabe shoved him. Derrick didn't budge. "Go for it." Derrick dropped the ball, stopped it with his foot. "Punch for punch, chest or gut."

"Yeah, right."

"I'll even let you go first. Come on." A single bead of sweat dripped down his neck, soaked into the tank top. "You can ask it," Derrick said. "I know you want to."

Gabe looked around to see if anyone was within hearing range, where the closest camera could be. "I gotta go."

"I know everyone's talking about the rumor, what happened at my old school. Don't tell me you haven't heard it."

Gabe softly said, "You really do that to him?"

"He called me a faggot so I was justified. The judge didn't even trip, said I did the right thing."

Gabe was glad Derrick skipped the details. He didn't want to know if those things were true. "Look, I really have to go."

"You're coming back, right?"

"Yeah, but it might be a few minutes."

Derrick dribbled the ball between his legs. "I'll be waiting."

Gabe headed up to his porch, looked over the top of his house. The skies, usually gray, had gotten worse since the Blocks sprouted up.

Gabe's mom was already at the door, her hair pulled back into a ponytail. She wasn't more than five feet two, but you could hear that voice a half-mile away. "What in the hell are you doing?" she said. "You scared me to death."

"Relax, Mom." Gabe patted her shoulder when he entered the house. "I wanted to walk."

"I called you five times since I got the message from the Transport. You pick up when I call, do you hear me?"

Gabe kept walking, headed toward his room. "My screen was off because of class. I didn't turn it back on."

"Hey! I'm talking to you."

At his bedroom entrance, Gabe stopped, turned to face her. "Mom, five calls in five minutes? Really? Think you might be overreacting?"

"No, I don't!"

Gabe went into his room, threw his bag on his bed, slipped off his shirt. "It's fine, Mom. Not a big deal. I'm going to play basketball, just wanted to warm up with the walk."

"With who? A boy?"

Gabe heard the fear in her voice, but didn't look at her. He put on his Vex-Stretch t-shirt. It sucked in the small ring of fat around his waist. He said, "It's just a guy from school."

"Well, who is it? You know our rule."

Gabe unbuckled his pants. "Do you mind?"

She turned away but didn't leave. "So who is it?"

Gabe shook off his pants, took the pink card out of his envelope and placed it on his dresser, next to a black plastic bag of magazines. He pulled on his shorts and said, "A friend. Derrick, he just transferred."

She was looking right at him. "You're not going anywhere until we meet him."

"The sun's going down in two hours. We're just going to play a few games of 21." Gabe snatched the plastic bag, threw it and the girly magazines into the trash.

"Don't be like that. I know it can be embarrassing to buy those. Nothing to be ashamed about."

He pushed past her. "I don't need them."

His mom shushed him, followed him into the living room and nodded at the wall screen. She kept her back to it and mouthed, "Don't even joke."

Gabe smiled and said, "I'll be back before dark." He hated the screen, but it served a purpose. All she did was sit in front of it and watch the news, while someone watched her.

"I didn't say you could go. I want to meet this boy."

He headed for the door. "Maybe after the game."

"Did you take your pills?"

"Of course, Mom. Now I have to go."

"You're already on your second warning. Next time—"

"I know! Stop, okay? I'll be back." One more violation meant The Program. Gabe didn't need to be reminded of what that meant. He'd been hearing stories since he was a little boy.

Derrick was waiting at the corner. He stopped dribbling, took a crumpled black mask from his back pocket and slipped it over his mouth. "You got one?"

Gabe searched the light posts for a camera. "You can't hide your face."

"Dude, relax, we're not protesting anything. I'm protecting my lungs. And we're just going to play a game."

Gabe wasn't so sure that was true. "I don't have one."

Derrick reached back into his pocket, pulled out another mask. He tossed it over.

The mask was just as crumpled as the other one, but this one was grayish-white. Gabe said, "You've been sitting on it all day?"

Derrick started down the street and called over his shoulder. "Yep."

Gabe slipped it on, smelled cheap cologne and something sour. It was weirdly intoxicating.

Derrick slowed down so they were back side-by-side, a slow dribble that blended in with each step. "So your mom trip on you? You seem kind of pissed."

Gabe bit the inside of his cheek, then lunged for the ball. Derrick crossed it over to his other hand.

Derrick said, "You guys losing the house?"

"Not yet, it's not in foreclosure. I hear them talk all the time, though, how much they're behind, how much they've been offered. But my dad won't take it, says it's not enough."

Derrick said, "What about heading for the Hills, working for one of the families?"

"My dad would never move into a Block. He'd die first."

Derrick turned down a dark road. Gabe hadn't been on it in a very long time. "I thought we were headed to the Rec Zone?"

"That place is crawling with Controllers."

Harrow Park was just down the hill. It'd fallen into disrepair. Thick brush crept onto the paths. Dying branches hung over the rusty playground. Strands of ivy covered the fences around the courts, turning them into secluded caves. A few men hung around the baseball dugout, another two by the bathrooms. Gabe thought about bleach attacks, he asked about criminals.

"Stop worrying. I told you, I'll protect you."

"We shouldn't be down here." The men were all fit, muscles showing under tight shirts, but no one seemed to be here for sports.

Derrick opened a small gate and slipped onto the basketball court. The sun filtered through the ivy. It was private, but not as dark as Gabe had imagined. The sky was still bright and gray above.

"We try to keep it clean," Derrick said.

Gabe noticed a condom wrapper in the corner.

"Full court or half?" Derrick asked and took off his shirt.

"We only have until dark."

"That only gives me an hour or so to kick your ass." Derrick chucked the ball. The sharp sting of it slapped against Gabe's palms. Derrick's bright blue eyes pierced through him. He crouched down defensively. Gabe dribbled, angled his body to block Derrick from the ball. He tried to move right. Derrick cut him off, forced him left, Gabe's weakest hand. Derrick whispered, "Come on, faggot."

The words seared through Gabe's mind. He dribbled faster.

"You can't beat me, faggot."

"Shut up."

"Why, faggot?"

All it took was a rumor to get you put into The Program, and Gabe already had two warnings. Anyone could be listening: undercover cops, Controller camp kids, snitches sent in as lures. Maybe that's what Derrick was? Gabe glanced up, expected to see a closed-circuit camera in the sky or hidden in the ivy.

Derrick whispered again. "Faggot."

Gabe picked up his dribble. Derrick smacked the ball out of his hands, pinned Gabe against the fence, slowly pulled down Gabe's mask.

Derrick said, "What about me? You think I'm a faggot?"

Gabe wanted to run or throw a punch. Why weren't his pills kicking in? Derrick's face was so close to his.

Gabe's voice trembled when he said, "Please."

Derrick took off his own mask, leaned in, the cologne and sweat so strong. Their lips pressed. Gabe closed his eyes. All the dreams, the fantasies he'd blocked out coming true. He opened his mouth, kissed back, rough but gentle and frightened.

A man shouted, "Shit! Controllers!"

Gabe pulled away, his lips still burning.

Derrick peered through the ivy. "Oh no."

Gabe rushed next to him. Four patrol cars. Two men being tackled next to the bathrooms.

A young Controller stepped onto the court. He had a perfectly plastered part in his blond hair, his jaw clenching like he'd been waiting all morning to crack someone's skull. "Well, what the fuck do we have here?"

Derrick stepped in front of Gabe. "We're just playing basketball."

"Yeah, right." The Controller ignored his electro prod, went straight for his plasma baton, the blue pulsing current flowing up and down the wand.

Derrick threw up his hands. "Hey, man, we don't want any trouble. We're just playing a game."

The Controller's fingers tightened around the handle. Derrick clenched his fists. Gabe knew what was going to happen, but he couldn't move, couldn't reach out to pull him back. Derrick lowered his shoulder and charged at the Controller, who raised the plasma baton. Derrick beat the blow and tackled the Controller. They rolled over and over until Gabe heard the crackling of burning flesh, the Controller's scream. Derrick pressed the blue pulse to the man's neck. Gabe closed his eyes, the sizzle echoing in his ears.

"Go!" Derrick said to Gabe.

Gabe couldn't look away from the gaping black ditch in the Controller's throat. "W-what did you do?"

"You have to go!"

Gabe saw the open gate, another squad car pulling up. He still couldn't move. Derrick ran over, shoved the mask back onto Gabe's face.

"You don't have a choice. You won't survive The Program."

Gabe stood frozen, kept whispering, "No."

Derrick grabbed him by the arm, yanked him towards the gate, shoved him onto the path. Another Controller was barreling down the hill. Derrick squeezed the plasma baton. "Go!" he screamed, then ran for the Controller. Gabe watched for a second, turned, then angled away from a screaming man with two Controllers kicking him in the gut and face. There was nothing between Gabe and the trees. His face was hidden. There was nothing left to do but run.

Eleven Times More Likely

August 16, 2049

Justin helped Emily into the elevator and pushed the button for the forty-fifth floor. She leaned against the back wall, her yellow maternity dress dingy from being outside and all the hands that had felt her stomach.

The shower had been too much, but people would've been suspicious if they hadn't thrown one. Justin held up the bag full of gift cards, deposit slips, and an old fashioned check from Emily's uncle. "At least this will help with Irene."

Emily wiped away her tears, smearing mascara across her splotchy cheeks. "Can we even trust her?"

Justin held up his finger to shush her then realized he'd just made the situation worse because the overhead camera should've switched on with the trigger word. He scratched his nose, acted like that's what he'd meant to do from the start. "She'll do a great job. All those other couples loved her."

The elevator opened and Justin walked Emily down the hall. Outside their unit, he let Emily go so he could place his palm on the reader and his eye to the Controllers' override scanner. Their door buzzed open at the same time as the one directly across from them.

Justin had Emily step inside the apartment before he turned toward Landon, their floor's True Resident for Peace. "What can I help you with?"

The pimply-faced eighteen year-old had a two-bedroom all to himself and didn't need to worry about the weight limit. His smug smile said it wasn't a bad deal for reporting a few dissenters here and there. "Just wanted to say hi. See how your wife is doing."

From over Justin's shoulder, Emily said, "I'm fine, it's just been a long day."

"Yeah, I noticed you guys haven't left together for quite some time. Thought maybe you were sick or had an early delivery."

Emily stepped beside Justin and patted her stomach. "Nope, still here."

"So what was the special occasion today?"

Justin held up the bag and told him about the baby shower.

"In town?"

"Our vehicle's chipped," Emily said. "Everywhere we go is logged."

True Residents weren't to be questioned and Landon's face showed it. "You've been crying," he said. "Did someone hit you?"

Emily shook her head. "No, I'm just very tired."

Justin told Emily to go lie down and waited until she was out of hearing range. "It's been a tough pregnancy."

"This isn't her first?

"It is," Justin said as Emily called his name. "I'm really sorry, but I have to go now."

"Sure thing," Landon said. "We'll be talking."

Justin got inside the apartment and locked the door. Emily stood at the end of the hallway, back to the wall, pointing at their bedroom. Justin took his time, expecting a cockroach, maybe a rat or a spider. Not the woman lying on their bed.

Emily whispered, "Who's that?"

The brunette looked familiar, but Justin couldn't place her. "Probably a junkie squatter. She's out."

"Look at her skin."

It was pale blue, the area around her bright red lips a deep purple. Justin ran for the kitchen. "I'll get the Controllers."

The black panic button was beside the fridge. Directly below it sat a balding man with sunglasses and a semi-automatic pistol. The right side of his face was a soft pink.

"And I always thought you were the smart one," he said.

Justin tried to steady his voice. "Who are you?"

The man looked up, his skin an ashy gray, lips cracked and bloody. "Don't recognize me?"

They were only twenty-nine, same parents, same genes. Feeling like he was staring into a twisted mirror, Justin said, "Jeremy. Holy shit, are you okay?"

Jeremy took out a speckled handkerchief and wiped his mouth. "Never better."

Emily stayed in the hallway where Jeremy couldn't see her, palming her miniature cell phone. "Your brother?"

Justin told her it'd be okay then saw Jeremy had his glasses off. His right eye was melted shut, his left one cloudy, colorless, a sure sign of an eleven timer. Even if Jeremy wasn't crazy, he had no business with a ballistic firearm. "What are you doing with that?"

"What do you think?"

Justin came a little closer. "Can I hold it?"

Jeremy laughed as he used the wall to get up. "No can do. Wouldn't want you to piss yourself."

Justin faked a laugh. "Seriously, just holster it. My wife's pregnant."

"No shit. Thanks for the invite."

"It's been eight years. You disappeared."

Jeremy pointed at the living room and told him to get moving. "Had to," he said. "I'm the one who fucked the world. Me and the Way. Think about that."

Justin went over to Emily and put his arm around her. He glared at his brother and said, "What do you want? And who's the woman?"

Jeremy nodded behind them. "On the couch. Both of you."

Justin squeezed Emily's hand and walked her past the dimmed images flashing across the wall-sized digi-screen. Jeremy sat in the recliner, arms resting on his thighs, gun pointing at the ground. The glass coffee table was all that stood between them.

Emily broke the silence. "Why are you doing this to us?"

Jeremy held up his finger and told her to hush. "You Connected?"

Justin said no. Emily said she was pregnant.

"That doesn't stop most folks."

"I care about my baby."

"One more question," Jeremy said, "You'd really press the button, call the Controllers?"

"What else could I do? I'm not getting a murder pinned on me."

"Relax, killer."

"Who is she?"

"Not important." Jeremy blinked twice and his face went slack, another sign he was just another number of the infected who filled the streets. He moved his head in small circles and said, "Listen to lies. Hear the truth. Lies. Truth. Listen."

Justin snapped his fingers. "Jay, you there?"

Jeremy focused on his hands. "I'm thirsty."

"I'll get it for you," Justin said.

Jeremy waved him down with the gun. "No, you lovebirds sit." He moved into the kitchen and poured a glass of water. "That's great, though, really. I'm happy for you two."

Justin held Emily's hand and hoped she understood it was best to play along. "Thanks, Jeremy. That means a lot."

Jeremy took a drink and gagged. He threw open the door below the sink and kicked in the water purifier.

Justin ran to the kitchen. "What are you doing?"

"A favor." Jeremy ran the water for a few moments before filling a new glass. "That thing isn't doing what you think it is."

"We paid close to ten thousand for it."

Jeremy sniffed the water and took a sip. "There isn't one under fifty that's worth two shits. All store models add Thorazine."

Emily looked to Justin.

Jeremy drank half the glass and set it down. "Just enough to keep everyone smiling."

"No one could get away with that," Justin said.

Jeremy waved him away and dropped the gun on the counter. He gripped the sink with both hands and doubled over, heaving a stream of red.

Justin thought of going for the gun. Instead he just stood there and waited for his brother to stop. "You okay?"

Jeremy took a swig of water and swished it around, spat it out. His hands shook.

It wasn't really a question when Justin said, "You don't decontaminate?"

Jeremy heaved again, his forehead smacking the faucet when he hacked out a long bloody rope of mucus.

"No bleach either?"

"You don't get it." Jeremy used his forearm to wipe off his face. "It's not the water. And bleach only speeds it up. They make money, get rid of the poor. All bullshit."

Justin went back to his spot beside Emily. Everyone knew drinking unfiltered water caused an eleven-fold increase in intestinal cancer, hallucinations, and a myriad of other conditions. As delicately as he could, Justin said, "What about the studies? You don't think you have any symptoms?"

Jeremy finished his water and went back to the recliner, gun in hand. "I know what I got, how I got it. Look at the soldiers. No pensions to pay when everyone dies by thirty-five."

Whether he had words or a sledgehammer, there was no stopping Jeremy once he got started. Emily had been told that story. Justin held her hand, hoping she remembered.

"Food, man. The meat."

"Pork?"

"That shit isn't pork. Not like it's supposed to be."

Justin didn't know enough about the hybrid to warrant an opinion, just that the FDA said the splicing was safe. "That's what's screwing everyone up?"

"One of many." Jeremy took a deep breath and blew it out, blood dripped off his lip. He wiped at his mouth and said, "I don't expect you to believe me."

"It's just a lot to take in. Think of all the people that would involve. And why would they kill themselves? Everyone eats that stuff."

"Not the ones who understand what it does. The research's out there, just got to dig."

"What does that mean? Why are you here?"

Jeremy set the gun on the coffee table and held out his hand to Emily. "I'm sorry to scare you like I did, especially with you so far along."

Emily scooted forward and shook hands. Sounding like she really cared and wanted an honest answer, she said, "Then why did you?"

"You two need scaring. Took forever to debug this place, set the Controllers' feed on loop."

Justin had no idea if Jeremy was making it up. "Where's the camera?"

"Are you serious?"

"Sorry I didn't go to spy school."

Jeremy pointed at the digi-screen. "Why do you think you can't shut it off?"

There had to be a reason. Justin couldn't remember what it was. "Are they going to see we tampered with it?"

"We have time. I'm no fool."

"Then get that woman out of here and undo everything you did."

"What happened to changing the world?"

"We tried," Emily said.

Justin put his hand on Emily's stomach. "It's too dangerous. Especially with a family."

"Why I'm here." Jeremy closed his eye and rocked forward, caught himself then sat back up. "Just listen."

"If you tell me who she is. Who the hell's that lady?"

Jeremy blew out a breath and dabbed at his cracked lips. "Friend of a friend owed me a favor."

Justin said that wasn't good enough.

Jeremy threw up on the coffee table and fell from the chair. He said he was sorry and dug a small syringe from his pocket. After he slammed the syringe into his neck, his cloudy eye became a little clearer. "It gets worse."

Justin wiped the back of his hands on the couch, looked away from the lunger oozing down the table's edge. "We're listening," Justin said. "What's so important?"

Jeremy got back in the recliner. "Realize what's out there, what you're up against."

Emily said they had a pretty good idea.

Jeremy said she was wrong. "And that's just stuff going on. What's in the works? Truth tunnels, mind rape, everyone bound to the Way."

Justin changed the way he was sitting to get a few inches closer to the pistol.

Jeremy nodded at it and told him, "Go ahead. It's yours."

"The punishment for ballistic…"

Jeremy held up his hand. "Listen to one more thing, then decide. The Way camps."

"We're keeping our child," said Emily.

"That's great," Jeremy said. "I'm interested in how."

"I'm not going to drive anymore," said Justin. "We'll use the money we saved for the waiver. We can afford it."

Jeremy nodded. "Good, 'cause you can't buy those kids back any more. Can't even visit in most states."

Emily asked Justin if that was true. Justin didn't know.

"It is, but that shouldn't bother you, right?" Jeremy's smile was all wrong, bloody lips and missing teeth. "You guys got it all figured out and are going to keep him. Or is it a she?"

"We want it to be a surprise," Emily said.

Like it was a matter of fact, Jeremy said, "They still told you."

Justin picked up the gun, its cold steel not making him feel any safer. "What does it have to do with anything?"

"One of each," Jeremy said. "I'd say that's a bit of a problem."

Emily's nails dug into Justin's thigh. He asked Jeremy who told him that.

"Controllers' database. Blood tests are automatic. Hope you didn't pay much trying to keep it quiet."

Justin felt sick. "They know?"

"Before you did."

Emily sobbed. "What are we going to do?"

Jeremy asked them what the hell they were thinking.

"We hired a midwife," Justin said. "Heard she was reliable."

"They're regulated."

"We've saved a lot. All she has to do is keep quiet and then we could dress them the same, only take one out at a time."

Jeremy kept shaking his head. "Sorry, brother. No one's risking twenty years' hard labor."

Justin said they'd find someone. Emily cried they wouldn't.

"It'll be okay," Jeremy said. "That's my present to you. A chance, if nothing else."

Emily sat up. "What kind of chance?"

"A fighting one. There are groups to the east…"

Justin put the gun on the table. "We're not joining a militia. We don't believe in violence."

Jeremy laughed; a red mist fell to the carpet. "Next you'll say you believe in God. Time to grow up."

"Screw you."

"Take the gun, protect your wife and children. There are other groups out there, past the old highways. The Controllers leave them alone for the most part."

"We can't just leave without approval. They'll track us wherever we go."

Jeremy reached into his pocket and pulled out a small black case, opened it to show the steel instruments. "I'll take out your chips. Just no coming back."

The light bounced off the scalpel. "Is that woman even pregnant?" Justin said, "She could never pass for Emily."

"This place is wired to blow in one hour. There won't be enough left of her to say otherwise."

Justin held Emily close. "We haven't even discussed it."

"What's there to discuss? Mom and Dad raised you better than that," Jeremy said. "You'd never send your kid to the Way. How could you ever decide which one?"

"We have no idea what to do. She's due in two months."

"You figure it out as you go. That's all you can do. Head east and find the others. They'll help."

"We have to try," Emily said.

"That's right," Jeremy said. "Now go pack, one bag, maybe two, can't look like you're moving."

Jeremy waved Justin down then sat beside him. He took Justin's hand and laid it across his lap.

"Hold on," Justin said. "There isn't another body, is there?"

Jeremy held the scalpel to the light, not the slightest shake. "Just promise me one thing. Don't name your boy after me."

Six Hail Mary's

June 26, 2050

Terrance Potter, pastor of St. Luke's, shook the rain off his jacket and hung it on the sacristy coat rack. After running his hands through his wet, thinning hair, Father Potter dried them on a hand towel and entered the dimly lit church. He stood in the sanctuary and saw the building was empty, just as he'd expected on a weekday afternoon. The only problem was that the attendance for Sunday Masses fared only slightly better than the nonexistent congregation. And if the Way had anything to say about it, that number would be the same.

Father Potter headed down the main aisle, his footsteps echoing off the walls. As he came closer to the back door, Potter spotted the outline of an imposing figure standing in the shadows. He'd almost forgotten Wayne would be on duty, that the church was never empty.

When Potter reached the end of the aisle, he nodded at the big man, noting the bulge under Wayne's sport coat. Potter moved toward the confessional they had recently built against the eastern wall. He tried to think not of Wayne's weapon, but of the man's faith instead. Wayne had once been a trusted assistant to Reverend Murphy and now he watched over Potter's diminishing flock, the Way tattoo on his arm erased, a true sign he no longer believed their lies.

Potter entered his half of the wooden confessional and took his seat. If people like Wayne could see through the Way's propaganda, maybe there was hope. Maybe the false church's stranglehold on all other religions would loosen. Maybe the government would realize they shouldn't be working hand-in-hand, a supposedly mutual relationship that only aided the Way by giving them the financing and advertising that Potter and so many other churches truly needed. Probably not, though. Potter had faith, but he was also a realist and a mathematician. The numbers didn't lie.

While the soft patter of rain played on the roof, Potter waited. Confessions were down, but they often brought in some of the church's special visitors. And if he were able to help at least one of them, Potter would gladly sit all afternoon.

Thirty minutes had gone by before the door of the adjacent box opened. Potter waited in silence, wondering if he would recognize the penitent. He couldn't see through the mesh wall dividing the two halves. After thirty years of serving the church, he was very familiar with nearly all his parishioners, and didn't need to see them to know who was there.

The confessional door closed. The person on the other side of the wall chose to kneel instead of sitting. Potter took this as a sign that the person was giving themselves up, trying to get closer to him, and through him, to the Lord. But he also understood that sometimes people would do it so they wouldn't have to speak as loud and risk anyone overhearing their sins and learning their desires.

The soft, timid voice of a distraught man drifted through from the mesh wall. "Forgive me, Father, for I have sinned."

"How long has it been since your last confession?"

"Far too long."

"Any idea, my son, as to how many months it has been?"

"Not since my wife passed away. It's been seven years." After a brief pause, the man whispered, "The Controllers killed her."

Potter sat upright. He needed more information, but it was dangerous speaking about the government, even in a confessional. If the man had come for help, Potter couldn't turn him away.

Potter pretended he hadn't heard the criminal outburst, hoping the man would understand that it wasn't safe to speak so openly. "I'm sorry to hear that. Be comforted that she is now in a better place."

"Thank you, Father, but I came here because I have a sin to confess."

"I am listening."

"I have an eight-year-old daughter and a quadriplegic brother that I care for. They rely on me, but I am only one man and my job does not provide well."

"Go on."

"I'm becoming sick and don't know how much longer I can continue to work. I can't afford much of the uncontaminated food, so what little I do get, I give to my family."

"That is very thoughtful and brave of you. The Lord looks kindly on your sacrifice."

"I can't keep it up. I worry about what will happen to them if I die. I don't know what else to do. My sin is that I've had the desire to steal food. I'm tempted to break the law and go against the Controllers' restrictions. Please forgive me."

All doubt was removed from Potter's mind. This man was obviously new to the confessional. Whether he knew the correct procedure, he had come for help.

"I understand and, of course, God forgives you." Potter said the secret code, "For your penance, you must say six Hail Mary's."

"I understand."

"Now for the next few minutes, I want you to quietly reflect on your sin so you do not commit it again."

"I will."

Father Potter activated the recorder taped to the underside of the bench. His prerecorded voice said, "I want you to think about your sins and your resolve to never commit them again as we say these prayers. Please say the words with me." After a brief pause, the prerecorded Potter began reciting the Hail Mary with Wayne following along in the background.

When the first prayer neared its end, Father Potter pressed the small button beside the recorder. With a slight squeak that Wayne would have to fix, the mesh wall slid to the side allowing Potter to see the gratitude in the dying man's tear-filled eyes.

The tape continued rattling off the prayer. Potter held his finger to his lips and motioned for the man to follow him. Instead of exiting the door leading back into the church, Potter pushed open a secret door that led to the old rectory.

He placed his hand on the frail man's bony lower back and guided him into the dimly lit building. After quietly closing the door behind them, he whispered, "Continue straight ahead. We don't have much time."

As they hurried down the hallway, the man said, "Thank you so much, Father. I didn't know if the stories were true."

"In there." Potter pointed at the door to their left. "Inside."

The thin man entered the room which had once served as the priest's dining area. Each of the four walls was covered with stacks of canned foods. On top of the table in the middle of the room were boxes of powdered milk and bags of bread, and although the bread was over a week old, it was made from clean wheat.

The man's eyes went wide. "I've never seen so much food. Where does it come from?"

Potter wouldn't give away information that could only lead to trouble. "I have helpers. Grab a box from over there and fill it quickly. Take what you need, but remember there are others like you that come here."

"I understand." The man picked up a cardboard box and filled it with green beans, chili, corn, tuna, and beets. When he spotted the mandarin oranges and crushed pineapples, he gazed at Potter. "My Vanessa's never had fruit. She's going to be so happy."

Potter checked the time on his pager. "That's good, but hurry."

He piled a few more cans into the box. After placing a bottle of milk and two bags of bread on top of his supplies, the man said, "I'm Enrique Salazar. I will forever be thankful for this."

Potter moved into the hallway and headed for the door leading outside. He peeled back the curtain and stared past the bushes concealing the entrance. The rain had stopped.

"Which car is yours? I'll run out and put the box in your trunk." When Enrique didn't respond, Potter assured him it was all right. "No one will see."

"I have no car. Never got my license."

Potter didn't give in to the panic. "That's fine. I'll place the box outside the door two hours from now. Come back then. You'll want to transfer the food into a duffle bag or something less suspicious before you leave here."

Enrique checked his watch. "Two hours."

"And if you're caught, you didn't receive the food from here. Understand?"

"Completely."

"Okay, set it down right there." Potter's pager chimed.

"I haven't seen one of those in years."

Potter looked down the hallway. "It's attached to the confessional. When you first entered the confessional you locked the door behind you, didn't you?"

Enrique nodded.

The pager continued to chime. "You're sure?"

"I turned the switch just like they told me to."

Potter held up his finger to silence the man. He took a step toward the church and heard voices besides those on the tape. The Controllers were on to him. And they'd gotten past Wayne.

"Hurry," Potter said. He ran for the exit, unlocked the deadbolt and pushed the door open. Someone pounded on the confessional door behind them. "Take the box and run."

Enrique slipped out the door and squeezed through the bushes. Potter worried the man would be too weak to get away and went after him to help.

The hallway door went flying off its hinges. "Freeze right there," a voice barked from the confessional.

He'd known the day would come. Potter put up his hands in surrender, but then a black hovercar raced into the parking lot and dropped inches from Enrique, the bright red San Angeles Controlling Force decal blazing on the door. Before he knew what he was doing, Potter ran at the car, yelled at Enrique to move.

The driver's door opened and the agent stepped onto the wet asphalt. Potter flew by Enrique and flung his body against the car door, crushed the agent's calf and chest.

Enrique froze, stared at the crumpled agent. Potter yelled for him to run.

"Stop! Both of you!" The agent from the rectory and his partner struggled to get through the bushes, their black body armor snagging on the branches. "Stop!"

"Go! Go!" Potter screamed at Enrique who was finally on the move. He considered jumping into the Controllers' car and speeding off, but he knew he'd be electrocuted when the steering wheel didn't register his thumb prints.

The agents from inside emerged from the bushes. The taller one told his partner, "Get the runner."

The agent took off toward Enrique. Potter tackled him around his legs. As they hit the ground, sliding on the rain-slicked asphalt, Potter held tight knowing every second he kept this agent on the ground increased Enrique's chances of getting away.

The agent struck at Potter's face with the back of his fist, trying to break the priest's clench. He hit him again and again, but the only thing to break was Potter's nose.

While Potter struggled to keep the agent's legs pinned to the ground, the taller agent ran at him. Potter braced himself, but did not let go. Potter felt his ribs break when the agent kicked him the third time.

"Let him go!" The agent shouted over the hum of his electroprod. "Now!"

Potter accepted his fate and held on. The agent raised the electroprod and brought it down. Before it struck Potter, a loud blast ripped through the afternoon and the agent was knocked to the ground, his head shattered, the electroprod skipping across the asphalt.

"Go, Father!" Wayne pulled Potter off the agent. "Go."

Potter faced him. Wayne's left arm was gone, the proton particles from a Controller's gun eating away at his shoulder.

"Now, Father. I'll take care of them." Wayne pulled the pistol from his waistband, aimed at the agent Potter had tackled.

"Enough blood has been shed."

Wayne said to move. The agent by the hovercar fired a particle beam into the back of his head.

Potter watched as Wayne's head disappeared. He barely heard the hum of the electroprod before he felt its shock, his body convulsing as thousands of volts coursed through him.

The agent turned off the prod and pulled out a retractable baton that cops had carried years before. "Father Potter, you shouldn't have disobeyed. You left us no choice."

Potter found he could not speak. The shock had stunned his body and he couldn't move a muscle.

The agent looked at his dead partner then back at Potter. Potter could only stare at him as the agent extended his baton then brought it crashing down onto Potter's upper arm again and again. The agent continued to strike the arm after it was already shattered. It wasn't long before the other agent joined in and began pulverizing Potter's legs.

As the baton blows continued to rain upon him, Potter prayed through the pain, praised the Lord's name. It didn't matter that his operation was destroyed and his life sentenced to prison. And even though Wayne and an agent had died, an innocent man had escaped. God worked in mysterious ways. Potter forced himself to believe that God had plans for Enrique, that the man would do great things. All it took to change the world was one man. As another bone snapped, Potter hoped with all his heart it was Enrique.

Twenty-Four Hour Bullshit

November 1, 2052

Kent Hollister took his place behind the news desk and looked over the revised script. He'd only seen the originals for a few seconds, but he recalled every pre-redacted word—one of the perks of being Unlocked. Three months ago, when Kent and his son, Kaiden, got the implants to become Connected, they elected for the surgery to free up an extra twenty percent of their brains. They thought it'd make life easier, but they were wrong. The revised report said enemy combatants stockpiling chemical weapons were terminated, no longer any mention of the children murdered for hoarding unauthorized food supplies.

The floating auto-stylist tried to powder Kent's forehead, but he swiped it away. The whirring mechanical bot wobbled and nearly collided with his co-anchor's auto-stylist. But Candice Northridge didn't flinch. Her baby blue eyes opened wide as the little mechanical arm applied mascara.

"Okay, let me see," she said. The auto-stylist rose up toward the lights so Candice could see her bright, sparkling face on the transparency. Her lips stretched into that trademark smile, a cheetah ready to pounce and devour.

Kent kept reading, shook his head with disgust. "Have you seen Bernie?"

Candice kept her smile, talked through her teeth. "Unh-unh."

A young guy in a silver suit came out of the control booth. The suit hung off him like he'd borrowed it from an older brother. The facial recognition software gave Kent four lines of info on the new program director. His name was Egan Tolbert, a Disciple in the Way even though he was only twenty-two years old.

"Where the hell's Bernie?" Kent asked.

"Gone."

"What do you mean *gone*? He was just here."

Egan shrugged. "Everyone's replaceable, right?"

Kent looked over at the exit door, and Egan grabbed the papers off the desk. Kent reached out.

Egan shook his head. "These are old. The new version's downloading."

That meant having to get it through the Connect, something he hadn't done in a long time. He only trusted his memory. "I need to see the pages."

Egan's eyes went cold. "Too fucking bad. We're rolling in one minute." Egan turned to Candice, his eyes soft and flirty. "Have a great show."

Candice powered down her stylist. "Count on it."

Egan headed for the booth, and Kent swiped one of Candice's hairs off the desk. No one spoke to Kent like that, at least not until the Way started showing up at the station. They'd purchased the network six months before. The news division was told the Way preferred a hands off managerial approach, but that proved to be just as manufactured as their recent news reports. Still, Kent believed he had a duty, that his voice still mattered. Seven nights a week, he entered every suite inside the Blocks and over half of the private residences across the country. If he stopped reporting the news, any hope for the truth would die.

The line producer's voice came across the intercom and told everyone they had thirty seconds. Candice gently squeezed Kent's thigh. He kept his eyes on the camera, but shifted in his chair. She loved to pull this shit just before air. He'd warned her to stop, but she liked watching him squirm. Becky had already threatened to leave him. One more slipup would send her out the door, and he'd lose Kaiden forever.

Kent closed his eyes to intensify the Connection and cut distractions. He used the focusing techniques Kaiden had taught him and located the reports, committed them to memory.

Egan's voice replaced the line producer's and started the countdown. Kent's eyes snapped open and he gave his practiced nod. Candice moved just enough to make her breasts sway. Together they greeted America.

The top story had been swapped out for a report on tainted drugs coming in from Mexico. An unidentified study linked the side effects to increased outbreaks and the rise in mental illness.

Kent's mind flashed back to the last dozen unidentified studies he'd mentioned in the past few months, each one claiming to explain the disease. He wondered how many people at home remembered what he'd told them just last week.

Candice pointed at the camera and said, "So just remember, get caught with any drug and you'll be sent straight to prison." The camera zoomed in on her full lips. "And that goes for you kids too."

"Great advice," Kent said. He delivered the revised report on the kid massacre word for word. His chest felt hot. Sweat beads trickled down the back of his shirt, but he pressed through.

Candice said, "Now here's a heartwarming story of a young man and a dog."

The image on the screen didn't match her words. A smoldering crater, that'd once been Signal Hill, filled the screen. At first Kent thought someone had screwed up, but Candice said, "I'm sure all of you remember this terrible event, the atrocious act of domestic terrorists." A chubby teenager's face appeared on screen. "Gregory Weedle, a True Resident for Peace in Block 3187 sure did. Early this morning, his quick, decisive actions, stopped a terror plot and saved a dog from being killed."

The camera zoomed out to reveal the trembling Chihuahua in Gregory's arms, its tiny little paws scratching at his chest. There were four piles of clothes behind Gregory on the sidewalk.

Candice continued. "What was the plot? How many people were targeted? Scary questions, scary answers." She turned to Camera 2. "Later, reporter Trisha Yorling will take a closer look at using the Connect. She'll talk about a growing call for a kill switch, and she'll teach you and your family the skills to keep you safe."

Seeing Camera 3's red light flash, Kent smiled and said just how right she was. "And now for the second installment of our six part series, where we give you an inside look into the Way Camps, witness these young citizens inspire us all by caring for society's unwanted. Tonight, we're taking you into one of the forty elderly units across this country."

The video showed boys in red uniforms helping older residents into black and red vans. "Every day, these boys take men and women, many of them grandparents, around the city for last goodbyes, sometimes even stopping at the memory bank for downloading in case their relatives can one day buy them a new body."

An old, wrinkled man stood by the back doors of the DMV. His face filled the screen. "Both my children are still alive. They got good years left," he said. "I've done all the gallivanting I need. I just want them to be happy. Isn't that what a parent is supposed to do?" After a few seconds, the man slowly entered the DMV.

Candice wiped away a tear and said, "Now…that's a good father." She was supposed to transition into the story on sterilization, but she leaned to the side. The tear had caused the mascara to run into her eye. Kent took over. He spoke about the new poll, which showed the majority of people were for lowering age requirements, even though he'd never met a single person who would be.

Candice pulled herself together and relayed the new round of home scale waivers. "There's no guarantee how long they'll be offered, so officials are recommending the ten-year certificates."

This went on for another thirty minutes. There were warnings of contaminated food and tips to make the world a safer place. The second the red lights blinked off, Kent stood up, told Candice to have a good night, and hurried over to the elevator before she had a chance to tell him about whatever trendy restaurant she was dying to try.

"Mr. Hollister. I need to see you for a second." It was Egan, followed by a leggy blond in a tight blue skirt. Her name was Shawna, all other details hidden. Someone with money was clearly paying for her privacy.

"I just wanted to say, great show," Egan said. He offered his hand. "And how glad I am to be working with you."

Kent pressed the up button and said, "Yeah, likewise."

"No, really," Egan said. He casually dropped his hand. "I'm sorry about earlier. The tension of my first show, new rules, all that good stuff."

"Not a problem," Kent said. "I've been in the business a while. Seen plenty of suits trying to make their mark. Just try not to cause the crew to revolt." The elevator opened and Kent stepped inside. "I'll see you guys tomorrow." He pressed the button, but Egan threw out his hand and helped Shawna inside. "Actually, Shawna will be flying with you tonight. She can help you get accustomed to your new Connect protocols."

Kent said it wasn't necessary. "I think I can figure it out."

"It's not a request." Egan had Shawna step in. The smell of her filled the elevator, peaches, breath mints and the faintest hint of sweat. He was glad the studio was only ten floors.

They'd just reached the top when Shawna said, "I thought you looked great as usual."

"That's very kind, but you might want to reserve the chance to recant once we step into the sunlight."

Shawna smiled and lightly touched his arm. Why the hell was he flirting? The door opened and Kent jogged across the rooftop, slipped into the luxury helicopter and out of the foul air. He took his usual seat on the plush leather recliner and pushed the button to slide open all eight cabin windows. Each view was the same, black solar panels of the massive Inner Blocks on either side.

Shawna took the seat across from him and crossed her legs, nearly every inch exposed.

Kent closed his eyes, threw himself into the Connect—images and videos, a full history of the Inner Blocks.

The helicopter rose and he turned toward a massive steel structure that was built to withstand a ballistic missile attack. Shawna said, "Mr. Hollister." Her finger was on the window button. "You don't want to look at that."

"I prefer them open." They continued up and over the Block, all of San Angeles spread out below. What fascinated Kent was the hundred-foot tall tide wall that ran the entire coast.

Numbers began flashing in Kent's mind. The ocean level had apparently risen ten feet in the last month. Kent recalled the stack of papers he'd seen in Bernie's office. He'd only caught a few lines, but they were about rising ocean levels. There was a mention of the tide wall, a scenario where it could be breached.

Kent suddenly felt cold. It was like his scalp was turning to ice. It spread from the back of his skull toward his eyes, which he couldn't seem to open.

"You shouldn't be poking, Mr. Hollister." The woman's voice was soft and soothing. Kent could make out a woman dressed in all white. It was Jeneal, his Connection assistant, in her sexy, librarian glasses, her body like Becky's before she had Kaiden.

Jeneal suggested an array of posts and pictures, proof the wall was perfectly safe. She asked, "Would you like me to show you?"

Kent was in Bernie's office. He saw the paperwork on the desk. Bernie was on the phone shouting. He was angry and a little frightened. Kent stepped toward the papers, saw the line about rising sea levels, but suddenly the letters began to jumble and bleed, spilling off the pages and onto the carpet.

He tried to practice the focusing techniques Kaiden had taught him. Breathe. Zero in.

A new voice came through. "Just relax, Mr. Hollister." Something caressed his head. "It's just the new protocol system."

Kent tried to open his eyes again. Light exploded, but he knew his lids were still shut. He was in a Tahitian bungalow and Shawna was sprawled on the white silk sheets. He started walking forward but stopped, knowing his feet were still on the ground, not moving. It wasn't real.

"You need to relax," Shawna said. "It doesn't have to be painful. It can actually be rather pleasurable. All you have to do is let go."

Kent knew what it could be like. He'd gone there with Candice before she became co-anchor, the most intimate encounter he'd ever had, better than sex without all the mess. It's what sent Becky wailing into the night. Kent looked everywhere, but it was his boss, Bernie, who found her in the Blocks. She'd gotten Connected. Bernie brought her home.

"It's okay to want this," Shawna said. She ran her hand over the sheets beckoning him to sit. He found himself moving closer, unable to resist. Her fingers slid up his chest to his face, her thumbs finally resting on his eyes.

A flash of awareness. She wasn't seducing him. She was probing for information. The papers he'd seen in Bernie's office had been backed up in his mind. Kent focused on the firewalls Kaiden had installed. He walled off the last meeting with Bernie and wondered exactly what his old boss had uncovered.

"That's what we're going to find out," Shawna whispered. It echoed in his mind. She was heading for the firewall, a sizzling current racing through his head. It was getting brighter. And just as Shawna started to peel away at the fiber optics, an electric pulse fired in his mind.

He opened his eyes and broke the Connection. Shawna was slumped back in her seat, her eyes closed. He started to inch forward, wondering if she was dead. But her eyelids fluttered open. She looked out the window like she was lost. "How'd…we…"

"Are you okay?" Kent asked. He looked over at the bar. There was a particle gun hidden under the cabinet. "Do you need something to drink? I can make one."

Kent started to rise, but Shawna grabbed his wrist. "No, I'm fine. I…" She shook her head. "I have to implement the new protocols."

The last ten minutes or so had been wiped from her banks.

"You already did," Kent said. "Are you sure you're alright?"

"Yeah, I'm...sorry." She pulled out a scanner. It showed the protocols had been successfully uploaded.

They were getting close to the foothills, the air cleaner, blue skies streaked with white trails. Shawna left the cabin and didn't come back. Kent got off the helicopter the second it landed and hurried to the pickup parking. The network paid for the hovercar and driver. Domenico rarely spoke and had his info sealed, the gun at his side meaning either off-duty Controller or the Way.

Kent switched on his internal music, made sure it was loud enough to drown out any rogue thoughts. It took five minutes to enter the gated community, another two to reach the summit of the hills, where Kent's house was the envy of every neighbor. The front door was unlocked, which meant Kaiden was home. Kent shut the door harder than he needed to then set the alarm.

Kaiden was in the kitchen getting a drink. Kent threw his wallet on the kitchen counter and saw Becky on the couch. Kaiden disappeared down the hallway. Kent grabbed the whiskey and filled a glass, didn't bother with the ice.

When he looked up, Becky was standing in the doorway. Her eyes were puffy and wet. Kent asked what was wrong, but she just stared right through him. He called her name and snapped his fingers. "Goddamn it! Turn that off."

Becky finally disconnected and blinked away the tears. "Bernie's dead."

Three Sacred Truths

August 12, 2053

The sun beat down on Kaiden Hollister's back, the hundred-plus heat absorbed by the black. Pants, shoes, shirt. That's what all the Initiates wore. No hats.

It was all boys on the sorting line, four staggered on each side, Kaiden at the end. They'd been up there since seven, had only come down for a five-minute lunch. Kaiden didn't know how much more he could take. The smell of curdled milk and runny shit seeped through the toilet paper stuffed in his nose. His mouth was a parched hole sucking in air, trying not to taste it.

The trash was bunched up at the start of the conveyor. Kaiden glanced over the edge, into the mouth of the compactor below. He wondered what Fielding felt those last few seconds.

The sun bounced off a piece of glass and Kaiden went back to his game, his right hand a black hawk swooping in and grabbing the shard, dropping it down the green hole. Kaiden shook the double-vision, picked off one piece then another. The top of a tin can burnt the left hawk's beak. The right hawk scooped it up and saved the day, circled back to snatch the scrap of aluminum before it disappeared over the edge.

Time went by dreadfully slow. Kaiden never had any idea when it was. He didn't know the temperature. The pollutant count. He didn't know anything. It didn't matter that he was Connected. The source had been turned off inside the fenced-in main portion of the Camp.

It'd only been a month since the Controllers' late night visit. It seemed like a year. The first week at the Camp had been recovery, simply surviving the vaccines. The last three weeks, Kaiden worked his way up the sorting line, waiting for the day they were going to tell him they knew he was just as guilty as his parents.

The pieces of trash were slowing down, further apart. His hawks perched on the ledge, the layer of filth allowing them to withstand the sizzling metal.

The last bit of garbage dropped into the compactor. Kaiden raised his right hand and spoke as loud as he could, his lips cracking. "Elder Mason. All finished."

A whistle blew and the conveyor stopped. Kaiden turned around and sat on the walkway, his back to the line.

Like all Elders, Mason wore red, boots to cap. The seventeen-year-old got up from the folding chair and left the shade, headed over with the tray of tin cups. Like most Elders, Mason was predictable, starting where he always did, down with the little ones.

Kaiden bunched the top of his drenched shirt into his mouth and sucked out the sweat while he reached into his pocket and pulled out three peanuts, a bruised grape, and a bit of burnt meatloaf. He stuffed it into his mouth, two chews, one swallow. Not enough to survive on, but less of the Camp food he'd have to eat. He'd already lost fourteen pounds and couldn't afford too much more before they started asking questions.

There wasn't much to be seen inside the electrified fences. Mountains of trash to the left, concrete-encased trash bales piled on the right. On the other side of the fence were three towers, Elders in red with plasma rifles so there was nothing to fear. The Preacher watching over his flock, ready to eradicate.

Kaiden went back to the concrete blocks and wondered which one Fielding was in, if maybe he'd already been picked up and dumped to the bottom of the sea as foundation for another island.

Mason slapped Kaiden's leg with the back of his hand and told him to grab the tin.

The others were sipping their water. Nelson, the bony sixteen-year-old beside him, could barely hold the cup to his lips. When Mason walked around the line, Kaiden filled his mouth and swished it around.

The water was one of the sweetest things Kaiden had ever tasted, but he didn't swallow a drop. He put his shirt to his lips and let the water run down his front, blend with the sweat. Even if Bradford hadn't warned him about the dangers, Kaiden knew better. He saw the blank look on the long timers, how they moved so slowly.

Most of the Initiates came from the masses, the rest with Health Index scores too low to be wanted. They'd been in the Camp their whole lives. It was all they knew, nothing of the outside.

But that wasn't the only thing that made Kaiden smarter. His parents had thought it'd be a good thing to do and allowed the surgery that unlocked a portion of his brain, made his memory a trap. He knew too much, but had to pretend like he didn't, too goddamn smart for his own good.

And now he was sitting in filth with no idea how many more days he could make it. All because of a girl.

If she hadn't joined his quest and rescued him from the orc ambush, Kaiden wouldn't have paid her any attention. But she did save him, looking hot as hell in her dragonskin bikini, her dripping short sword. She whispered she liked to get close and told Kaiden to follow her. It'd be fun.

Kaiden was Connected at a coffee shop with no restrictions. He said why not and locked on to her, went along for the ride.

Her face stayed in front of his as she took him through a dozen doors, site after site after site. The scenes became more peaceful then slowly went dark.

The light crept back, layers of orc slayer melted away and the girl's true face appeared, nothing special, her eyes a dead glaze. The camera panned out, her face slack while some guy pumped in and out between her legs. "Can you hear me?" she asked without moving her mouth. "You like this?"

Kaiden couldn't look away from her eyes. He didn't know the words for what he felt.

"Come on and stay," she said. "Twenty dollars a minute."

There were two other teenage couples on the couch, one on the floor, pushing and pulling, oil rigs up and down.

Something hit Kaiden's leg, knocked him out of the memory. It was Nelson struggling to his feet. He said, "It's time."

Mason pressed a button and dumped the trash bin, Unit 7 painted across the side, a reminder they better be thorough. Most of the trash was picked off before it got to Kaiden, little scraps here and there flicked into the holes.

Kaiden's mind drifted off, back to the girl who didn't want to be there. He'd asked her why she did it, where she was at. His family had money, maybe he could help her.

The girl gave in and took Kaiden's hands, her face back to the slayer's. The first scene was a giant lodge, people picnicking on the lawn. The second was a glimpse of a chapel, the Way's cross cutting through the clouds. The last was an unmarked building, white walls, no windows. She took Kaiden inside, showed him things no one should see. Her sister was in there with an abomination growing in her womb.

Like she'd been on a string, the girl went flying back to the couch, her eyes still glazed, but popping out. Her face purple with the guy's forearm crushing her throat.

The guy was well above the weight limit, muscles too big for his body, short spiky hair visible when he spun to the camera and told Kaiden, "I know you're there."

The conveyor kept rolling and there it was, a fleck of yellow amidst the grime. Kaiden's hand shot down and broke off the pencil's tip, buried the lead behind his dirt-filled fingernail. He held up his hand and called for Mason.

The whistle blew and everything stopped. The metal walkway dug into Kaiden's knees when he got down and placed the pencil inside Mason's glass container.

Mason told Kaiden good job and returned to his shade, sipped the water from his pack. "The rest of you give me twenty."

The walkway shook as everyone but Kaiden fell to their chests and got back up, counted each time. When they got back to their spots, Nelson started wheezing, his sunburnt skin the whitest it'd been.

Kaiden concentrated on the trash, his hawks moving faster because Nelson was just standing there, hands by his sides. Nelson's eyes rolled back and he fell face first onto the conveyor.

Both boys were going into the compactor unless Kaiden did something. With one foot braced against the railing and the other on the machine, Kaiden lifted Nelson off the conveyor and stood him back in his spot.

Mason yelled for everyone to get back to work, but Nelson was back to being a zombie, shit dripping off his face.

"Come on, man," Kaiden said. "You okay?"

Nelson glared at Kaiden and nodded. Then he took two steps back and flipped over the rail, landed with a loud crunch. He was looking up, but not at Kaiden, the angle of his neck all wrong.

Mason didn't move from his chair. "Hollister. Check him."

Kaiden lowered himself over the edge and dropped to the concrete, picked up Nelson's wrist. "His pulse is weak. Maybe a broken neck."

Mason nodded and radioed the infirmary. "One headed your way from RC." He pointed at Engle, a seventeen year-old slob with clumpy brown hair. "Help carry him. Head back to your units when you're done."

Kaiden got his arm under Nelson's neck, saw right away it wouldn't stay straight. Engle used the ladder at the front of the line, took his time walking over.

Kaiden lifted his end, couldn't believe Nelson was so heavy. "Let's go, he's all jacked up."

Engle brought up the legs, held them so Kaiden carried most the weight. "He shouldn't have fell."

Kaiden figured he'd walk faster backward than Engle would forward. He led them out of the recycling yard and into the hallway, toward the rest of the main campus.

Even though Kaiden's grip was slipping, it was Engle who stopped, dropped Nelson's legs the second they were out of Mason's sight. "Go ahead, superhero," Engle said. "Fly him to the rescue."

Kaiden kept his voice down, afraid the hallway would echo. "Pick him up. He's dying."

Engle shook out his arms and black flakes floated to the floor. "You seen his eyes. It's what he wanted."

"His heart's beating. Don't do this." Kaiden didn't think before he said, "I'll yell."

Engle stood there, crossed his arms. "You would, wouldn't you?"

Kaiden said to hell with it and hauled Nelson higher on his chest, secured his grip and dragged him backward. "What if it was you?"

The infirmary wasn't that far. Kaiden hoped he could do it on his own or at least get to where the towers could see him if he fell out. Not that they'd do much besides radio Mason so he could order someone to help Engle.

Engle stood still, his eyes darting around nervously as Kaiden came close to stepping from the shadows.

"Hold on," Engle said. He caught up with Kaiden and scooped up Nelson's legs, held them so no one could move. "You gotta slow down."

Kaiden nodded and headed out of the shadows, the sun shining bright. The Elder in the east tower was turned their way.

The concrete campus looked deserted. Everyone was still at work. They turned at the back of housing Unit Five and took the path between it and Six. The units were long, sixty rooms per wing. Three and Four were next, One and Two right past them.

They began the last stretch, passing the building where sterilized girls made uniforms, helmets, ammo belts and armor. At the end of the path was a wall of green, the open gate just big enough for a golf cart. An Elder in red stood on the other side.

Kaiden's arms were on fire, both boys in danger of toppling over. Nelson's heart thudded. "We're almost there," Kaiden said.

An Initiate Kaiden had never seen headed to the units. The grease on his arms and face appeared as black as his shirt. The boy barely moved out of the way.

When they were close enough to the gate, Kaiden shouted, "One from RC to Infirmary."

The brown-skinned Elder said to hold on. He finished patting down another Initiate and pushed him through the gate. One look at Nelson and the Elder pointed up the road. "Better hurry."

They walked past the Initiates lined against the ivy fence, not one of them offering to help. The road continued another hundred yards, the canines housed way down at the end. All along the left ran the two-story windowless building, its slick white wall impossible to climb.

That was the building no one talked about. Kaiden knew what was in there. After the girl had given him the glimpse, he went digging, found files he never should've seen. It was where all the unsterilized girls were assigned. The building Kaiden told his dad about, the real start of this nightmare.

They passed the last Initiate and came to the tunnel between the lab and the infirmary. Kaiden slowed to fix his grip, felt the soft pull of his Connection come to life.

On the other side of the tunnel was a street like he had back home, green grass around the picnic tables. To the right was the gym Kaiden had only heard about, the male Elders' complex, the pool beside it. The female complex sat across the street, the orc slayer's lodge a short path away. Straight ahead lay the chapel and a glorious mansion, only the best for the Anointed.

There was a door halfway down the tunnel. Kaiden jerked his head at it and said, "It's closer."

Engle asked if he was stupid, nodded at the faint blue light buzzing across the top of the tunnel.

The infirmary's front door opened and a voice called the boys over. The young man's red uniform had seven silver stripes on his shoulder, one for each year as an Elder.

The cold air gave Kaiden the last burst of energy, got him past the row of monitors, the empty sick bays. A one-way mirror ran along the other wall, a glimpse into the fish tank, puny kids huddled up in blankets, fighting the vaccines. Most wouldn't make it.

Four young men in white coats waited around the steel table. They looked too young to be doctors, but Kaiden knew if they were Connected, had the will, determination, and extra brain capacity, they could learn anything. Kaiden hoped it would be enough as they heaved Nelson onto the table.

The doctor in charge put two fingers to Nelson's throat and flopped his head to the other side. "Good job, boys." He told the Elder to start up the birds.

The Elder put one hand on Kaiden's back, the other on Engle's, and guided them to the water cooler. "Grab a drink and close the gate on your way out."

Kaiden followed Engle, waited patiently for his turn, jumped at the whopping thump-thump-thump coming from the other side of the wall.

The Elder sat in front of a large screen which showed a row of miniature black helicopters. He opened up a black journal and said, "Ready."

The doctors had slipped on plastic covers, strapped down each of Nelson's limbs. One scanned the right wrist and said, "Peter Nelson. Number 470302."

The Elder said copy and wrote in the journal. Something clicked to Kaiden's right. Engle stood on the other side of the closed gate, middle fingers raised.

The buzz of the saw drowned out the choppers. The whine got wet as the blade tore through skin, ate at bone.

One doctor held open a bucket, wisps of dry ice flowing over the sides. The other removed the heart and set it inside. He checked the clock and called time of death.

Another box, another organ. Six altogether before the doctors ran them outside, loaded them in the helicopters.

Kaiden shook the gate and tried to keep his voice calm. "I got locked in."

The Elder called him an idiot and pressed a button, clicked open the gate. When he got outside, Engle was gone with the rest of the Initiates. It was just the Elder sitting on his folding chair, enjoying the shade of his umbrella.

Kaiden stopped for his pat down. "One Infirmary to Unit 6."

He didn't bother getting up, just nodded at Kaiden. "I've heard good things. Keep it up."

Kaiden trudged down the path, thought about the water he'd forgotten, the ragged buzz he never would. He checked in at Unit 6's front desk, He waited for Elder Dawkins to unlock the wing and slide open the door to his room.

The room was a quarter the size of the room Kaiden had back home, just enough space for the steel bunk bed, toilet-sink, and the two-drawer dresser. Bradford was in black shorts and a T-shirt, down on the bottom bunk. The fourteen-year-old worked the culinary, knew what was safe and what was not. He asked if Kaiden was okay.

Kaiden said he was and nodded at the toilet.

Bradford went to the door and got on his tiptoes to block the window.

Kaiden took a sock from his drawer and sat on the toilet, bent over in case the overhead camera was on. He dangled the sock into the half inch of water over the trap and put the sock to his lips, then sucked down the water.

When he had enough, Kaiden sat on the bunk and Bradford took a piss, the only way to make the toilet flush and refill. He sat down next to Kaiden and slid him a rolled up slice of meat.

It was gone in two gulps. Kaiden remembered the lead and dug it out of his fingernail, handed it over.

Bradford didn't smile much. Twelve years with the Way, his billionaire mother dead, the inheritance gone just like that. But he smiled at the lead.

Kaiden felt a little better with the water and got up to block the window. Bradford ducked beneath the bunk, started sketching on the metal. Kaiden couldn't see it, but knew it was Bradford's mother: the gentle strokes, the slow blink, the softness of his cheek.

The wing door opened and heels clicked. Kaiden threw Bradford the damp sock and their door opened. Kaiden peeked out and saw a spiky haired Disciple in a silver suit, an Anointed in white behind him.

The muscle-bound Disciple hurried down the hall and got in Kaiden's face, no question he was a killer. "Hollister, Kaiden. Step back to the wall."

Kaiden considered going for the Disciple's plasma pistol. He backed up until his hands touched the warm cement.

The Disciple ordered Bradford to wait outside. He followed him out of the room.

The Anointed came in with his white cloak, a black scarf striped silver and red draped over his shoulders. He said his name was Portelson and told Kaiden to have a seat.

Kaiden did what he said, but was thinking of Lafferty, the Anointed that had awakened Kaiden with a tap on the shoulder. Told him everything was going to be okay a split second before the gunfire. He said Kaiden didn't have to worry, his parents would never hurt him again.

Portelson moved in front of Kaiden, his sparkling white hands clasped in front of his cloak, the faintest hint of flowers. "You've been brought to our attention."

Kaiden waited for the verdict.

"Truth is, they think you're a little old to be sorting through rubbish. You're smarter than that."

It sounded like a trap so Kaiden just nodded.

"Would you agree?"

"I believe I can do whatever is asked of me."

Portelson laid his hand on Kaiden's shoulder. "You can walk the path of the Way? Answer the questions truthfully?"

If Kaiden turned them down, they wouldn't come back. His voice cracked when he said, "I can."

Portelson brought forth a white ribbon, laid it on the dresser. "Get cleaned up." On his way out the door, he said, "Report to the tunnel in fifteen minutes."

Bradford returned and the door slid shut behind him. He pointed at the ribbon, sat down next to Kaiden and whispered, "You think you're ready?"

"The Preacher is ruler above all else. I believe that with all my heart."

Bradford looked like he might cry.

"What he does for us, for all the unwanted. Just think about it." Kaiden took off his clothes and threw them down the chute. He said the words so he could believe them. "The Preacher is willing to sacrifice all to make this world a better place."

Bradford wished him good luck and Kaiden said the same.

Elder Dawkins buzzed Kaiden through for the minute-long sand blast of a shower, which made his skin red and raw. By the time Kaiden was dressed and out the front door, the campus was back to being deserted, everyone tucked away in their rooms waiting for dinner.

The sun had dropped enough that the walk to the front gate wasn't so bad, each step an echo of the Preacher's triumphs. There were four female and three male Initiates lined up by the tunnel. Kaiden took his place at the back of the line and blocked out the nervous whispers. The source felt more powerful, the Connection stronger with each step.

The kid in front of Kaiden told him to watch out. Kaiden backed off him and said sorry, ran through his prayers, and praised the Preacher. He noticed the tall brunette at the front of the line, the white ribbon clutched in her hand. The way she leaned forward, she had to be Connected.

She was staring at the patch of grass at the other end of the tunnel. She was in there somewhere, just a matter of searching. Inside the virtual world, Kaiden called out the number on the back of her dress until they Connected, told her to hold on as he led her down to the blade, to the dirt, life itself.

When it was just the two of them, she asked if Kaiden was ready for the tunnel. He said he hoped so and wished her luck.

Everyone stood at attention, ruined the weak Connection. A black jeep with two Disciples parked at the end of the tunnel. The Disciple from earlier strode down the tunnel, the blue light dancing off his silver suit. Halfway down, he banged on the door. By the time he got to the Initiates, the sound of whirling blades filled the air.

The Disciple loved his job, the gleam in his eye undeniable. "Okay, boys and girls." He smiled and said, "This is it."

Kaiden took a breath and blew it out, asked himself what the hell he was doing.

"Ladies first," the Disciple said. "One line across."

They did as instructed and stood at the edge of the tunnel, holding hands.

"Come forth and answer these questions," the Disciple said. "Does the Preacher speak the word of the Lord, he's the voice of God that can't be questioned?"

The girls entered the tunnel, their professed love and devotion echoing off the wall. Three steps in, the rail-thin blond on the right gave one twitch then fell to the floor.

The Disciple walked backward without a pause. "Is the Preacher the Chosen One, the ruler above all else?"

A resounding yes filled the tunnel, all three girls continuing forward.

The Disciple approached the far side. "Will you forever follow the Way, offer your body, your blood, your soul?"

The short girl on the right convulsed for a second, dropped with a thud. The infirmary door opened and doctors dragged her and the blond inside, the door closing behind them just as the last two girls reached the end of the tunnel. The Disciple in the jeep waved the brunette to get in the back. A live-in for a Disciple, the best job she could hope for.

The Disciple waved the boys forward. It was time to speak the truth. Kaiden walked inside, blue lights above. He would not disobey. The Preacher was his master.

Seven to Go

August 31, 2054

Robert Edgefield sank into the wheelchair and gathered his coat. He hated being pushed around by others, but he no longer had the strength to do it himself. His older brother, Troy, never complained about his new role as caregiver, but Robert felt nothing but humiliation, especially as they entered the air-conditioned lobby of the animal hospital. The two remaining employees were just about to lock up. They barely glanced in Robert's direction. There was only one reason anyone showed up here without a pet.

Dr. Cooper appeared in the doorway and held up his bloody gloves. "I'll be ready in a minute. I just need to clean up." Dr. Cooper forced a smile before disappearing into the back, leaving the two brothers alone in the room.

"You sure about this?" Troy asked.

"Where else am I going to go?"

Troy wheeled Robert by a plant and took a seat on one of the red plastic chairs. While Troy flipped through a magazine, Robert stared at a poster of a kitten pawing into a goldfish bowl.

Troy's nostril whistle was only adding to Robert's stress, so he told him to go drive around, that he'd call when he was ready to be picked up. Troy just kept reading his article. Robert didn't push it. Troy had finally stopped trying to pay for Robert to see a real doctor.

Robert hated himself for bringing his brother into this mess, but there was no one else he could trust.

Dr. Cooper strolled into the waiting room and quickly shut the blinds. "Sorry about the wait, Mr. Edgefield."

"Oh, no worries."

Dr. Cooper asked if he was ready, and Robert nodded. He hadn't eaten in days and Robert found it increasingly difficult to carry on conversations.

Troy started to stand, but Robert waved him off, said he was fine. Dr. Cooper let Troy know they'd be about an hour then gripped the handles and wheeled Robert past the receptionist's desk. When they entered the hallway, a wave of delicious smells filled Robert's nose. A hint of mesquite and the hearty aroma of steak. It was coming from the bags of dog food lining the wall, but it didn't stop him from salivating. If he had more energy he would've torn open a fifty-pound sack and poured the entire thing down his throat, consequences be damned.

But Robert quickly came to his senses. He was fortunate, blessed with a beautiful child, and he wouldn't risk her safety. Teresa, his adoring wife, had already been taken by the Controllers, another number chalked up to the goddamn Reduction Act. If it came down to it, Robert swore he'd never eat another bite. He prayed it wouldn't come to that. There was talk legislation might be passed to loosen the requirements. But even if the lawmakers actually pulled it off, Robert knew it wouldn't happen before tomorrow at three o'clock.

As they neared the swinging double-doors, a huge cockroach scurried out from under a bag of dog food. Robert thought how lucky the little bastard was, able to eat whatever it wanted, right before the wheel of his chair crushed it. But even then, he couldn't help envying its quick death.

They passed through the swinging doors and entered the main kennel. Dr. Cooper stopped the wheelchair in front of the floor scale they used for large breed dogs. "Do you need me to help you get undressed, Robert?"

Robert wanted to say he was a grown man, to leave him the hell alone, but he didn't have the strength to pull himself out of the wheelchair, let alone unbutton his shirt and pants. When Robert nodded, Dr. Cooper helped him out of the chair and had Robert lean against the wall for support.

As soon as Dr. Cooper removed Robert's jacket, Robert began to shiver. By the time his pants and long-sleeve shirt were on the floor, Robert couldn't stop his teeth from chattering.

"Jesus," the doctor gasped.

Robert laughed. "I'm just getting ready for my modeling career." His bones looked like they were trying to carve through his skin. Robert slid his hand over his sunken stomach.

"I'm sorry. I just…I'm sorry." The doctor helped Robert step onto the scale. After a second, Dr. Cooper said, "That can't be right. Scoot over here a second while I check it."

Robert sighed. "Don't bother. It's right. Same as I was at home."

The doctor looked up at Robert. "I don't understand. Last year you made weight and you weren't nearly this thin."

Robert motioned for the doctor to help him back in the wheelchair and cover him with his coat. "Yeah, well, that was before June." That's when the Controllers dropped the weight requirement another ten pounds.

"Right, right," Dr. Cooper said, as if he wasn't well aware of this. "Seven pounds is a lot though, Robert. You sure you're up for it?"

"Does it matter?"

"Yeah, I need to hear you say it."

Robert pulled a thick envelope from his coat pocket. "Here's your answer."

The doctor took the envelope. "You know what they'd do to me for this."

"I know. I'm sorry. I thought they were going to pass the height exemption."

Dr. Cooper fingered through the hundred dollar bills. He slapped the envelope against his palm and asked Robert one last time if he was sure.

"I have a three-year-old. Just do it."

"Okay, well…you know your brother is going to have to take care of you for a few weeks. Is that going to be a problem?"

"It'll be fine."

"Is he still at the prison?"

"Yeah."

"Because you need—"

Robert cut him off. "I have it covered, and if you can't get on with this, I doubt my brother will have a problem reporting your little operation."

Dr. Cooper clenched his jaw then wheeled Robert over to a steel table. He helped Robert up, laid him face down with his shoulders and head hanging over the edge. Dr. Cooper rolled over a surgical tray stand for Robert to rest his head on.

Shaking from the cold, Robert asked, "Any way you could turn off that AC?"

"Sure." He hit a switch on the wall and picked up a syringe from the counter. "But after this, you won't be feeling a thing." He flicked the syringe. "Ready?"

Robert felt his throat close, simply nodded. The doctor plunged the needle into Robert's right shoulder and injected the bright green solution. Cold rushed through Robert's body. Dr. Cooper was right. Two seconds later, Robert couldn't feel anything.

"Let's see if it's working," Dr. Cooper said. He sounded like he was getting a kick out of it.

Robert turned his head as the good doctor picked up a scalpel and stabbed the meat of Robert's left calf.

"Anything?" Dr. Cooper asked.

Robert shook his head, queasy as he watched the blood spill out of the incision.

"Good." He set the scalpel onto the tray. "I'll be back in a minute. Give the drugs some time to fully kick in."

Robert grunted, part of him wishing he'd get this over with, the other part wishing the doctor would never return and just leave him alone with his thoughts of Teresa. How thin she looked before she stepped on that scale. One pound. That's all she was over. You could see every bone in her body, but at six-foot-one she wasn't skinny enough for the State.

Robert replayed every meal, every drink he allowed Teresa the week before her death. Then the month. Then the year. So many chances to take away her plate. All he had to do was not cook three meals, and she'd still be with him.

A loud clang woke Robert from his dream. He saw the acetylene torch Dr. Cooper had just dropped onto the surgical tray. The studded dog collar and leashes in the doctor's hand.

"Oh, don't worry about these. They work better than anything else I've tried."

"Yeah…"

Dr. Cooper wrapped the collar around Robert's thigh and cinched it tight. The leashes went around Robert's chest, waist, and legs, right above his knees. "Last time you moved too much. These should keep you still." Dr. Cooper pulled the leashes again, tied them under the table. "I don't need to restrain your arm, do I?"

Unsure if the doctor was trying to be funny, Robert told him to start the procedure.

"No sensation, right?" Cooper asked.

Robert had to look to see the doctor was lifting his leg off the table. "Nothing."

"Good, because seven pounds means we're going to have to go deep."

Robert remembered when he had boulders for calves. His legs had been so strong he could dunk at fourteen. When the whine of the saw shook Robert from his thoughts, he said, "I used to be small forward for the Bruins. All-conference three years in a row."

"That must have been fun. Were you looked at by the pros?"

"No, my knees were shot. And the NBA was pretty much dismantled by then."

"One explosion. Who'd have thought that's all it would take."

The saw's whine grew louder. Robert saw the flesh and blood flying and splattering. Robert closed his eyes and continued talking about designing his own sneaker when he was getting recruited in high school.

"They were going to be in every mall."

Dr. Cooper had to stand to get the leverage to carve through the bone. "My parents were just glad I was getting an education," Dr. Cooper said. "They were so happy to have a doctor in the family. Even if I was just a vet."

"I'm sure."

"They died a few years back. I stupidly mentioned bleach would damage their intestines, so they never decontaminated their drinking water."

Robert was surprised to find himself sympathizing with the man sawing through his leg.

"Is that why you do this? Risk everything?" Robert said. "I mean, ten grand won't buy you anything these days."

Dr. Cooper's eyes narrowed and his lips pursed as he applied more pressure to the saw. He'd hit the center of the bone. Feeling nauseous, Robert lowered his head. A few moments later, he jumped when he heard a loud pop followed by a splashy thud. Dr. Cooper apologized. Robert lifted a bit and looked. The blade had gone clean through his leg and imbedded in the table. The thud must have been Robert's tibia hitting the floor.

Dr. Cooper picked up the torch. "Cover your nose. We're almost done."

When Robert came to an hour later, he found himself strapped to his wheelchair. Troy was sitting next to him in the little room.

"Hey, Bro. How you feeling?"

"I don't know. I don't feel much."

"That's good." Troy held a glass up to Robert's lips. "Have a sip."

Robert let the water touch his lips then pulled away. "I better not."

"Don't worry. You're three pounds under and that's with your bandages. You're going to be fine."

Robert stared down at his gauzy stumps, the right one slightly shorter. It started to finally sink in. He'd never walk again, but at least he'd get another year with his little girl.

Robert said, "Let's just hope the Controllers don't drop the weight limit again." He wiggled his left stump of a shoulder. "'Cause I'm running out of options."

28 Blocks

September 30, 2055

Frank Hollister strode through the shadow of Inner Block Four, sixty stories of steel and black solar windows. The particle pistol holstered under his jacket did little to ease his nerves. It wasn't the residents. The smell from the aqueduct kept all but a handful inside the massive complex covering almost three square miles.

The demonstration was supposed to go down next Sunday night, but Gabriel had pushed up the meeting to eleven o'clock today. Gabriel had been acting paranoid. Frank hoped he just wanted to go over the plans one more time to be safe.

Frank stepped inside and joined the masses. All Blocks were designed exactly the same, fifty-nine floors of wall-to-wall dorms, one entrance on each side of the building. The first floor was the bazaar – clothing stores, electronic stores, a grocery store, movie theater, church, bank, and even a casino. Everything provided. No reason for anyone to ever leave.

Gabriel called it their prison. Everything could be locked down in sixty seconds.

Two teenagers stood off to the side of the stairs, both wearing black armbands. Neither looked familiar, but Frank hadn't met everyone in the faction. Something wasn't right with these two though. Something about their eyes. They seemed to be looking at nothing.

Frank moved through the bazaar, surprised how crowded it was, a sea of black and gray, the end color of everything. Usually he came in on Transport. It took him to the basement. He'd walk straight to Kyle's room for briefing.

Today Frank was coming from Controller Station #56. He worried someone had been following him, knew he'd been working as a snitch. Maybe this was a setup.

Frank slowed, let others bump past him as they hurried into the market, joined the fast-flowing stream to the pharmacy. Up ahead giant glass elevators sprouted from the middle of the open floor. Frank turned back. The two teenagers were gone.

Around the corner was the Confessional. A line of sinners snaked through the bazaar. Today was the day to pay dues or give names. It was easy to tell from the way most were standing which one they'd picked.

A Controller in black body armor stood at the Confessional's entrance checking wrists.

A hand clamped down on Frank's shoulder. "Hey man, how you doing?"

Frank spun around, already reaching for his gun, but stopped when he saw it was Steve Cooper, a guy he hadn't seen since high school. Frank forced a smile, talked softly so Cooper would keep it down. "I'm good, I'm good. You scared the hell out of me though."

Cooper laughed, looked smug in his shiny blue suit. "You live down here?"

"No, just here to see some friends."

Frank's little cousin, Kaiden, came over the Connect, a voice only Frank could hear. *Exactly. Now get to it.* Kaiden had just been promoted to Disciple and transferred to the Controllers. He clearly relished this new power over Frank, who used to torment him as a boy.

Frank ignored him and asked Steven, "How about you? You living here?"

"No, wife and I have a house on the skirts. Trying to stay close to my dad's clinic." In high school, Steven used to get the best drugs from his old man's office.

"Skirts, huh? You should probably be heading home, right? Rush hour and all."

"It's Sunday, Frank."

Today was only supposed to be a demonstration, but with Gabriel moving up the meeting, Frank feared this could get dangerous.

Kaiden warned Frank to be quiet. Frank eased open his jacket, exposed the butt of his pistol. "Head home."

Before Steven could say anything, Frank walked off, tired of Kaiden bitching him out. *You follow instructions, Frank. You hear me?*

Frank turned down the controls so Kaiden could only hear what was spoken, not Frank thinking he was an asshole. Taking orders from a spoiled seventeen-year-old was becoming unbearable, but Frank was in too deep to speak up.

The liquor store was next to the Confessional. Frank thought it fitting as he headed to the back of the line. Gabriel and Kyle were standing right where Gabriel said they'd be, not thirty yards from the Confessional entrance. They were definitely on camera, but didn't seem to care.

The Controller's Station looked empty, but Frank knew it wasn't. Six Controllers ran the complex of holding cells, another six on patrol. A dozen agents for 80,000 residents.

Frank turned up his Connect and thought, *Gabriel's here. With Kyle. Both in black coats.*

Kaiden acknowledged him, told him to stop looking suspicious. There was a glass mechanical eye on the pole in front of him. Everything always on camera.

Frank noticed two more of Gabriel's guys hanging by the fence.

Kaiden was no nonsense. *Approach the faction leader.*

If Gabriel heard those words, he'd laugh. He never saw himself above the resistance, just another body for the cause. Frank slipped out of line and stood in front of Gabriel, blocked him from the station's camera. Frank forced a smile. "So, what's new?"

Gabriel said, "There's a change of plans."

Frank had known Gabriel since they were young, but a lot had changed in the last seven years, and it wasn't just the beard.

"What's up?" Frank prayed to The Preacher that Gabriel was calling off the demonstration. Even a simple protest typically ended with people hurt, harsh warnings for lasting reminders.

Kyle, a stocky blonde punk with an eye patch, stepped forward. Gabriel's right-hand man that never left his side. "How about we stop talking out here?"

They moved through the crowd and into a stairwell. Gabriel closed the door and said, "Things have escalated. We're taking over the Block."

Frank thought to Kaiden, *Are you getting this?* No response. Frank said, "Taking over how?"

Gabriel pinned a thumbnail camera to Frank's jacket, patted him on his shoulder. "Don't worry. Your job's the same. We have two minutes. Are you in?"

Frank's mind scrambled for an excuse, a reason why he had to leave the building. "What happened to the demonstration?"

Gabriel opened his jacket, gave a glimpse of all the weapons strapped underneath. "All you have to do is film. Take the internal as backup and don't stop rolling."

Frank thought, *What should I do, Kaiden?*

Still nothing. Frank figured this stairwell was blocking the connection. Maybe they'd brought him here because they knew who he was.

Frank looked up the stairs, didn't see any more of their guys. "I still don't understand what's happening here."

Kyle said, "All you have to do is film. Can you handle that or not?"

Frank didn't need the recog software to know Kyle didn't trust him, that Kyle would kill him if he knew Frank was a snitch. He said, "I can handle it."

Gabriel zipped up his jacket. "We're putting an end to this. The word will spread. We're broadcasting everything."

"What about Cameron?" Frank asked. Cameron was supposed to be filming too.

"Cameron got scooped up this morning. He'll probably talk. That's why it has to be now."

"Okay, look," Frank said. "Even if we take over, what then? If the other Blocks don't participate, it means nothing."

Gabriel said, "They'll see the video and join. I have each leader's word. Once this goes out, everyone will follow."

Frank wanted to say no one would see the video, that the Controllers had already blocked the signal when they heard about the demonstration. Nothing would be transmitted until it'd been through their filter. Instead, he nodded along to Gabriel, glanced at the door. The Controllers were just outside. Frank wondered how far they were going to let this go.

Gabriel pressed a panel on the wall next to the stairs. A secret door slid open. A lanky kid in a trench coat stepped out, along with five other teenagers. Gabriel looked at Frank, rubbed his scraggly beard. "How do I look?"

"Determined." *Naïve.*

Gabriel opened the door. His men filed out, clearing a path for Gabriel. Frank moved left to get the Controller's Station behind Gabriel, just like they'd planned.

Frank thought he'd hear Kaiden's voice, but there was just a light buzzing noise. He wondered if Gabriel had jammed his Connection.

Gabriel raised both arms, a particle pistol in each hand. "Ladies and gentlemen, welcome to the revolution!"

The Station's door slid open and four Controllers rushed out, ran right for them. A circle of rifles aimed at their heads, the Controller in the middle shouting, "Get down! Get down on your knees."

A crowd circled to watch the show, a wall of bodies behind the Controllers. Men and women inching closer. Gabriel kept his smile and slowly turned around. He shook his head. "No, you get on yours."

"Drop your weapons!" a Controller yelled.

The wall of bodies came to life, a dozen men dashed in. They were all wearing black armbands, driving knives into the Controllers' throats.

The resistance swept up the rifles, ran towards the Station, Gabriel and Kyle right behind them. Frank stood there shaking. "Holy shit." The pooling blood spread across the tile, flowing around his boots.

Don't be stupid. Just do what you're told. Keep filming. Kaiden's voice was back. Or had it been there all along? *You want your parents getting a late night visit?*

Frank chased after them. Kyle shattered the glass, tossed in a grenade. The blast cleared, and six resistance fighters slipped inside, shots fired. All but one came back out, announced it was clear.

Gabriel turned to Frank. "You getting all this?"

Frank could only nod yes.

"Follow me!" Gabriel led the way into the station, pushed aside the dead body on the chair, sat at the monitor. He looked at the camera on Frank's chest. "The first step is separation from the Controllers. We don't need you." He punched in a code to seal the doors. Then he turned off the Transport. "No one will be leaving this building, no one will be entering."

Kaiden, you there?

Gabriel rose. "We will no longer be controlled. We will no longer pay for our own enslavement."

Gabriel stepped out of the station, two rows of men keeping the civilians back.

Frank positioned himself so he had Gabriel's profile. A bead of sweat running down his forehead, Gabriel addressed the audience. "They created these Blocks to keep us contained, to keep us under their control. But these Blocks don't belong to them. They belong to us!"

Some in the crowd cheered. Others looked uneasy, slowly backed away.

One guy in the front shouted. "They'll kill us."

Gabriel laughed it off. "They already are. They sent our brothers and sisters into South America to die for nothing."

"What are you talking about?" the guy said. It was clear they had no idea what really was going on with the war. The confusion turned to anger. A woman said, "They're going to be coming for us now!" Someone else shouted, "They'll send in the drones!"

Panic rose. Screams, chaos, people pushing.

Gabriel told Frank to keep the camera focused on him. "This is for the good of our brothers and sisters. You have to see that."

A little girl began crying. Gabriel was losing control.

Keep him talking, Kaiden said.

Gabriel's face was bright red. More screams in the distance. Gabriel spoke of chemicals in the water, of microchips, and government spies among them. "Their lies are everywhere! But it all comes crashing down today!"

Yes! Got it.

Got what? Kaiden, where's the cavalry?

No response.

Gabriel stopped midsentence. The panicking crowd was dispersing. A man fell. Trampled.

"Are we still broadcasting?" Gabriel said. "Frank?"

Frank turned away from the poor man and nodded, even though he knew they weren't.

A deep voice came over the Connect. *Third back on your left, gray hat, recogs. Stop him!"*

Frank turned, searched the crowd, found the guy, who pulled out a particle pistol.

Frank went for his holster, tore out his gun. He was about to fire when he noticed the guy wasn't aiming at a person, but at a silver orb hovering near the fourth floor.

Lankford, take him out!

Who the hell is Lankford? Frank thought.

A man with a black armband emerged from the crowd, fired three shots. The gray hat fell to the floor.

Seemed Frank wasn't the only infiltrator.

The voice said, *T-minus ten seconds.*

Frank kept his gun out, steadied his shaking hand. *Who is this? Where's Kaiden?*

Nine.

Frank went deeper into the Connect, saw Gabriel's face on monitors around the city.

Eight.

Gabriel was speaking, his words already edited.

"Welcome to the revolution!"

Seven. Six.

"These Blocks don't belong to them."

Five.

"They belong to us!"

Four. Three.

"And today…"

Two.

"…it all comes crashing down!"

Oh God.

The first explosion came from the second floor. A cloud of plaster and glass rained down on the bazaar. Another blast hit the front entrance as a group of people tried to escape. More charges started going off everywhere. A family of three flew through the front of the electronics store. A shard of metal sliced off a woman's arm. Everything slowed. Frank fell flat on his back, rolled to his side as Gabriel ran for the little boy, both of them buried under a collapsing wall.

What had they done?

Eight Out of Nine

December 17, 2056

Vanessa entered the waiting room. The door slammed shut behind her. The lock clicked. Four rows of girls turned as one to see the new girl. Vanessa clutched the faded gray robe to her chest and slipped into the last row of blue plastic chairs. The center's over-sized slippers slapped the tiles as she made her way past trembling knees. She didn't look at their faces, giving them the privacy she so desperately wanted. Halfway down the row, two girls clutched each other's hands. Vanessa wondered if they knew each other before today.

The coarse robe scratched her bare flesh. Vanessa hurried and sat down on the last chair against the wall. The girl two seats down whispered something like hello. Vanessa nodded and stared at the Sweet Fourteen slip in her hands. Her bright red fingernails were chipped. She'd need to touch them up before she returned to work. This was the first time she'd rather be at her job. The crumpled card had her information printed on the front and the penalty for not appearing on the back. She tried to steady her hands, search for some loophole, a mistake she missed or a word they got wrong.

This was the first piece of mail she'd ever received, the only one that would ever matter. Eight out of nine. Those were the odds every girl was given.

The rectangular waiting room had no windows. The walls the color of a gray winter sky. The door she'd entered was behind her and locked. The massive metal door they'd all eventually walk through was directly in front of them. Vanessa tried not to think of the things taking place on the other side.

She'd never seen the inside of a slaughterhouse, but that's what she pictured. Her father had told her stories before he died. He worked in one back when it was still safe to eat meat. He always said he felt sorry for the helpless creatures. It was like they knew what was coming. The way her parents must've felt the last time they went to the DMV.

Vanessa tried to remember her father's face. It used to be so clear in her mind. She only knew her mother from the faded picture her father carried in his wallet. Part of her wished they were in the other room with the rest of the parents, all anxiously waiting to take home their little girls. But another part was glad they weren't around to see this.

Large, red letters scrolled on a continuous loop across the electronic display box above the steel door. "Joanne Weaver." Vanessa wondered if Joanne was already on the other side of the door or if she was here waiting, cowering in her chair, clutching the last shred of hope they'd forget her and move on to the next girl.

Vanessa looked around the room for Joanne. Every girl was different: none fat, but all degrees of skinny. Some were pale and ugly, others a little beautiful, even though they were crying. One girl with blond hair just kept smiling. Vanessa wondered if the girl's mother had told her they might pass her over if she looked pretty. There were dark-skinned girls, and blue-eyed girls; there were tall ones and every shade of hair.

But while every girl was different, every girl was the same. Some hid the fear better, but no one wanted to be here, not on her birthday. Vanessa used to look forward to the little party her father and uncle would give her. They never had money, but they'd sing and split a stick of gum. When she turned eleven, Vanessa's uncle took her to a field to shoot tin cans with a particle pistol. Vanessa hated the whirring noise it made when it was charging, but it made her giggle when the tin can would evaporate.

That was the last year girls had options, back when the Controllers actually paid those who volunteered.

The box above the door chimed and a mechanical voice said, "Michelle Jackson." A homely girl in the front row stood before her name finished scrolling across the display box. Her legs shook, but she held her head high as the metal door slid open and the guard clad in black entered the room. He was tall with a shaved head and thin goatee. He grabbed Michelle's card and studied it.

Vanessa eyed his electroprod and shiny particle pistol. It looked nothing like the old-fashion one she'd fired with her uncle. She didn't understand why a man twice Michelle's size needed a weapon at all. With those giant hands he'd kill her with one punch.

Michelle walked through the door, her head still held high. Vanessa hoped she'd be just as brave when her name was called. If Michelle had been attractive enough to find a decent husband who could support a family, would she still have been so quick to get up? Maybe Michelle never dreamed of being a mother. Even though Vanessa had never met her own, she always thought one day she'd have a kid, do all the things she could only imagine growing up, like story-time or learning to put on lipstick. The woman who taught Vanessa told her to cake it on so men wouldn't focus on her wide nose.

The girl two seats down was suddenly next to her tapping on her leg. Vanessa hadn't realized she was shaking. Not from cold, not from fear, but out of anger. The Controllers had taken everything, her mother, her father. This was all she had left, and it'd be gone in the next fifteen minutes.

"Relax," the girl said gently. "They say it doesn't hurt."

Vanessa stared at the girl's hand, the bright red fingernail polish a clear sign they were both in the same line of work. Vanessa always told herself she was better than the others. She had her uncle to care for. All she had in common with the girl next to her was a birthday and the same shitty luck.

The speaker called another name. When no one stood, the speaker blared the name again. "Karen Chen. Stand up!"

The tiny girl seated in the second row shot up, beautiful black hair halfway down her back. She wavered slightly, looking like she might faint when the door slid open and the guard walked toward her.

Karen screamed as they dragged her through the door.

The girl next to Vanessa said, "It's for the best. My sister just had a kid." She lowered her voice and said, "She refused to give him to the Way. Now she's got to come up with five hundred a month for the orphanage until he's adopted. Believe me, this is better."

Vanessa nodded, trying to force herself to believe that was true. If she ever got pregnant, she knew she'd sacrifice everything. She'd be a good mother. Her dad always told her that, said Vanessa had the same heart as the woman she never knew.

The box chimed again and the speaker buzzed to life. "Vanessa Salazar." A hiss of static then nothing.

Vanessa's name scrolled across the box in red letters. The speaker squawked her name again. Vanessa bit her tongue. She wouldn't yell or cry or let them see the fear. She could hold onto that.

The door slid open. The guard that had taken the other girls away appeared in the doorway, his cold eyes searching the room. If he wanted to take her, he'd have to come and physically rip her from the seat. Vanessa wanted him to grab her. She'd claw his eyes, rip out his throat, and escape. She was small and he'd underestimate her, not ready for the fury raging inside.

The guard called her name. Vanessa wanted to rush him, but that'd only work if the rest of the girls would follow. There were enough, but if she called them to arms, she knew most wouldn't budge. She needed the element of surprise. She'd wait until the prick was inches away.

"Population Control Cards out. Names up," he ordered.

The guard walked down the first row, read each girl's slip. At the end of the second row, he got on his transmitter. "Barnett here. I'm gonna need Williams."

Barnett grabbed another card, read it and shoved it back to the girl. Halfway down the third row, Vanessa could see his forearm muscles twitching, the excitement in his eyes. He lived for someone to resist. Dragging innocent girls into the back, sticking his hands underneath their robes, having his way with them. Why else would he work here?

Barnett moved down her row. His hand rested on the butt of his pistol. She tried to remember what her uncle had taught her. Arms locked. Shoulders square. But he'd never taught her how to disarm anyone, and if she couldn't get it from him, the prick would kill her.

Vanessa no longer cared. She'd be with her parents. She'd never have to go back to work. Her uncle would understand. She kept telling herself that, even as the images of him starving to death fired off in her head. Gasping. Too weak to even take his own life.

The guard stopped in front of her chair. "Turn over your card."

Vanessa stared straight ahead.

He ripped the card out of her hands and waved over the fat guard walking through the doorway. Barnett pointed at the display and asked Vanessa, "Are you deaf?"

She shook her head, not understanding why she couldn't move her arms and go for the gun.

"Then get up."

Vanessa couldn't. She tried to stand, but her legs felt like they were filled with cement.

Williams walked over, knelt in front of her, his eyes surprisingly soft. "Look, Vanessa, you have to get up. There's no choice."

"She's not getting up. Grab an arm."

"Give me a second." Williams lowered his voice and whispered, "If you don't stand up, they'll make us use force. And if you fight, they're going to do what it says on the back of your card. Trust me, you don't want that."

Vanessa didn't believe his kindness. It was a trick. His eyes were probably always watery. No one cared about her, at least not in this place.

"Just walk with us," he said. "You'll barely feel it."

Barnett tapped Williams, who finally got up and moved to the left. They each took hold of her arms. Their fingers dug into her flesh. They yanked her from the chair, dragging her toward the door. She opened her mouth to shriek, but couldn't make a sound.

Pretending like he wasn't enjoying her terror, Williams grunted and told Barnett, "You still wonder why I'm transferring to the prison?"

The tips of Vanessa's slippers bent backward on the tiles as they neared the door. They crossed the threshold and the door slid shut, her body suddenly awake. She'd been mistreated by men, but never like this. She felt their hands loosen. They thought they were safe. Vanessa flung herself from their grip.

Barnett grabbed her by the hair, reached for the electroprod on his belt. "You better relax."

Vanessa spun, the hairs ripping from her scalp. She launched a knee at his groin, heard the crunch. He let go of her and dropped to the floor, but Williams was right behind him. Vanessa took one step back and braced herself for his attack.

Williams stepped toward her. "Hey, let's calm down."

Vanessa ran at him and raked his face with her fingernails. Her fingers found a chain around his neck and ripped it off when he pushed her away. The crucifix at the end of the chain hung in the air for only a moment before Vanessa snatched it and plunged the long end into Williams' cheek.

Williams screamed, one hand on the cross, the other reaching for Vanessa. Vanessa ducked under his arm, flipped the tab, and ripped the pistol from his holster.

Barnett was back on his feet, the buzzing prod in hand. "Drop the gun" he said. "Or I'm gonna have fun with you."

Vanessa backed against the wall, the gun aimed at Barnett's chest. There was a hallway to the right. She inched her way over, her thumb fumbling for the safety. It wasn't where it had been on her uncle's pistol. Finally, she found it. Whirring filled the air. Barnett's hand moved toward his own pistol.

"Do it and I'll shoot," Vanessa said.

Barnett's hand steadied, hovered over his pistol. Vanessa's gun was fully charged. She couldn't tell what Barnett was going to do, but then his eyes narrowed. There was no way he'd let her go. His thumb slowly flipped open the tab and Vanessa squeezed. The force shot her back, nearly sent her to the ground. When she opened her eyes, she saw Barnett's arm vanish under his sleeve. He flailed and slammed against a gurney. She turned, saw the emergency exit down the hall. Barnett's scream cut through the buzzing in her ears. Vanessa passed a small room with a tray of sharp instruments, the girl on the table with her legs in stirrups, ankles strapped down, towel stuffed in her mouth.

There wasn't enough time to save her. She heard other guards coming.

Williams called out to her. He'd pulled the cross from his cheek. Blood poured from the gaping hole. "You can't run forever."

Vanessa shot the lock off the emergency exit and kicked open the door. "I can try."

Eighteen is Enough

May 8, 2057

National Guardsman Cody Bradford walked down the shaded Path of the Way, rifle at the ready. Everything was deathly still, not a student to be seen or professor heard. He'd survived sixteen years in a Way Camp, but this was somehow more terrifying.

Sunlight flickered off a shrine up on the left. Five sets of benches surrounded an enormous statue of the Reverend holding his bible in the air. His other arm was spread wide, welcoming the gray skies and dead grass, bodies scattered across the campus, piles of shoes and scraps of burnt clothes everywhere.

Cody paused at the start of the hill and turned the amplifier in his right ear to its highest setting. On top of the hill he saw a giant set of stairs leading to the looming eight-story Murphy building. Cody had to hurry. People were depending on him.

He continued up the path, kept close to the trees. When Cody got to the stairs, he threw his back against a brick column, slowed his breathing and prepared for the ascent. Something touched his shoulder and he almost screamed, but felt foolish as the dry breeze blew a faded brown shirtsleeve off the column and into the air.

The penalty for going AWOL was automatic death. Cody still didn't see a soul, but he had no choice but go forward. To head back risked being spotted. And he'd made a vow, committed to the National Guard. Cody couldn't turn his back on the men he'd trained with, even after all he'd witnessed.

Cody checked the building's closed door and every window on the north side. He started up the stairs, one step, then two, his heartbeat thumping in his ear. He gripped the rifle. Someone was watching, but he didn't know from where.

He was exposed. One wrong move and he was dead, so Cody stilled his breath, listened. Leaves in the distance, but no footsteps, just the breeze. Then the slight rasp of a window being opened. Somewhere above and to the left. The sun flashed off the barrel of a gun four stories up. Cody's body swiveled. He aimed, fired three short blasts, the amplified reports shattering his eardrum.

A body fell from the window. Cody ripped the amplifier from his ear and threw it to the ground. The legs of the gunman splattered on the concrete with a wet, cracking thud, but Cody could barely hear it. It felt as if a knife had ripped through the side of his head, the blade twisting in his brain. There was no way he'd hear another window opening, maybe not even a shot.

Cody ran the last dozen steps. He sprinted across the landing and put his back to the wooden door. The searing pain made it hard to think. He took one Teflon-armored hand off his rifle and touched his ear. Clear pus coated the tip of his glove. His eardrum liquefied. He was just another member of the ever-growing ranks of the walking wounded.

He should've known better than to rely on the malfunctioning amplifier. The National Guard was never issued the best equipment. He should've had covering fire. If half of the military wasn't in South America fighting the worst guerilla war in history and the other half wasn't quelling riots in the former Canada and the rest of this country, maybe the National Guard could have gone into the university with more than twelve men. Maybe the rest of Cody's squad would still be alive.

But he couldn't change any of that. Cody still had a job, and if he was ever going to find out what really happened to his parents, then he needed to get his shit together. If they suspected him of anything, he'd be out or dead.

Intelligence said the squad that had been dispatched to the university two days prior was holed up inside this building. The last report was ten hours old. It'd come just moments before La Causa had accessed the mainframe and knocked out all communication.

Cody wiped off his glove, gripped his rifle with both hands, and faced the door. If someone was inside the building they already knew he was out here.

Friend or foe. He was about to find out.

Cody banged twice on the door, then moved three feet to his left. Nothing. No sound at all. Cody feared he hadn't knocked hard enough. His ear still pulsing. He was about to repeat the process when the door shook against his shoulder. Two knocks. Friendlies inside giving him the go.

If it was a trap, it was too late to do anything. Cody knocked twice to signal he was coming in, pulled open the door, and entered the dimly-lit lobby. A group of four guardsmen were huddled in the shadows, guns aimed at him and the staircase. A swarm of flies hovered over someone on the ground. A San Angeles Controlling Force agent lay motionless, his face a bullet-riddled mess.

Fuller, the senior officer, looked more like a kid than a first lieutenant. He held the hand of an injured guardsman on the hardwood floor, a backpack propping up his head.

Cody said, "Private Bradford reporting, Sir."

Fuller asked where the rest of his squad was. Cody clenched his jaw and shook his head.

The guardsman closest to the staircase said, "Don't believe this douchebag, LT. Sabotage runs in his family. He probably shot them all himself."

Cody realized the guardsman was Todd Jaworski, one of his asshole instructors from the academy. Cody told the lieutenant about the snipers in the parking lot, didn't mention how eight of the dead had been Initiates with him at the Camp.

Fuller said, "You two know each other?"

Jaworski said, "Yeah, this guy's dad's the one who fucked the world."

Cody couldn't control his volume, his head splitting from the earache. "You don't know what you're talking about."

"Yeah? Well, his crazy-ass mom tried to pin it on us, said it wasn't the Muslims. Fucking nut-jobs, the whole family."

"Knock it off, Sergeant." Fuller let go of the injured man's hand and stared at the bloody pus from Cody's ear. He pulled a small syringe from his med kit and motioned Cody closer.

The tip of the needle touched the side of the ear canal. "Look at me," Fuller said. "You'll be fine."

The needle went in and cold fluid filled Cody's ear, numbed the pain and muffled the ringing. Cody glanced at the black teenager sitting on the floor, back to the wall. His stomach and right leg were wrapped with field dressings, most of the white fabric stained dark red.

Two injured, three healthy, not good odds for a safe retreat.

"Are we waiting for reinforcements?" Cody asked. "Last I heard, my squad was it, so it'd probably be a while if anyone does show up."

"We can't wait for that," Fuller said.

Cody motioned toward the guard on the ground. "Do you want me to cover you guys or carry him?"

Fuller shook his head. "We're not going anywhere. They'll pick us off one by one before we're halfway down those stairs."

"I took one out. Didn't see anyone else."

"They let you up," Jaworski said. "Probably saw your name tag and figured you were on their side."

Not caring that Jaworski was his superior and almost twice his size, Cody got in Jaworski's face.

"I told you two to cut the crap," Fuller said. "Jaworski's right about them letting you up, but it's because they want us to leave. We're fortified here. Once we're out those doors, we're easy pickings."

Fuller was right. Cody asked him, "So what do we do?"

"The job we were sent to do," Fuller said. "We clear this building and rescue any hostages that might be alive upstairs."

"Let's kill us some fucking Spics then," Jaworski said.

The guard on the ground kept his eyes closed when he spoke for the first time. He sounded even weaker than he looked when he called Jaworski an asshole.

"I didn't mean you, Gonzales. It's just the rest of your banditos I could do without."

With his eyes still shut, Gonzales said, "*My people* know what happened in Canada."

"Yeah, yeah, yeah." Jaworski was no longer watching the stairs. "Fuck you, Gonzales."

"Enough," Fuller said. "You all need to shut your mouths and do as I say if you want to get out of this alive. Understood?"

After everyone copied, Fuller turned to Cody. "I want you and Jaworski up those stairs. Clear this building and bring back any hostages."

"Are there any hostages left?" Cody asked. "It's been three days."

"Are you questioning my order?"

"No, not all, just asking, Sir. Just want to know what I'm going into."

Fuller suddenly looked older, his eyes cold. "You got three seconds to get up those stairs."

Cody said yes sir and Fuller tossed him a bright blue vial. Jaworski bit the cap off his syringe and spit it out.

"You better watch my back, you little shit." The needle disappeared into the side of Jaworski's neck. "And do your best not to kill me."

Cody had never zeroed in before, but he'd done the walk-through in training. The instructor had warned if you did too much, your brain would pop. Some guys couldn't get off the stuff after they returned home. But worrying about getting hooked was pretty stupid right now. Reaction time was the only thing that might save his life.

Cody slammed the syringe into his neck, felt the cold electricity enter his veins, everything so bright, so focused. The syringe fell to the ground, both his hands on the rifle. He said, "I'll take lead."

Jaworski grabbed Cody's arm. "Settle down, jitterbug." He stepped over the rotting agent and started up the stairs, his boots squelching in the congealed-blood coating each step.

Flies swarmed, and Cody could make out each flap of their wings. Jaworski gave a signal and Cody took the right side of the stairs, stayed three steps behind the Sergeant. Cody's finger hugged the trigger, Jaworski's heavy breathing sounded too rapid. Cody wondered if he'd taken too much.

Jaworski paused at the second floor landing, his rifle trained on the doorway. Cody crept past him and crouched in the corner, covered the third floor landing. Jaworski left Cody by himself and checked the hallway.

Sweat trickled down Cody's forehead as the seconds ticked by, each one felt like a minute. This was why they said getting zeroed in was like hitting a pause button. Every sound distinct, every detail so clear. From the hallway someone yelled in Spanish. The blast of Jaworski's repeater boomed several times against the rat-a-tat-tat of machine-gun fire. Then everything stopped and a few moments later, Jaworski appeared back on the landing, holding his right arm, bright red blood pumping through his fingers.

Jaworski squatted next to Cody. "Floor's cleared."

Cody looked for something to plug Jaworski's hole, but the Sergeant swatted him away. There was movement up above.

On the third floor landing, a young boy leaned over with an Uzi. Cody yelled for Jaworski to move, but the kid had already squeezed the trigger, covered them with a blanket of bullets.

Cody fired blindly up the staircase as bullets bounced off his helmet and shoulder pads. Something warm sprayed Cody's cheek. Then a thud. Jaworski lay flat, two bullet holes punched through the side of his face.

Finally, the shooting stopped. Cody's proton pack was empty, so he grabbed Jaworski's rifle, yanked it from his lifeless fingers. Cody looked up. The kid was gone, just a pile of smoking clothes where he'd last stood.

Fuller called from below. "Jaworski! Bradford!"

Cody yelled that the sergeant was dead. He hoped the lieutenant would shout for him to come back, they'd wait for reinforcements. But no orders came, so Cody said, "I'm heading up."

Fuller said nothing. Cody's proton pack flashed green, so he switched out the rifles and headed up, the blue drug steadying his shaking hands.

He was only one man, but one man could ruin the entire world. That's what Jaworski had said about Cody's father. A lot of people did. If Cody wanted to find out who was really responsible for his father's death and sending the Americas down the drain, he had to act like a soldier and clear this building.

Time seemed to stop and rush by all at once as Cody checked every hallway and cleared each classroom. He stepped over bodies. Students, teachers, and agents, all rotting as one. Piles of clothes proved that the agents had dealt some damage, as well.

Cody felt confident on the fifth floor, enough to distract him, even on the drug. He passed a sign for the physics department and thought of his father.

Two men jumped into the hallway and opened fire.

Cody dropped to his stomach as bullets sailed overhead and ricocheted off the wall. He fired a particle beam to the brown bandanna wrapped around the taller one's face. The shorter one was hit with three beams, not much left of either man by the time they touched the ground.

The rest of the fifth floor was empty except for dead bodies behind every door. Cody found the same on the sixth and seventh floors, decaying flesh, curdled blood, body parts. It was hard to imagine this is what the revolution wanted, but it's what they got.

Hoping the last floor was just as empty, Cody climbed the final flight of stairs. He was halfway down the hall when he heard the hushed voices. Definitely Spanish.

Cody peeked around the corner. Two men with assault rifles stood outside the last door on the left, both of their backs turned, easy targets. They were the enemy and had to be eliminated, but Cody had never shot a man in the back. These two were soldiers. They deserved the opportunity to surrender.

Plus, Cody didn't want to risk his proton pack draining. The room might be La Causa's headquarters. A dozen resistance fighters could be behind the door.

Cody pulled a vaporizer grenade from his utility belt and armed the timer for two seconds. With only his eyes exposed, Cody yelled for the men to drop their weapons. They turned and opened fire. He tossed the grenade.

A silent flash ripped through the hallway. Cody stayed down until the bullets stopped. He crawled out. The men were gone, their clothes and weapons bunched on the floor, the walls undamaged. Cody felt guilty. At least with the primitive guns of the resistance, bodies could be buried. Cody just erased his enemies.

He kept his rifle aimed at the door, headed down the hallway. Standing to the side of the door, Cody tried the knob. It was locked. Fine. If they didn't want to come out, he'd go in.

Cody stepped in front of the door and kicked it. The door flew open and he rolled into the room. A man in black armor stood behind an overturned desk, his arm around a dark-haired Hispanic girl's throat, a rag stuffed in her mouth.

The man fired. A particle beam slammed into Cody's chest, and he stumbled back. His armor absorbed the protons. The man tried to fire off another shot, but his pistol had lost its charge.

Cody took aim.

The man held up his gun and shouted, "Cease fire! I'm American. Controlling Force Agent."

The teenage girl's hospital gown was ripped and bloodied, her left breast exposed. Her face was battered and turning the same shade of blue as the dress draped across the desk in the corner, two high heels on the floor.

Still zeroed in, Cody's mind puzzled together the scene. The two resistance fighters outside weren't protecting this room. They were trying to get in.

Cody asked the girl, "Are you La Causa?"

She shook her head.

"Of course she is," the Controlling Force Agent shouted. "Now, lower your weapon." His pistol was almost charged. He began to aim it, but not at Cody. The barrel was heading for the girl's temple. Her eyes wide and terrified.

Cody squeezed the trigger, the agent's face gone.

The pistol clattered to the floor and the girl collapsed onto the desk. Cody stepped over the disappearing agent and undid the girl's gag, helped her to sit. She curled into a ball, her back rising with each deep breath.

Cody looked over at the dress in the corner. "Did he do that?"

"Yes."

"You're okay now. You're safe."

She looked at the pile of the agent's clothes. "They brought me here. They said tests or termination." The way she kept curling into herself told Cody he didn't want to know what they'd done.

"But La Causa came to rescue you?"

The girl nodded.

"How do you know?"

The girl shook with fear. Cody knew it was true. He looked to the left and saw the control room, the smoking computers and particle beam-charred equipment. He saw the examination table, the stirrups.

Fuller started shouting. Maybe five floors down. Not much time. Cody saw a man's body in the corner. A professor, his face bloodied and mangled, like he'd been beaten with a pipe.

Fuller's voice. Four floors down.

"Help me," Cody said to the girl. "Grab that." He pointed at the agent's armor. She dragged it to Cody, who threw it over the professor's head, slipped in his arms.

Three floors.

The girl finally realized what Cody was doing, helped him dress the professor.

Two floors.

Cody saw the professor's loafers. Quickly flung them off, reached for the agent's boots.

One floor to go.

Cody crammed in one foot. Started the other when—

"Bradford!" From down the hallway. Fuller said, "Answer me."

Cody pushed the girl in front of the desk and told her to stay down. "In here, Lieutenant. Everyone eliminated."

Fuller stepped inside the room. "No survivors?"

Cody noticed the agent's heel sticking out of the boot. He stepped in front of it and told Fuller no one. "They even got one of the Controlling Force Agents."

Fuller looked down, saw the mangled face. He started to bend down. Cody saw the girl's fingers on the floor.

"The building's clear, but we should move. There could be more coming," Cody said.

Fuller nodded, stood straight. "It all goes." He tossed Cody a yellow package. "Take out the entire level."

"Yes, Sir. Once you're all clear." Cody pointed to the window. "I can cover you from here to the parking lot. It's our best chance."

Fuller was slow to answer. "You're a hell of a soldier, Bradford. You make your country proud." It was like he was reading lines from some Controllers' pamphlet.

Cody thanked the lieutenant and walked him out the door. At the top of the stairs, Fuller said, "This stuff we see, you can't let it bother you. And you can't talk about it either. La Causa blew the building."

"I understand." Cody waited until it sounded like Fuller was down at least two floors. When he returned to the testing room, the girl was still in a ball. He forced his way into the storage room next to the control panel and came back out with a bag of clothes. He went over and threw in the blue dress. Cody set them in front of the girl. He noticed her plastic wristband: VANESSA SALAZAR.

Cody walked to the far side of the room and opened the yellow package. "We don't have a lot of time so get dressed." She sat there holding the dress to her breasts.

"I'm not going to look," he said. He gave her space and packed strips of the explosive into all four corners.

The girl wasn't wearing the blue dress. She had on a pair of jeans and a shirt two sizes too big. "You're going to let me go?"

Cody walked up to her. "No, I'm going with you."

"They'll kill you."

Cody took his spot at the window and watched Fuller hobble down the hill with the two injured men. "They'll figure it was the explosion. We won't be missed."

"But I have nowhere to go," Vanessa said.

Cody looked to the mountains covered in the gray mist. "There are groups. We just have to stay hidden until we find them."

Twenty-Twenty

November 4, 2058

Eric Norvak reread the letter then checked the postmark on the envelope. He had hoped the woman had simply mistyped the date, thought a six instead of an eight, but there it was stamped on the back: June 1, 2056.

The towering stack of letters on his desk had to be a hundred high. Eric wondered how many he had handled in the last twenty-one years as the Preacher's personal assistant. How many obsessive fanatics had he dealt with? How many disenchanted nutcases threatening violence? How many women claiming they had a damaging secret worth millions to keep quiet?

The smart thing to do would be to stick this letter at the bottom of his stack and eventually get to it. He should forget about it, let it go, but he couldn't. It was eating at him like the cancer ravaging his intestines. Something needed to be said.

Eric left the small room he shared with his son, walked up three flights of stairs, and entered the pulsing red Hallowed Hall. Twenty-four-carat golden angels lined both sides, their fiery swords raised high overhead, casting the corridor in orange-crimson. People around the world were starving, for food, for space, for guidance, but not here. The world's problems never stepped foot inside the walls of the palace.

Eric cleared his mind. He wasn't afraid the Preacher would read his thoughts, as he often claimed he could. If Eric spoke calmly, clearly, he might get his message across. Eric had known Kenneth all his life, for years even thinking of himself as a good friend, but now it seemed his advice no longer mattered. He wasn't even sure how safe it was for him to have an opinion.

There was never a good time to interrupt the Preacher, especially right after breakfast. Eric knocked on the door anyway.

Nathan, the Disciple with no neck, bulging shoulders, and a spiky blond crew cut opened the door wide enough to show his face. "What do you want?"

Eric still felt strange calling Kenneth by his self-appointed name, but he had no choice. "A word with the Preacher."

Nathan twisted his nonexistent neck for a moment, then back to Eric. "Make it quick."

Kenneth sat behind his desk in satin pajamas, his flaming red hair brushed back. He didn't even look up. "Yes?"

"I was hoping for a few minutes of your time."

"Yes, I suppose." Kenneth scribbled something in a golden notebook.

Eric turned to Nathan. "Would you mind giving us a minute?"

Kenneth said, "He'll stay."

Nathan stepped behind Eric, practically nudging him.

"I…have a question about a letter."

Kenneth sighed, his pen still scribbling. "Of course you do."

Eric started to place it on the desk, but when Kenneth didn't make a move to grab it, Nathan snatched it. "It's from two years ago," Eric said. "I think it might have been put in my pile by mistake."

"Nathan doesn't make mistakes when it comes to sorting my mail."

"No, Your Grace."

"Of course," Eric said. He bowed his head. "It's just that we have so many cases and…"

Kenneth looked up. "And what? Do I give you too much work? Is it too hard for you? Not rewarding enough?"

"No, it's fine," Eric said. "I only asked because this letter is different from the others. She's not talking about your son."

Nathan said, "The Preacher told you there wasn't a mistake."

"Well, I'd like to hear it from him."

Kenneth scratched his chin. *"Him?"*

"I would like to hear the *Preacher's* answer."

Kenneth glanced at the envelope and went back to writing. "Not that it matters, but I did consult on that letter. I know what it says. I know blackmail when I see it."

"But has she written back in two years? If so, then maybe, but if not, then she's obviously not a threat."

Kenneth held up his hand to quiet Eric. "And you know this how exactly?"

Eric knew better than to speak.

Kenneth said, "We do not question God when He tells me what will pass. This woman intends to harm me and our beloved church. She must be stopped."

Eric apologized for questioning him.

Kenneth pushed back from his desk, pulled out a nail file. "See, it's not just her that's the threat. Just imagine what others will believe. If they say her son shares my blood, he'd have a right to my crown. They'd strike me dead. Kenneth III is just a little boy. If something happened to me today, my son couldn't take over for another fifteen years. But someone born of my bloodline could."

Eric said he understood.

"So you'll take care of her first thing."

"Of course."

Eric had barely taken a step when Kenneth said, "And take Nathan with you."

"That's not necessary."

"Did you see the cute way she spelled her name? That's reason enough for reinforcements."

Nathan laughed on cue. Eric forced a smile, knowing Kenneth no longer trusted him. The seeds of this mistrust were planted when Eric brought back Michael five years before. Eric had been careful, waited a month before bringing home the baby he said he'd rescued from an orphanage. Kenneth had his suspicions, but allowed him to keep the boy. Eric knew Kenneth would one day recognize himself in Michael. Maybe it was already too late.

"We'll leave at once," Eric said. "I'll grab my gear and meet him by the hovercar."

Kenneth said to make it ten. "I'm not done with Nathan."

Eric left the room, headed downstairs, and went straight to his closet, careful not to wake Michael. He pulled his particle pistol from the top shelf where Michael couldn't reach. After slipping the gun into his holster, he took down other tools from the shelf and clipped them onto his belt. It'd been a long time since he'd used the laser saw, tiny torch, or sonic hammer. He'd swore he'd never use them again.

The gut-twisting nausea forced Eric to take a seat on Michael's tiny bed. Eric concentrated on his son, the only thing that kept him going, the only reason he'd never left the palace. He'd been foolish enough to believe he could keep Michael safe.

He still had five minutes. Maybe they should run. Michael stirred, and asked what was going on. Eric kissed his head. "I have to go to work."

Michael rolled over, fell back asleep.

Eric told himself he'd be back, that if he did what was commanded, he'd regain Kenneth's trust. Michael would be fine.

Eric packed the rest of his gear and walked to the gates. The heat was sickening, so he waited inside the air-conditioned hovercar.

Ten minutes turned to twenty before Nathan lumbered out of the palace in his silver suit. Ahmer, a dark-skinned Disciple, walked beside him dressed exactly the same. They slid into the back seat, their TV blaring a moment later.

Eric leaned his head against the window, watched as the ocean passed by beneath them in a blur. In a half an hour they crested the top of the tide wall. The chip in the dashboard enabled them to use the devoted Way's lane. It wasn't long before they pulled to a stop in front of a rundown shack in the slums of Beverly Hills.

Nathan and Ahmer were chuckling like idiots at their show. Eric got out and Nathan told him not to move.

"I can handle it," Eric said. "Just finish your program."

The Disciples got out of the car. Eric slipped on his windbreaker to cover his gun and gear.

"Really, I've got it."

"We'll make sure," Nathan said. "You know, never can be too careful, right?"

"Then at least wait here until I get inside. She won't open up if she sees all three of us."

"Then we'll open it for her," Ahmer said.

"There's no reason for that."

Ahmer said, "What does that matter?"

Eric's jaw clenched. "You want to force her into a corner? It's going to take hours to get her to talk. Is that what you want?"

Nathan pulled Ahmer back. "Let the old man do it his way. He's not going anywhere." He told Eric he had ten minutes.

Eric went up the front porch, held onto the railing for balance. Once he had his legs back under him, Eric knocked.

Footsteps hurried toward the door. A well-built blond in a red polka dot sundress opened up, her voice painfully sweet. "Well, hi there."

Eric gave his best grin. "Hello, ma'am."

"*Ma'am*?" She laughed, covered her mouth like a shy teenager. "You're funny. What's your name?" Before he could answer, she held out her hand and said, "I'm Vickii with two I's."

They shook hands and Eric gave his name, no need to lie.

"Good God, it's hot out here." Vickii fanned her chest and said, "You want to come on in for a glass of water?"

Eric said that'd be nice and entered her house. It was never this easy, but he made sure to turn back to the Disciples to give a little nod to show them he knew what he was doing.

Vickii flicked on a switch. "You'll need some light to see my hall of treasures."

Although her body could have passed for a twenty-year-old's, the lights showed the rest of her was nearing sixty. She'd had work done, but the plastic surgeons seemed to have only been paying attention to her body.

Eric felt it happening, but there was nothing he could do to stop the violent hacking coughs. It sounded like his throat was coming apart.

"Oh my…" Vickii's hand slid around his lower back, helped guide him to a seat.

"Here, I'll get you that water." She poured a glass pitcher. The water looked clean, but there was no way of knowing. Eric guzzled it. She said, "You shouldn't be out in this mess. It causes all sorts of nasty stuff."

"I'm…fine." Eric forced himself to his feet. His legs were wobbly, but he was feeling better.

Vickii pointed toward the framed photographs lining the right side of the hallway. "These are from when I was younger."

Eric couldn't help but admire her scandalous snapshots. Each one more provocative than the last. Her long hair cascaded over her low-cut dresses. He could see why the Reverend had been attracted to her. He was even in several of the pictures. Things weren't looking well for Vickii.

"A big fan I see," Eric said.

"Oh yes, he was a great man."

She showed him to the dining room, where she took a seat. She offered one to Eric but he waved it off, finished the last of his water. Eric couldn't help but stare at her parted legs, long and silky. Vickii covered her legs with a blanket, kept her hands underneath. "Sorry if it's too chilly. I like the air all the way up." She stared at him and smiled. Way too calm for this sort of thing.

"You know who I am, don't you?"

"I'm old, not dumb. But I've done nothing wrong. Did someone say that I said something blasphemous? You know how women can be. Jealous bitches." She held out her wrist to expose her chip. "Scan me."

"I'm not here to check that. But it is nice to see you're a member."

"Of course I'm a member. And I pay my tithe. It may not be much, but check my records."

A loud click from the hallway made her jump. "It's okay," Eric said.

The Disciples walked into the living room. Eric knew it hadn't been ten minutes. Or had it? This damn cough.

"Would you gentlemen like something to drink?"

"You get anything yet?" Nathan asked. He looked nervous and angry, like he'd just gotten a call from Kenneth berating him for letting Eric go in alone.

"We're getting to that."

"Getting to what?" Vickii said.

"You know damn well what," Ahmer said.

"You claimed to birth the Preacher's brother," Eric said. "You said your son is so very smart and good looking and would be an asset to the Way."

"I never had any children."

Eric asked, "Why would you send the letter?"

"What letter? I never sent a letter."

"She's lying," Nathan said. "It's off your printer."

Eric knew he had to make this look good. He undid his jacket so the tools on his belt would show. "I'm sure she's just remembering incorrectly."

"My meds," Vickii said. "Sometimes I don't think straight."

Eric asked her what kind of pills she took. Before she could answer, Nathan said, "Tell us where your kid is!"

She trembled and slipped both hands under the blanket. "I don't know what you're talking about."

Eric didn't know if he could go through with this. He'd killed hundreds at the insistence of the Preacher, but that was before Michael and his mother, a fourteen-year-old altar girl who couldn't possibly disappear and take care of a newborn.

"Maybe there's something else I can give you." Vickii subtly hiked up the blanket, revealed more of her long legs. "I don't have a lot of money, but you can take anything you want."

Nathan and Ahmer were glued to her shiny calves.

"Why don't you two wait outside?" Eric said, "I work better alone."

"Oh, we know all about how you work." Nathan's hand rested on the butt of his gun. "Now get to it."

Eric studied Vickii and asked her if the letter was true. "Did you have the Reverend's child?"

Tears rolled down her cheeks and splashed off her breasts. "But I never knew him. I don't know his name. I gave him up for adoption after the delivery."

"See that wasn't so hard." Eric tried to think of some way get the Disciples to go outside. He could have Vickii strip down and hide, fire his particle pistol and show them the pile of clothes as proof of her death. He turned to Nathan. "She's talking. Let me handle—"

Nathan pushed past him. Eric tried to reach out, but stopped. A loud blast ripped through the room. The particle beam struck the side of Nathan's head, vaporizing his upper body before it fell against Eric.

Another blast. A loud *umphh* from Ahmer like he got punched in the gut. Eric stared down at the two empty silver suits.

Vickii aimed a gun at Eric's head.

Eric held up his hands and noticed his holster was empty. Vickii with two I's was a lot smarter than he'd given her credit for. "I was going to let you go," he said.

Vickii took a deep breath and blew it out. The gun never wavered. "Sure you were."

"I was going to fake it. That's why I was trying to get them outside. I'm not a killer."

"You just carry the tools?"

"I know how it looks, but you have to believe me. If I don't report back, then he'll send a squad of Controller Force Agents here."

"And if you report back without those two? What then? He'll just forget about it?"

"I can convince him."

"I already gave up my son once. I'm not doing it again."

"And you wouldn't have to. You two can leave, start a new life somewhere else."

"I'm afraid it's too late for that."

"Please, Vickii. I have a son, too. He's five."

Vicki's finger tightened around the trigger. "Then you understand."

26 Pills

January 21, 2059

Steven was half asleep as he carried his baby boy into the kitchen, his slippers dragging over the tile. He pulled his child against his robe and shushed him. "Come on, buddy," Steven whispered. "Not now, dude. It's too early."

Mattie whimpered, but got quiet when Steven took the bottle from the fridge. "Here you go, little man." Steven headed into the living room. The soft, electronic chirp of a cricket came from the black screen. He eased into the recliner and said, "Beach." The screen flashed to a sunny day, gentle waves lapping at the shore, deep blue skies above.

Mattie snuggled into Steven's chest, closed his eyes as he sucked on the bottle. This was their time, the few moments before work with his boy. Steven worked seven days a week to pay the mortgage on the house, but he'd need to work eight to hold onto it, especially now that he'd been stuck with his dad's legal fees. The man had been dead over a year, but the bills kept coming in.

Steven eased his head back and closed his eyes. The lull of the ocean and Mattie's soft breaths let Steven drift into the memory of when Loralei and he moved into the house. They drank wine on the floor and slept under a pile of winter coats. Loralei said this would be the place they'd one day die.

Tap! Steven snapped awake, the baby bottle plopped onto his lap. He turned to the window expecting he'd see the Controllers.

It was a bird, a kind he hadn't seen since he was a child. Nothing but crows dared the skies of San Angeles.

Mattie yawned, his eyes blinking to focus. Steven set the empty bottle on the carpet and eased his son towards the window. "Look, Mattie. It's a blue jay."

The jay picked up a nut from the ledge and cracked it in its beak. Steven checked for Mattie's reaction, but the boy was back asleep. The bird hopped off the ledge and flew towards the dying tree out front.

The clock said he still had forty minutes before he had to leave for work. He thought of going back to sleep, but decided to show Mattie the bird, that their neighborhood wasn't all death and gloom.

Steven set Mattie in the basinet, listened to the house for a few seconds – nothing but the lapping waves. He headed into the kitchen, reached on top of the fridge and brought down a small pill bottle, shook out the contents. Only four Coralmine pills left. There'd been 30 when he bought them five days ago.

The pills were free to every Blocker. They increased productivity. Loralei refused to have them in her house, said they caused too much stress and anxiety.

The tab dissolved on his tongue, the effect immediate, everything clearer in a rush. Not crystal, but so much better than the fog Steven stumbled around in.

He stepped over to the laundry and took off his robe, changed into the black shirt and pants, scuffed up leather shoes. The pill bottle went in his suit jacket he'd left hanging by the door. Steven swigged some stale coffee, grabbed a tiny filtration mask, kissed Mattie's forehead, slid the mask over his fine red hair. Mattie smiled through the plastic visor and opened his deep blue eyes. The left was a little lazy, just like Steven's father's, the man responsible for Mattie even being here.

Steven started to stand but was jerked back down, Mattie's hand clutching his tie.

"You're getting strong, buddy." He peeled off Mattie's chubby fingers and gave him another kiss. Steven wrapped the brown blanket under Mattie and said, "Come on, I've got a surprise for you."

The moment Steven stepped outside he felt like a new man. He ignored their yard of dirt and dead leaves, once a garden before the Block was erected and cut off all but a sliver of sun.

The Block's glimmering black wall was all there was to the east. It drew everyone in and never let them leave. *We're all moths.*

Steven reminded himself he'd come here to show Mattie something delicate and good. He walked Mattie into the yard, noticed the tree was empty. He checked the cables for the jay, ignored the buzzing of foot-long saucers peppering the sky. The bird wasn't up there either. There were no bushes to hide in for miles.

Steven, still looking up, kicked something, fell forward. He caught his balance. Mattie squirmed out of the blanket. "Oh God," Steven said. He'd tripped over the bird, lying flat, its left side a diseased mass. Steven nudged it towards the trash incinerator. He'd throw it in later with gloves.

Right now Mattie deserved a walk. The neighborhood was relatively safe, especially this early. Steven took the usual path, the one Loralei used to walk to work, back when she'd leave the house.

Mattie kept his eyes on his father, uninterested in the decaying trees. Steven searched for words of wisdom, something about appreciating everything around you. He tried to remember all the things his dad had told him. The man had risked everything to help them and died because of it. The burned out remains of the clinic were at the end of the street. The Controllers had torched the place after Steven's father had been charged with sterilization tampering.

Steven had spent so much of his life in that building. It's where he met Loralei ten years ago, the cute little tech who would smile, but hardly talk. His dad had trusted her with everything, loved her as his own. That's why he'd performed the surgery. She desperately wanted a child. Mattie was the final gift Steven's father would ever give. Six days after he was born, the clinic was raided and everyone arrested. Loralei's name popped up in the files. The Controllers scanned her, knew she'd been sterilized and it'd been reversed. They gave Loralei ten seconds to make a choice: testify or have Mattie taken away.

Loralei told them everything. Steven's father was executed the following week.

"Steven Cooper!" a deep voice boomed. "Return to the sidewalk!" It came from a metal speaker in the light post.

Mattie burst into tears and Steven leapt back onto the sidewalk. He didn't even realize he'd wandered off the curb. The pills usually kept him completely focused. He wanted to shout that there weren't any vehicles out, that it was safe, but it'd only make things worse.

The speaker on the light post said, "Jaywalking violation. Automatic withdrawal of $452."

"Of course," Steven muttered. He calmed Mattie down and crossed at the corner, tried to stay upbeat. He hummed a song his father used to sing to him.

They turned back onto their street. A woman paced their yard. Loralei. Her eyes popped and she sprinted at them, her robe flapping behind her. Loralei pointed at their house. "Get inside!"

Mattie cried.

"Lower your voice," Steven said.

She leapt for Mattie, her fingernails digging into Steven's forearm. "Now!"

Steven shielded Mattie with his back. "What is wrong with you? I could have dropped him."

"Why the hell are you out here? You promised!"

There was always someone listening, even outdoors. Steven yelled, "We were on a walk. Where do you think I'm going?"

Loralei forced him towards the porch. "We said no going outside. We agreed."

"It's not going to kill him."

She took Mattie. "It's okay, baby."

Steven said, "You need to calm down. You're scaring him."

Loralei took a deep breath and blew it out. "You promised you would never do this."

"He's my son, Loralei."

"Then act like it. Protect him!"

"You need to stop getting so hysterical and paranoid." Steven's hand was shaking. He felt sweat beads on his neck even though it was chilly.

Loralei stomped her foot. "I'm not paranoid! This is our child! Look at you," Loralei said. "You're jittering. You're on those God damn pills, aren't you?"

Steven clenched his fist. "Of course I'm not. Don't turn this on me."

Loralei shook her head in disgust, entered the house. Steven started to follow, but she slammed the door in his face. Steven grabbed the knob, almost threw open the door, but stopped. He could hit the baby. He backed off the porch, his heart thumping so hard he felt it in his head.

Still had another twenty minutes before he had to leave for work. He closed his eyes, breathed. Loralei would be upstairs in a few minutes, and he'd be able to get his stuff and go.

The diseased bird was still by the incinerator. He walked over to the garage, scanned his palm and it opened. He grabbed a pair of work gloves and a lead-mesh bag. The gloves were snugger than usual.

Steven walked back to the incinerator and squatted down next to the bird, its healthy side up. When he was a boy, he used to see blue jays like this all the time behind the clinic, back before the skies turned to ash. The news said it was due to a meteor shower colliding with the moon, the particles drifted into our atmosphere. That's what the newscasters said. But everyone knew it was the factories outside Zone 45. Black gunk poured out of the stacks night and day for over a year until they built the iron walls to hide the truth, forced everyone to move down into the valleys so they couldn't see what was being pumped into the sky.

A distant boom reverberated through the streets. A rumble shook the ground. Steven nearly fell onto the bird. He turned and saw flickering orange lights coming from the Block. He shielded his eyes, squinted, saw the black solar panels had been blown out about halfway up the massive wall. Fires inside.

Sirens blared, and Steven covered his ears, the rough fabric of the gloves dragging across his skin.

"Residents, return to your homes immediately," The speaker on the light post announced. "This is not a drill. All residents return to your homes immediately."

Steven stood and saw something racing out of the block. A motorcycle kicking up dust. It drew closer. Sparks flashed around the bike.

A Controller on top of the Block was shooting. Steven found himself walking towards the bike barreling over the hill and down his street. A bullet pierced the back tire. The rider launched over the handlebars and slid across the pavement, the mangled bike following, finally crashing into a parked car.

The rider tried to roll over but fell back. Steven ran into the street.

The speaker on the light post said his name. "Jaywalking violation. Automatic withdrawal of $452."

Steven knelt by the rider, saw his own reflection in the mirrored visor. "Just lie still." But the rider wasn't staying put.

"They're coming," a young woman said.

"Just relax."

"They're going to kill us all."

"Okay, just lie back. You could be bleeding inside." Steven looked around, didn't see any blood on the street or around her body.

"Resident Steven Cooper, step away from the fugitive," the speaker commanded.

"Please. Help me," the young woman said.

"It's okay. You're going to be okay."

"This is your second warning," the speaker said. "Step away from the fugitive."

Steven looked back towards the Block, saw three Controller vehicles zooming out of the gates.

"Take me inside," the young woman said. "You can't leave me here."

The Controllers were closing in.

Steven scooped her up and carried her into his yard.

"Resident Steven Cooper, you are in direct violation of security command."

"It'll be all right, it'll be all right," Steven repeated.

Loralei threw open the door. "What are you doing? Who the hell is this?"

"Get out of the way!" Steven pushed past Loralei and set the young woman onto the couch.

"Residents, a known fugitive is being harbored in home 1312."

"Steven, get her out of here. Now!"

The rider pulled off her helmet. She couldn't have been a day over sixteen. "Thank you."

"What happened to you? Why are you running?" Steven asked.

"Who cares? Get her out of here!" Loralei said.

"We were just protesting the new ordinance when the Controllers opened fire. They shot Timothy in the head. They just shot him. We weren't even doing anything. We just had some signs. We were singing a song, and they just killed him."

"This is your final warning," the speaker said.

Steven swiped hair from the teenager's eyes. "What's your name?"

"Kate." Her jaw clenched as she shook her head back and forth through the tears. "I'm so sorry. I couldn't help him."

"There's nothing to be sorry for. Everything's going to be okay."

Sirens grew louder. The Controllers had arrived.

Mattie cried from upstairs. Loralei must have put him in his crib.

"Oh God, they're coming," Kate said.

"Yes, and you have to go!" Loralei gripped Kate's arm, yanked her. Something popped in Kate's shoulder. She screamed.

"God damn it, let her go!" Steven said.

"I'm sorry. I'm sorry," Loralei said. She stumbled back towards the front door.

"Residents, you have ten seconds to send out the fugitive or we will use force," a Controller said through a megaphone.

"Tell me exactly what happened," Steven said.

"You can't send me out there. You can't!" Kate said.

"No one's going anywhere," he said. "Just tell me what happened."

"We were just singing, and people started gathering around. A family joined us."

Loralei threw open the front door, her arms raised. "This isn't what you think! She forced her way in. Please help us!"

"Get down on the ground!" a Controller yelled.

"They're going to kill me, aren't they?" Kate said. She was trembling, her eyes locked on the window. A buzzing grew louder. A steel saucer hovered near the dead tree. Two metal flaps opened underneath the saucer. A tiny missile.

"Loralei, get away from the door!" Steven yelled.

"Oh God, no," Kate cried.

Steven stood, ran for his wife who was refusing to get down.

"Just take her!" Loralei screamed.

Steven was only three feet away when he heard the whoosh of the missile cutting through the air. A blinding light filled the room as it rocketed inside their home. Loralei's head splattered into a thousand flecks, the ringing in his ears forced him to his knees. He looked down, saw the severed white bone of what used to be his left arm.

He tried to turn back to Kate, but stopped at the window. Another missile. Another whoosh. A flash.

Then nothing at all.

Two Minutes to Midnight

November 14, 2061

"You ain't gonna puke, are you, kid?" C.O. Campbell asked.

Troy Edgefield wasn't used to being called "kid." At thirty-six years old, he was bigger and badder than all the other correctional officers and most of the prisoners. Even as he caught his reflection in the gatehouse's bulletproof window, he looked nothing less than hard, and if he hadn't gotten the referral from his father, he'd be on the other side with the animals. The ones he was about to put down.

Troy hated Campbell for his cushy job, checking ID's, scanning for weapons, answering phones. "Why don't you have another drink?"

"All in good time, don't you worry." Campbell's head seemed to have a sunspot for each of his sixty years. He shoved a finger in his nose and glanced at his monitor. "In an hour, we'll both be done with this shithole." Campbell pulled his finger out and wiped a gooey booger on the control panel. After the cleanup it'd be the front desk of the new orphanage.

"So you're really going to retire?"

"The fuck do you think?"

Troy had nothing to say, but that was never a problem for Campbell. "Well, let's get this over with. I got a bottle waiting at home."

"I still got fifteen minutes."

"So do they." Campbell laughed. It was almost midnight.

Now Troy really did feel like he might puke. The higher ups had given Troy a choice: push the button or find another job.

Campbell stretched his neck, the rapid-fire clacking of vertebras. He groaned and sniffed. The old man had always disgusted Troy, but he'd give anything to trade places.

"Not going to happen, kid."

"I didn't say nothing."

Campbell leaned forward and put his grizzled face to the window. Troy realized Campbell had the reader on. All of Troy's thoughts were scrolling across his monitor.

PUSH IT FOR ME…

"You better erase that shit."

"I will, as long as you do your job. Now get to it before the LT calls and has both our asses."

The wrinkled old man looked like he'd probably have a heart attack within a week. Troy thought about all the things he'd do to Campbell's pretty young wife and headed for the door.

Campbell laughed. "In your fucking dreams, kid."

Troy didn't turn back, just waited for Campbell to buzz him through. The corridor was long and cold. Long enough to think about all the faces he was about to see for the last time.

Troy hit the end of the corridor, put his face to the retinal scanner. The steel door slid open and Troy braced for the screams. But it was deathly quiet. Had things calmed down since he left the unit or did Campbell somehow fulfill Troy's request?

Troy noticed the master silence switch was activated. He must have flicked it on before he walked out. If someone wanted to be heard, they'd have to push their button and wait for Troy to acknowledge. And that would not be happening.

Troy stepped inside the giant rotunda, but didn't look up at the four stories, the prisoners trapped behind their soundproof glass. He focused on the bubble in the center of the room, the common area known as the "pit."

The bubble, which looked nothing like the steel sphere his dad had worked in twenty years before, let Troy see everything. He could spin in all directions, move around the pit, even float to different levels to check on the inmates, but it also meant the animals could see him too. Raging eyes peering above the fogged-up glass.

No one would be getting out of his cell today, but even if one did, he wouldn't dare come within fifteen feet of Troy's bubble. The chip at the base of every inmate's spine and the pulsing electromagnetic field circling the station guaranteed Troy's safety.

He climbed in, locked the clear handle, and fired up his monitor. Usually Troy preferred working in the open, where he could see everyone, but tonight he wished for steel walls. Troy used to love the silence, it was soothing, but tonight it felt suffocating. The air seemed too thick. Troy undid the top button of his uniform, concentrated on the monitor flashing the status of every inmate.

Troy didn't have to look around to know the animals were screaming his name, begging for his attention. His father taught him to call them that, "animals," told him it's to remind the C.O.s there's a separation. "The inmates aren't us," his father had said. "But they need our care."

That's what Troy thought about as he stared at the white button.

At least he tried. Across the pit, Inmate Johnson knelt in prayer behind the glass of 1023. His tearing eyes locked with Troy's. He mouthed the words, "Don't do it."

Troy turned back to the monitor, clicked on the air, which only blew out this warm mist. He'd put in a repair request two weeks ago, but higher ups probably saw no reason to fix something that wouldn't be used after tonight.

"Visual confirmation required," the automated voice said.

Troy felt his throat swell. There was no way he could hover by each of their rooms, watch them pound their doors and scream. If someone had escaped, so be it.

But Campbell's voice clicked in. "Video's recording, kid."

Troy knew it wasn't live and there was no reason for someone to watch this later, but he couldn't risk altering protocol, not this close to the orphanage job. He hovered out into the pit, spun in a slow circle, pretended to count, but focused just above each cell, above the pleading fists. Then he rose. Second floor. 2097, old man Thompson, a pedophile rendered harmless, sat on his bunk, head drooped onto his chest. Third floor. 3016, Gomez, a leftover from the failed revolution. The guy claimed he had nothing to do with La Causa. A self-proclaimed peaceful man, he sat on his bunk rocking gently in prayer.

Fourth floor. 4058, Crawford, a wiry freak, pressed his naked body against the glass. Moved his arms and legs slightly up and down, doing his best impression of da Vinci's Vitruvian man. 4025, Hayden, a thirty-year-old on his final leg of a twelve-year stint. Hayden had burned down the weigh station that terminated his mom. Troy didn't blame him, but he couldn't tell the guy. Until yesterday, Hayden thought he'd be out in three weeks.

On the way down, Troy pretended to scratch over his eye, typed in the visual confirmation codes.

A loud thud rang out behind him. Afraid the unbreakable glass had finally given way, Troy spun and searched the wall. It was only Worden on the second floor. Generally, the walls kept in the noise, but Worden was determined to be heard…and seen.

Troy backed into his chair, stared at the bloodied glass in disbelief. Worden had already knocked himself out three times during the shift. Troy had called for medics, but Campbell said they'd already been let go for the night, the infirmary closed. Troy thought the last blow had finished Worden, but the stocky bull staggered to his feet, walked to the back of his cell. He smiled before he ran forward and smashed his forehead into the glass, crumbled to the floor.

The vitals showed Worden was still alive, but barely.

A loud thump came from the third floor. The new fish in 3045 ran over and picked up his chair, threw it again at the glass. Any other night that behavior wouldn't be tolerated, but Troy didn't see the harm in letting it continue. The chair would be the only thing to break.

Troy didn't know what crime the fish had committed, but guessed he wasn't a violent offender as the man still had all his limbs. Troy punched a few keys and checked the screen. The guy was an IP-lifter, hadn't hurt anyone, but it was his third offense and he'd been sentenced to five years. The guy had only been in for three days.

A handful of inmates were lying on their beds. Some were pacing back and forth, signing to the individuals in the rooms around them. Most were standing in front of the glass window screaming at Troy. He couldn't hear them, but he knew exactly what they were saying.

Each and every one of them knew what was going to happen. They were still allowed televisions, a right the Controllers would never dare take away. The inmates all knew they were going to die tonight. There were only four minutes to go.

Troy looked down again at the white button. It was so small, so easy to press. Even a child could've done it. One pound of pressure and the switch from prison to orphanage would begin. He'd have his job and a future for him and his wife. Troy closed his eyes and pictured her face. He could never tell her about this. It'd kill that beautiful smile of hers.

Ringing filled the bubble. Troy picked up the handset. He knew it wasn't the governor calling with a pardon. Even if it was, it wouldn't make a difference. Nothing could stop this. The Controllers had spoken. The decision was final. At midnight, the button would be pushed.

Over the phone, a man barked, "Did you hear what I said?"

"I'm sorry, Sir. Who am I speaking with?"

"Colonel Hayden."

Troy glanced at 4025, wondered if the name was simply coincidence. "Sorry, Sir. I missed it."

"I said, 'It's two minutes to midnight.' Are you ready?"

"Two minutes. Copy."

Troy hung up and brought the bubble down to the center of the pit. He turned to room 1006. Inmate Terrance Potter, the group's self-appointed spokesperson, was sitting in his wheelchair repeatedly pushing his call button.

Instead of turning away, Troy reached for Potter's intercom switch. Potter was one of the nicest men Troy had ever met, in and out of the prison. The former priest was guilty of running an underground Catholic church, sneaking food to the poor and faking sterilization papers. He was the kind of man that would have tried to help Troy's brother, Robert. The kind of man the Controllers abhorred, four severed limbs to prove it.

Addressing the man in a way he hadn't dared to before this night, Troy said, "Yes, Father."

The white-haired man gazed at Troy. "C.O. Edgefield, I understand that you have no choice in this matter, that you are only doing your job. I forgive you for what you are about to do, but I cannot speak for the others. Please look into your heart and let them speak. Let them say their piece even though it will fall on deaf ears." Potter motioned to his fellow inmates. "Let them speak to one another."

Potter was correct about Troy not having a choice. If Troy didn't do his job, he could be arrested, and someone else would push the button. Prisoners no longer had a place in society. But this wasn't the same as shooting an escaping prisoner. He'd promised his dad he wouldn't be like the others.

Still, he couldn't flick the communal speaker switch. Potter was one thing, but he wouldn't be able to face the onslaught of anger, the crying voices begging for mercy.

Campbell clicked in. "Aw, just let them talk."

"Negative," Troy said. "We're under two minutes."

"Kid, let them hear something."

"Why? It's not going to make any difference."

"Shit, nothing does."

Troy clicked off Campbell's voice. Fuck Campbell. The man didn't have to come back, face the empty cells, knowing what he'd done. The only sound in the bubble was Troy's breath. He clenched his teeth, pictured his wife, Laura, the woman who thought she married a decent man, a kind man.

One minute to midnight.

"Even animals deserve compassion," his father's voice played in his head.

How could Troy ever look at Laura again if he couldn't even live up to those simple words?

Troy clicked on the communal speakers. The rotunda's silence was shattered with shrieks and curses, a multitude of prayers rolling underneath the wailing. Inmates yelled for Troy to open their doors. Others begged for a phone call. Some said they forgave him. Most damned him to hell.

Troy wanted to close his eyes, wanted to run, but he owed them this, so he stared into their eyes. He brought the bubble high into the air as hatred showered him like a tidal wave.

Ten seconds left. Even if these voices would haunt him forever, Troy refused to think of anything else, to hear anything but their words.

The clock clicked. Midnight. The new day arrived with Troy pressing the white button. Cloudy gray gas poured from the ceiling vents in each cell. Most inmates fell to the floor and covered their mouths as the deadly fog descended. The brave ones stood tall until the gas hit their skin.

The Controllers had promised a quick, painless death. Not this. The men clawed at their frying skin, their fingers pulling off piles of melted flesh.

Troy blindly slapped at his control panel. Silence, but too late. The blood-gurgling cries echoed in his mind. He watched as the gas ate away inside and out.

Some of the prisoners wrapped blankets around their bodies. It was no use. The gas found them. It found everyone. It looked like when an egg cracks in boiling water.

The lucky ones died instantly from the shock, but others were still flailing, writhing for a minute…two minutes.

A few of those still alive were already on their way to the death chamber, but the rest were in for petty crimes. On the second floor, inmate Fulton, a father of three who'd embezzled for his kids' college, tore at his wrists with his fingernails. Inmate Baker had his head buried in the toilet as his back sizzled and split until Troy saw the man's spleen. He was one of the last to go, but he ended up just as dead as everyone else.

Troy's shaking hand picked up the handset and dialed the Controllers' headquarters. When the mechanical voice answered, Troy said, "This is C.O. Edgefield reporting from San Angeles, California, Prison 146, medium custody." Everywhere he turned, piles of blistering flesh. "I'm…confirming cleansing success." Troy slammed the phone and looked around the bloodied cells. Four hundred lives in less than three minutes.

The map on his monitor blinked over San Angeles.

Troy ran the figures of the two continents combined. Little lights blinking everywhere. Over twenty-one million people.

One Last Bedtime Story

February 1, 2063

The local news flashed across the holographic platform. Tammy Longley snuggled in her husband's arms. John told her to keep flipping, but her finger didn't move, eyes glued to the screen. John tried to grab it. She stuffed the remote between the couch cushions under her leg.

"Come on, the game's starting," John said, all tired and whiny.

Tammy was already welling up at the Child of the Day, a button-nosed boy named Phillip. "Oh, he's so cute."

Phillip's height, weight, IQ, and Health Index Scores scrolled across the bottom of the image. He had two weeks until he turned five. The news anchor said that as an older child, his chances of ever finding a home dropped drastically each day.

John scootched back and sighed. "Why do you watch stuff that makes you feel like shit?"

Tammy wiped at her tears. "Because that boy doesn't have anyone."

"I know, and it's awful. But there's nothing we can do. Now please, just turn the channel."

Tammy kept facing the image, but she wasn't watching. "Can we talk about it?"

"I can't do this tonight, Tammy."

"But we can help." Before John could even open his mouth, Tammy cut him off. "We have the money. And you teach from home. We always eat in. Hardly spend a dime. We'll be here to raise him – or her." Tammy put on her little girl face, the same one she'd used to get John to agree to the dog.

"But don't you like our life just the way it is? Bella might get jealous."

"She's not going to get jealous, and I love our life, which is why I want to share it. You know we'd be good parents."

"Of course you'd be a good mom, but…me?"

She touched his cheek. "You'd be the best."

"You don't know that. Come on, I'm lazy. And you said it yourself, I'm a hermit."

"Which means you'll be here to play. You two can watch sports, build forts, and I'll never watch the news again."

"*Never?*"

"Never." Tammy put her hand over her heart. "Swear."

John shook his head. "Tammy, I'm sorry, I'm not doing this. I know you want it, but I don't."

Tammy bit the inside of her cheek. "Why?"

"Because…I'd screw him up, okay? All the shit I live with in my head, I can't put that on a little kid. I can't…" John looked over at the wall.

Tammy pulled his chin toward her. "You can't keep doing this to yourself. You're a good man, and you've got a good heart. But you're killing us."

John didn't say a word, his cheeks burning the same shade as his hair.

"What if your parents hadn't adopted you?" Tammy said. "I never would have met you."

"Maybe that would've been better."

Tammy stopped breathing for a few seconds, just stared at him. "Is…is that what you think?"

John clenched his teeth, shook his head a little. "Of course not."

"I just want us to have a life, John."

"And I don't?"

"We have to stop living full of fear and worrying what might happen. We can do this and make a difference. What good's our life if we don't?"

John blew out a deep breath, closed his eyes. "Alright."

"Yeah?"

"Yeah."

Tammy threw her arms around him. "Oh, I love you, love you, love you…" She sat back with the biggest smile, couldn't remember the last time she'd been this happy.

"But we're going to be smart, we're not going to rush."

"No rush."

"And if we don't find the perfect kid, we'll—"

"We'll keep looking."

"You promise."

"Promise, promise, promise."

# # #

They pulled into the orphanage's giant parking lot. Tammy pointed out there was only one other car. John didn't say anything, just pulled into a stall.

The trip took had taken two hours, even though the Reduction Act was supposed to decongest the highways. The DMV denial rate had even been bumped up to fifteen percent. Still, nothing changed. It was, in fact, worse.

John stared up at the four-story concrete building, the sun shining off the narrow window slits cut into the domed top.

Tammy asked if John was okay and he said he was fine.

John shook off whatever was bothering him. "This is going to be sad. You sure you're up for it?"

Tammy took his hand and led him to the steel doors. His limp was more pronounced than usual. They entered the drab, gray building and headed to the bulletproof window.

The young blond sitting behind the desk jumped when John said hello. She gave an embarrassed smile and set down her magazine. "I'm so sorry. I didn't hear you guys come in. Can I help you?"

Tammy said, "Well, we're thinking about adopting."

"Oh, that's so great," the receptionist said. "Let me call Troy so he can show you the kids."

"I thought there was an interview first," Tammy said.

"Interview?" The receptionist laughed. She clicked her headset and told Troy to report to the front for visitors.

John looked around the lobby. "Don't we, uh, have to fill out paperwork before we do anything else?"

The receptionist whispered into her headset. "…No, I'm not joking. Now get down here."

Tammy shot John a look. He'd promised not to intentionally stall.

"Oh, the kids are going to love this," the receptionist said. "You should see how excited they get. Even the little ones seem to realize this might be their chance. It's so cute." She pulled out a single sheet of paper. "You do have to sign one of these. It releases us from any liability and transfers ownership of the child."

John looked it over. "You mean right now?"

"If you like, sure. You just pick out the one you want, and I can have you out of here in five minutes."

There was so much white space on the page. John said, "I thought there would be more to it."

"Well, a social worker will make a scheduled visit once a year to check on everything. If the child's gone with no explanation there could be a fine."

"*Fine*?" Tammy said.

"Yeah. Unfortunately, some people adopt just to get their hands on fresh organs. It's so gross."

Tammy gasped. John didn't look surprised.

Troy Edgefield staggered into the room, his gut threatening the structural integrity of his uniform buttons. His white shirt had food stains, his face showed a few days of beard. The only thing that looked professional was the sleek particle gun holstered on his thigh.

"This is Troy," the receptionist said. "And these are the…"

"Tammy Longley, and this is my husband, John."

John stepped toward Troy, but didn't shake his hand. He stood straighter than Tammy had seen in a long time.

"You look familiar," Troy said, his speech slurred. "I know you?"

John's casualness sounded forced. "Doubt it. Just here to browse."

Troy turned around, nearly fell, and led them down a long hallway. While they waited for the security system to read Troy's retina, Tammy glanced at John, wondered why he was acting so strange. Before she could get his attention, the door opened and they walked into a huge, circular room that reminded Tammy of some gothic circus tent.

They followed Troy to the workstation located in the middle of the rotunda. It was so quiet. Tammy looked all around the room, shocked to see so many little faces staring back at her from the other side of glass walls. She spun slowly, mesmerized by the hundred tiny eyes filled with hope, anxiety, defeat, and despair.

This wasn't a circus. "It looks like a prison," she said.

Troy took his seat at the computer console. He didn't even look up when he said, "Used to be."

Tammy covered her mouth and turned to John, finally realized why he was being so peculiar. She whispered, "This isn't where Peter…?"

John nodded toward the fourth floor. "Cell 4025."

Troy's fingers hesitated for a split second before he went back to typing.

Tammy turned to John. "I'm sorry, I didn't know. Do you want to leave?"

John shook his head. Tammy apologized again and held his hand. When she noticed Troy looking at them from the corner of his eye, she smiled and noticed there weren't any kids outside their cells. "Are their doors locked?"

Troy kept clacking away. "During visits it's protocol. But if you see one you like, I can let you in. Oh, and I'm supposed to ask. You got any requirements?"

"Oh, uh…" Tammy sputtered.

"Race is the main one." Troy let out a little burp. "Predetermined height's a big one. So is IQ. Not too many people want to adopt a retard. I can plug in whatever you want though. Narrow it down. We've weeded out most of the ones with anything terminal."

"*Weeded out*, huh?" John said.

Tammy didn't like the way John was acting. "Can we look around?"

"Yeah, browse away." Troy scratched at his fat neck waddle, a tan line on his ring finger.

Tammy asked John where he wanted to start, but John just kept staring at the back of Troy's head.

Troy pointed. "Infants and one-year-olds are down here, two-year-olds got the second floor, threes on the third, and fours on top."

Tammy pulled John toward a cell of babies in their cribs. Their cries silent behind the glass. A video screen listed off names and statistics, illnesses highlighted in red.

The babies were adorable and cute, misshapen and ugly. Some were smiling, others sleeping, the rest screaming.

"I don't know if I want a baby," Tammy said. "I kind of want to talk to them."

"Did you say *them*?"

"You know what I meant." She turned to Troy. "Can we go upstairs?"

"Yeah, I'll buzz you."

A gate opened. A metal staircase zigzagged all the way up to the fourth floor.

As they made their way up, Troy snuck a drink from a little flask.

"This place is just so awful," Tammy said. "How can they lock them up like this?"

On the second floor, little tykes wobbled around in their cells. Some played with blocks covered in bite marks. One kid just kept spinning until he fell against the wall. After a few minutes, Tammy and John decided a two-year-old would also be too much work. They went up the next flight of stairs.

Most of the three-year-olds were standing in front of the glass. They smiled, trying to look so cute. Tammy cooed, and John rolled his eyes. A little girl stood behind her glass and posed like a ham, her chin on her folded hands, bottom lip stuck out in a little pout.

Tammy covered her mouth. "These kids know how to work it."

John looked down into the pit at Troy staring blankly at the wall.

"What do you think?" Tammy asked. "Do you see anyone you want to meet?"

"I don't know." John looked down the long row of cells. "What about that kid?" He pointed at a little boy sniffing his armpit.

As they started walking, Tammy kept looking up at the fourth floor.

"Tammy, at four, they've been… They've just been here a long time."

"But is there *really* a difference?"

"I don't know."

Tammy batted her eyes.

"If you want to look at four, let's look at four."

Tammy dragged him back toward the stairs, her heels clanging against the metal. She hurried to the first monitor, read the boy's name. Brian, four years, three months. A beaming smile pasted on his face, his arms awkwardly hanging at his sides like he didn't know what to do with them. Then there was Gabriel, sitting on the toilet with his pants around his ankles, his face flushed a bright red. They quickly moved to Tommy, juggling two orange balls. When one fell, he started punching the wall. An angry little man.

They hardly stopped at Victor, the largest kid in the place, rocking on the edge of his bed, screaming so hard his face was the color of Tammy's purse.

Tammy didn't even realize John had moved ahead two cells. He was staring at a blond boy sitting on his bed, a book in his lap, a pair of broken eyeglasses on the floor, tears coursing down his cheeks.

"He's beautiful," Tammy said. "Do you want to go in?"

John's voice cracked when he said, "It's Peter's room."

Tammy didn't know the whole story about John's cousin. He never wanted to talk about it. She looked down into the pit, but Troy was no longer at his monitor.

"You find one?" a voice said.

Tammy jerked back. She hadn't heard Troy come up, but there he was standing right behind them.

"Yeah, can you open 4025?" Tammy said.

Troy pressed his thumb against a scanner. Tammy read Matthew's stats. The kid had a high IQ, but his health index was low. But most importantly, tomorrow was his birthday.

The door slid open. Tammy and John walked inside the room and knelt in front of the child. She picked up the glasses from the floor and asked, "Is this your only pair?"

He nodded, eyes down.

"That looks like a really neat book. What's it about?"

Speaking barely over a whisper, he said, "Billy gets lost at the amusement park and his Mommy looks for him all over but he joins this group of pirates who rescue her from this evil king."

"That sounds like a great story. Would you mind if I read it to you?"

Matthew mumbled okay and wiped the tears from his face.

Tammy sat next to him. "Well, Matthew, I'm Tammy and this is my husband, John."

Matthew said hello then looked into Tammy's eyes. "Do you like to read?"

"Very much." Tammy scooted closer, and for the next five minutes, she read the book. By the time she was finished, Matthew was cuddled against her side.

Tammy closed the book and handed it to him. "Did you like that story?"

"It's my favorite. Can you read it one more time?"

She looked up at John and he said, "Maybe later."

"Come on, John." She turned to Matthew. "He does really good voices. Especially pirates. Would you like to hear them?"

Matthew nodded with excitement.

Tammy waved John over and he finally sat down and took the book. When he finished telling the story, putting extra flare on Captain Blackbone, John gave the book back to Matthew and told him this was now his favorite story, too.

"Matthew, do you mind if John and I go outside to talk for a minute?"

"Can you read one more time?"

"When we get back we can. We'll only be a minute."

Matthew threw his arms around her leg and squeezed. He whispered something about not wanting to go to sleep.

Tammy sat, held him tightly. "It's too early for bedtime. Don't worry."

Matthew violently shook his head, nearly cracking into Tammy's jaw. John noticed a digital clock on the wall. It was ticking down. Two seconds…one second…

An alarm blared on Troy's watch. "I'm sorry. Visiting time is over. You two have to leave. Matthew, remain seated."

Tammy looked to John. He was standing, a few feet from Troy.

"We're not going anywhere," John said.

Troy shouted, "Leave the room! Now!"

Tammy asked why the clock hit zero. "He doesn't turn five until tomorrow."

"I'm not going to ask you again," Troy said. His hand hovered over his particle pistol.

John, the man who'd never been able to stand up to anyone, got in his face. "We're not done with the visit."

"You have five seconds."

John walked over, took Matthew's hand. "Do you want to go home with us?"

Matthew nodded.

Tammy saw Troy pull out his gun. "What are you doing? We want him. Let us fill out the paperwork."

"I can't do that. Protocol." His gun aimed at Tammy's face.

"Just call the receptionist," Tammy said.

John scooped up Matthew . "They're not going to hurt you."

Troy blocked the doorway. "Put him down."

"We're taking him," John said. "I'll sign whatever we have to, but he's not staying." He started to move past Troy, who put the gun to John's head.

"Put down the boy!"

"You don't have to do this," John whispered.

"Yeah, I do." He pointed at the vent in the ceiling. "Now, they're either going to find one body, or they're going to find three."

"I remember you," John said. "My cousin was here."

Tammy begged Troy to stop this. Slowly, John set Matthew down, told Tammy to take him. Then John turned so the barrel of the gun was flat against his forehead.

A small white mist began to pour out.

"I have to close the door," Troy said. He reached his other hand toward a remote on his belt.

Matthew was crying, his arms wrapped around Tammy's neck. They both coughed.

"It's burning!" Matthew screamed.

John stared at Troy. "What happened here? Come on, these are just kids."

Troy's finger tightened around the trigger. John closed his eyes and Tammy held onto Matthew as she crouched on the floor, trying to stay away from the mist, her skin itching, then sizzling.

"On the first floor, there's a back door," Troy whispered. He slipped something hard in John's hand.

John opened his eyes, saw Troy's ID card. Troy stepped to the side. John pulled Tammy, who was still holding Matthew. They hurried out. The door slid shut. Tammy turned back as Troy walked into the mist.

Twelve O'Clock High

November 14, 2066

Residential Recreational Zone 44 was practically deserted. A few kids played tackle soccer, filtration masks strapped around their little heads. One kid drove his shoulder into a spindly boy, slamming him onto the scorched field. The sole parent standing on the sideline clapped weakly.

Colonel Charles Hayden was the only person not wearing protection. He kept staring at the gates, checked his watch. In their two years of retirement, Andrew had never been late to their Sunday chess match. Charles wondered if it had something to do with the date, five years to the day since they'd done the unthinkable.

Charles was sitting at one of the concrete tables surrounding the pond. Just looking at the black water caused an itch in his throat. He hacked up a mouthful of bloody phlegm, spat it on the ground, and wiped his lips with his once-white handkerchief.

This used to be a great fishing spot. The rod holders attached to the benches around the pond were now rusted. Even the fish had gone the same way as most everyone Charles had known.

Charles arranged his gold and silver pieces on the chessboard painted on the concrete top. Two old men were sitting a few tables down. Their eyes squinting in concentration behind their fogged up plastic masks. One guy's muffled voice asked Charles if he wanted to play winner, but Charles said he was waiting for someone.

Andrew was the most punctual person that Charles had ever known. Charles tried to tell himself Andrew was home sick, unable to call because the black lung had progressed. Last week, he seemed fine, coughing much less than Charles had, but now that Charles thought about it, Andrew had been acting strange. They never spoke of the unthinkable, but that afternoon Andrew was dancing around it, mentioning people who'd been in the command center, the officer who'd patched through every call. Andrew seemed agitated, distracted, actually lost every match. Something that had never happened.

While Andrew had never mentioned the calls specifically, that's all Charles could think about. They'd made hundreds that night, given the commands to correctional officers.

Charles reached under his chair and pulled out his mahogany case. He carefully set it on the concrete table, so as not to scuff the wood. Charles thought back to Andrew saying several of the officers had been found dead. Charles had reminded Andrew the streets had never been safe, especially for old men.

Although Charles wasn't too concerned about his safety, leaving his chess pieces out longer than necessary was asking for trouble. He put away the back row of gold pieces on Andrew's side first, wondered if maybe his friend had reached the first stage of insanity. The black lung progressed differently for everyone. Some killed themselves during the paranoia.

Charles placed the pawns in the felt-lined case. So many pawns and only one king.

Charles checked the park one last time. A couple by the fence gathered their items and hurried toward the back exit. Two of the Way's missionaries had just entered the premises.

They wore filtration masks and black shirts instead of the crisp white ones of old. Even the highest quality white fabric couldn't keep its brilliance in San Angeles' air, and in their line of work, wearing white wasn't a good idea.

The Wishionaries, as Charles called them, walked toward the two old men playing chess. It didn't matter that the Way had more members than any other religion, that nearly every political leader, including the President, was a member. They still pounded the pavement, searched for new recruits who would be willing to accept the promises that never came true.

Their Preacher said he'd reshape the Americas, make a healthier, happier, more prosperous nation. He said he'd lead them to salvation. The one true religion delivered through the one true voice.

Charles used the back of his sleeve to wipe the sweat from his forehead. It wasn't even noon and already in the 100's. The gray sky blocked out the mountains, cut skyscrapers in half, made it so he could barely see the top of the tide wall surrounding the city.

Charles was grateful he had no children to leave with this shit when he died.

A voice from behind said, "Good morning, Resident."

Charles took his time turning around. Both of the Wishionaries were standing there. One held a bible, the other a scanner. Both had particle pistols on their hips.

The taller of the two spoke through his mask, but his words were unmuffled, a nice feature of the more expensive models. "Are you with the Way?"

Charles rolled back his sleeve to expose the tattoo, twenty-five years of dedicated worship.

They seemed disappointed. The stubby one with the scanner asked Charles for the name of a disbeliever.

"Sorry, I don't know anyone."

"Surely there's someone you know that needs guidance."

Charles motioned at his empty table. "Does it look like I got any friends?"

The tall one straightened his back. "You know the rules, Brother. Give us a name or it'll be a mark."

"Mark away."

The stubby one scanned Charles's wrist. "I'm sorry, Colonel. You…have a good day."

Charles closed the case. The sun played off the gold plate stamped into the top. January 1, 2064. In Recognition of Forty Years of Honorable Service.

Honorable, right.

He'd been on the President's Council, the highest position he could have reached, but when the orders came down, it didn't matter. Charles didn't have a choice. He didn't even try to argue to get out of making the calls. He'd learned his position didn't mean a damn thing when not even his wife was excused for failing to make weight. All it got him was this stupid chess set.

Charles looked toward the park's clock. The Wishionaries were escorting a muttering old woman through the gates. A man and a young boy walked past them, each holding a cellophane-wrapped bouquet of flowers. The man had the noticeable limp Charles hadn't seen since he retired.

Charles was excited to see his nephew, John, but not about to let it show. John had aged in the last five years, his red hair too gray for a man in his forties.

John placed his hand on the young boy's shoulder and signaled him to stop a few feet from Charles' table. "Good day, Colonel," John said through his filtration mask.

Charles nodded.

John introduced the boy as his son and told him to say hi. The frail boy softly muttered a hello while staring at his shoes.

The boy looked around seven or eight, too old to be John's biological son.

Charles felt the phlegm rising, tried to stifle it, but couldn't. Hacked the bloody goop in his handkerchief.

John said, "You shouldn't be out here without…"

Charles waved his nephew off the subject. A filtration mask wasn't going to wipe out the darker-than-the-sky, fist-sized spot on Charles' lung.

"Why are you here?" Charles said.

"I was worried about you."

Charles figured it had to be his nosy neighbor, Betty. The woman couldn't keep her mouth shut, and she was one of the few who knew about their Sunday chess match. Charles, of course, had a tracker implanted from his days of service, but only top-level officers had access.

John set his flowers on the table and unfolded a flatscreen he pulled from his pocket. "Have you been watching the news?" John pressed a button on the screen then handed it to Charles. "I recognized him right away, I met him at your house."

A photo of Andrew in full dress uniform appeared on the screen. It was from years ago, back when Andrew had a full head of hair. A reporter described in grisly detail the condition of the General's body. The Controllers found it in the parking lot of the orphanage, which the reporter mentioned used to be a prison. The Controllers were looking into a connection between his death and the murders of ten other high-ranking officials. Charles recognized all of the names. He'd worked with each of them at some point in his career. Charles couldn't be sure, but they had probably all played a part in the eradication.

The video stopped. John took back the screen and put it away. "I'm sorry."

Charles cleared his throat. "He lived a long life."

"I just thought I should find you. If there's someone out there—"

"There's not. And if there is, I'm too old to be hiding."

"But you could stay with us."

Charles turned away and coughed. A young couple entered the park. There was a man in a black jumpsuit by the bathrooms. A longhaired teenager slipped change into the vending machine. Suddenly, everyone looked suspicious.

John said, "I saw your eyes when you read their names. You know it's real."

Charles ran his fingers across the smooth edge of the chess case. He smiled at Matthew, hiding behind John's leg. "Did you pick out these flowers?" Charles asked.

Matthew nodded then ducked back behind John. John eased him back out and said, "We're going to visit the cemetery. You should come."

"Nah, I need to get going." Charles hadn't been there since Peter's funeral, the worst day of Charles' life, standing there knowing he was the one who'd made the call.

Charles stood and glanced at the man in the black jumpsuit still watching them. "It was nice seeing you, but I'm running late."

John blocked Charles' path. "Just come with us. You'll be safe." John lifted his shirt to reveal the grip of a ballistic firearm tucked into his waistband.

Charles started laughing, which sent the bloody phlegm shooting up his throat. This time he just spat it on the ground. "Should we smile for the pictures?" Charles asked. There were cameras everywhere. The man in black had moved to a bench, but was still watching them. He was trying to be discreet, definitely ex-military.

Charles grabbed the case, bent down next to Matthew. "Do you know how to play chess?"

Matthew shook his head.

"Well, that's a shame because your dad is an expert. When you get home, he's going to teach you how to play just like I taught him." Charles held the case to Matthew.

Matthew looked to his dad for approval. When John nodded, Matthew took the case and mumbled a muffled thank you.

"Just come with us," John said. "I know Tammy would love to see you."

"No, I have an appointment." Charles couldn't look at John. It was too painful. He tried to remind himself that if he hadn't made the call, he would have been executed for treason. That's what he'd been telling himself for five years.

John put his hand on Charles's shoulder. "You can't keep blaming yourself."

Charles gave a little nod and walked off, angled across the park, headed for the south gate. He turned left onto Seventh Street and headed for the bus stop three blocks down. He wished he'd kept his car, but when he'd retired, he forgot to sign up for automatic renewal of his driver's license. The DMV's denial rate was up to twenty percent, so public transportation was Charles' only option.

When he reached the end of the second block, he looked behind him. The man in black was a block back. Charles quickened his pace. The 11:50 bus was pulling away from the curb.

Charles tried to make it look like a leisurely stroll. He kept thinking about the Western reruns he used to watch with his father, showdowns at noon. Only Charles was running away from instead of stepping into the street. If the younger Charles saw this, he'd puke.

The bus pulled over half a block ahead. Charles ran as fast as his tired heart could handle.

Charles stepped through the doors just before they snapped shut. His heart thudded against his ribs. Charles pushed his way through the crammed bus. He was stuck between two teenagers. The bus began to move, and Charles started breathing. They made it a few feet when the brakes squeaked and the doors swished open.

He couldn't see who the driver had stopped for, but inched further down the jam-packed aisle until he was up against the emergency exit. The doors slammed shut and the bus pulled into its dedicated lane. A low murmur made its way toward Charles – people complaining about someone pushing.

Buildings zipped by. Charles looked at the emergency chord, but even if he did make it to a Controlling Force station, what would he tell them, that some guy got on the same bus as him?

The crowd was getting louder. Someone said, "Watch it, asshole!"

Charles saw the library coming up on the right. He yanked the cord and was out the door the second the bus stopped.

Charles hurried up the stairs. He reached the front door, threw it open, and checked behind him. The man in black jumped out of the back of the bus and was walking toward him. His right hand was buried in his pocket, probably gripping the same gun he'd used on Andrew and the others.

The library was cold and quiet. Charles headed for the elevator. The digital indicator said the car was on its way down from the third floor. Charles looked to the front door, saw the man in black reaching for the handle. The elevator dinged open. Charles slipped inside, his finger mashing the top floor button. The doors closed, but not before he saw the man in black's blue eyes.

When the elevator opened, Charles ran down the hallway and into the stacks. There wasn't a soul in sight. "Hello?" Charles said as he entered one aisle, then turned down another. Lights flicked on as he stepped into each aisle, like overhead breadcrumbs for the man in black. Charles was suddenly confused, trapped in this maze. The elevator chimed. Charles crouched down. The mirror in the corner gave Charles a clear view of the elevator.

Without any hesitation, the man in black headed straight for Charles. He must have had Charles' tracker code. There was no other explanation. Charles saw the emergency exit, ran, pushed open the door, and climbed a flight of stairs that led to the roof. With some luck the killer's scanner wouldn't know whether he went up or down.

Charles slowly pushed the service exit and prayed there wasn't an alarm. He walked onto the roof. The only place to hide was the three-foot wide track along the front of the enormous billboard, overlooking the street. Charles stepped out looking everywhere but down. He grabbed the electronic screen with both hands and made his way to the center, felt as if the slightest breeze would send him plummeting to the pavement.

Charles finally opened his eyes, looked at the electronic image. It was an ad for The Way, the Preacher's bowed head directly above his.

The man in black poked his head around the edge of the billboard, his blue eyes and blond hair a rarity outside of the Way's top echelon. Charles suddenly remembered the face, but Private Cody Bradford had been reported dead. Charles blinked, wondered if he'd hit the first stage of insanity. But this was definitely Cody, almost the exact image of his father.

Cody said, "Aren't you a little old to be playing hide-and-seek?"

Charles kept his left hand on the billboard to steady himself. "Aren't you a little young to be chasing old men around the city?" Charles tried to sound tough, but he knew exactly what he looked like, hanging up here like a coward.

Cody's hand was in his pocket. "Come off of there so we can talk."

"No, I like it here. The breeze feels good."

Cody clenched his jaw and stepped onto the railing, causing it to sway. He no longer looked as confident when he brought his hand out of his pocket to balance himself.

Charles locked eyes with Cody. "So what is it you want to talk about, young man?" Charles watched as Cody started to reach inside his pocket. If Charles started rocking, he could probably send Cody over the rail.

"To hear you beg for mercy."

"Why don't I save both of us a lot of time by just letting you shoot me?"

Cody pulled out the pistol. "On your knees and beg!"

Charles blew out a long breath. Why the hell had he been running? He let go of the screen. "Begging just means I've got something to live for."

"You killed my dad. You and the Way."

"Son, I killed a lot more than your dad."

The pistol shook in Cody's hands. "You make me sick."

"Yeah, you and me both."

"You're not even sorry?!"

The gun didn't scare Charles. Neither did the angry young man behind it. "Why don't you just do us both a favor and pull that trigger."

The clock chimed.

"Shut the hell up. You think you're so smart!" He had to yell over the chimes. "You and your friends destroyed everything!"

"Yeah…I guess we did."

Charles turned and put both hands on the railing. He thought of Peter, his only son. If Charles would've refused the order, someone else would've made the call. But Charles had been scared to die.

"What the hell are you doing?" Cody yelled over the chimes.

"You don't need any more blood on your hands, kid. Trust me."

"Get on your knees."

Charles leaned forward, felt all the blood rush to his head, then his feet hitting the top of the rail, spinning him end over end. The sky, the ground, the steel building in front, the brick library behind. Then nothing.

Twenty-Two Pine Avenue

March 6, 2067

Nothing could be heard over the Controllers' civil-defense sirens, but Captain Fuller kept on the hovercar's horn as he flew a hundred miles an hour along the shoulder of the stopped freeway, the flood waters already reaching the windows of the abandoned vehicles. Citizens washing past the hovercar, the strong ones swimming, the weak or unlucky face down.

Fuller yanked the microchip off his helmet to override the autopilot. He took the wheel, swooping the hovercar from side to side, narrowly avoiding the bodies sweeping by. The car reported, "Eight miles to Twenty-Two Pine Avenue."

An accident up ahead blocked most of the shoulder. A half-submerged van smashed by a jackknifed big rig. Fuller yanked the wheel, whipped right, took the hovercar up the retaining wall. The bottom scraped the van's roof and slammed down on the water, continued skimming over it at an almost uncontrollable speed.

Johnson's voice came over his earpiece. "What the hell are you doing?" He sounded rattled. Johnson was never rattled.

"How bad? How bad is it?"

The crackle of static followed by silence. Fuller feared he'd lost the connection to headquarters. Then Johnson said, "The Twenty-Third District is gone. Same for most of the southern coast."

Fuller kept his eyes locked on the roaring river that used to be a highway. If he crashed, Susan and Nick were as good as dead. "How far along is the containment?"

"They're on it, but running into problems."

"Is it blocked?"

"Not yet. No one expected this."

Fuller doubted that last part.

The hovercar crunched over what Fuller hoped was an already dead body.

A new voice came on the headset. Chief Tolbert. "Get your ass back here now, Fuller."

"I cannot do that, Sir."

"The aquarium's gone. The initial wave ripped it apart."

Chief Tolbert had been standing there when Nick called saying he was going to the aquarium. Fuller saw the Chief's face.

"Turn around and get back to HQ. There's nothing left."

The car reported Twenty-Two Pine was only seven miles away. Nearly every non-hovercar on the freeway was completely submerged.

Fuller swerved around the top of a moving van and into the middle of the water-filled freeway. He was now topping one-ten. "I know they're alive."

"There are no reported survivors, Fuller." Tolbert's ragged breaths filled Fuller's headset. "I'm sorry. But we need you here."

Fuller maneuvered the car side to side to avoid the tops of taller vehicles, uprooted trees, and countless bodies. "And I'll be there just as soon I have my wife and kid."

"Goddamnit! The walls are almost up. If you do actually get in, you won't get out. Let the Controllers handle this. If they're alive, the rescue squads will find Susan and Nick."

"I'm not waiting."

"I'm ordering you to turn around!"

The car said six miles before Twenty-Two Pine Avenue. Johnson came on the radio. "That's not where the aquarium is—"

"Get off the goddamn radio!"

"Where is it then? My GPS visual is cutting out, but it keeps repeating this address."

More static. Fuller prayed Johnson would respond. He kept driving, thought about pleading to the Chief, but he knew that wouldn't get him what he needed. So he just sat there.

Finally, Johnson came back on. "A restaurant three blocks from the aquarium. It's on a hill. They might be alright."

Fuller was now racing at one-twenty, no longer worried about the cars several feet below him.

"Their bodies were probably washed there," Tolbert said. "You're going to get yourself killed."

Susan hadn't answered a single call, but she'd activated both of their distress signals. Tolbert kept yelling and Fuller threw his earpiece and career out the window. Fuller banked right. Supercopters filled the sky, each dropping a mountain of dirt. Landmovers the size of warehouses piled the payloads into a new wall. Corpses spilled over the top of the moving mountain, rolled down the sides. Fuller dropped the throttle. He had no idea where the incline would send him, but he knew he had to hit it fast. Three seconds before the hovercar hit the moving mountainside, Fuller realized some of the bodies weren't dead. He saw their eyes as they tumbled down.

Fuller closed his eyes and braced for the impact, but he knew without autopilot, he'd just drive straight through. His eyes popped open. Straight ahead of him was a woman with three children, huddled on their knees. To his right was a five-story building, two feet from the wall. He'd never make it through.

The girl screamed as the hovercar flew at her, stopped when it struck her stomach and slammed her head against the hood before sucking her under.

The car hit the top of the mound at too strong an angle and flew over the tangle of cars, the people crawling over each other trying to escape. The hovercar was forty feet above the water, then twenty, then slammed down so hard Fuller bounced up and his right kneecap crunched into the dash.

He'd never broken a bone before but knew it was shattered. He flipped back to autopilot, hoped HQ didn't have him in range on the other side of the mountain. His speed dropped in half and he tried adjusting the GPS picture, but it was nothing but flickering roads and coordinates.

Destruction in every direction. Single-story buildings were nothing more than rooftops, cement lily pads. The high rises remained. The hovercar passed over a sea of bodies floating toward the Landmovers. Suddenly, the GPS video came through. Susan and Nick's chips were still blinking at Twenty-Two Pine Avenue. A mile away.

Fuller took control of the wheel and hovered in between two towering steel buildings. The car announced the address again. Fuller was getting close, but he didn't see the hill, only a handful of tall buildings, the crumbled remains of the giant tide wall, and the never-ending waters pouring over it.

Fuller dropped his speed again, the car telling him he was point-five miles away, then point-two. There was only one building left on Pine Avenue.

Fuller shut off the thrusters and hovered. He didn't know what he expected to find. Maybe Susan and Nick sitting on the roof, waving him over to pick them up.

There wasn't much left of the second floor, the water devouring it inch by inch. The monitor said this was it. He stuck his head out the window and looked down. A car blocked the front door. One of the building's windows was open. Someone was inside. A woman.

The car kept announcing he was at Twenty-Two Pine. Fuller squinted, saw the woman's face drifting back and forth under the rippling water. When he saw those lips, even the shrilling sirens went silent.

Fuller slammed his fist on the dash. *Always late*, that's what Susan used to say.

The monitor kept announcing Twenty-Two Pine Avenue again and again. A small blinking light appeared. Nick's chip was still at this address. Still in the building. Alive.

Water was nearly to the roof, but there must be air inside. Fuller slipped on his goggles and snapped off the airjets, took a deep breath and threw himself out the door. The weight of his uniform and utility belt dropped Fuller past the marble columns. His shattered knee cracked into the car pressed against the building's front door. He couldn't see through the bubbles, so he blindly reached out, his head throbbing from the lack of air. His hand hit flesh. The door was only open a foot, filled from top to bottom with arms and legs.

Fuller pulled one arm then another. Nothing happened. Then he pushed the body at the top of the door and felt it give. One more push, and the man floated backward, leaving a space just large enough for Fuller to swim through. About to pass out, he unclipped his utility belt and pushed off the pile of bodies, his arms flailing for the lights above. He hadn't taken a deep enough breath. The light began to fade.

A hand grabbed Fuller's collar and yanked him out of the water. Fuller opened his eyes, the ceiling only three feet from his face. He was on a long wooden platform, the water just inches from its edge.

Fuller stared at the twenty-something black man. "Thank you."

"Yeah sure," the man said. "I'm Shane. I don't know his name."

Nick lay against the wall on another platform, eyes open, chest rising. But Nick just kept staring at the ceiling, at nothing.

Shane said, "His mom tried to get us out through the window. She…didn't make it."

Fuller nodded. "Yeah, I saw." He dragged himself toward his son. "Nick? Hey… Are you hurt?"

"Man, this shit's rising fast."

The water was lapping at the edge of the platform. In five minutes it'd reach the ceiling. Fuller tried to get closer to Nick, but the pain paralyzed him. He looked down, saw bone sticking out through his pant leg.

"Oh fuck!" Shane said. His face winced up like he was about to puke.

Fuller kept his voice calm. "You know this building?"

"What?"

"Do you know this building?"

Shane nodded. "Yeah, I'm a bus boy."

"Any way out besides the front door? Any roof access?"

The kid was scared, about to freak out. "No, man."

"How good of a swimmer are you?"

Shane looked at the rising water. "The door's blocked. I already tried."

"It's not, not all the way. I made it through. Can you help my son make it?"

"I don't know."

Fuller pointed at Nick. "Well, I need your help. Can you do that?"

Shane looked at the water then over at Nick. "Alright."

"Help me get him in the water." Fuller helped lift his son's head. "Come on, Nick. You have to help too." Fuller snapped in front of Nick's eyes. "Hey!"

Nick's eyes fluttered open. Shane pulled Nick's other arm around his neck.

"My hovercar's just outside, take it out of the district." Knowing they would be the last words he ever spoke, Fuller kissed Nick's forehead and whispered, "I'll always love you."

Before Nick could say anything, Fuller dropped into the water, tore through the bodies and found the door. More bodies had piled into the opening. He yanked on a woman's arm, used his right foot for leverage against an old man's chest. Finally, he cleared a small space just as Shane and Nick came into view.

Fuller's ears popped. His vision blurred as he felt the woman's arm yanking back. But she was dead. Fuller saw her leg was caught on the car. It was sliding down, threatening to seal the door for good. Fuller lodged his body into the opening, had to use his shattered knee. Shane swam through the opening, dragging Nick behind him. Something released inside of Fuller's chest and a small hand brushed past his cheek, through his hair, disappeared into nothingness.

Sixteen Acres

December 24, 2068

The hunt had never lasted this long. It was Christmas Eve, and for the first time in his life, Ben Adams stepped off the ranch. Any other year, Ben and his father would be sipping hot cider while the women prepared the feast, but something had spooked the deer, that's what Ben's father, Justin, said. Ben prayed his father was right, because if the deer had migrated or died off, they wouldn't survive the winter.

The three men and one girl sat with their backs to the mountain, a small fire blazing in the middle of their clearing. They hadn't seen a deer all day, not in the usual spots, and the rabbits could no longer be trusted. Six people had developed skin rashes after eating them.

Justin pointed at the underbrush on the right side of the clearing. "It's the splicers," he said. "They're scaring them away."

Miguel, the former Controlling Force Agent, ran his knife along the sharpening stone. "Splicers, my ass. No one's seen a single attack."

"If we could Connect, we'd know in five seconds," Ben said. He stared at his father. Justin had kept everyone off the grid for the group's protection.

"Kid's right," Miguel said. "We don't even know what's out there."

Justin didn't take his eyes off of the forest. "We're not risking everything for information that might not even help us."

Ben told his father, "We could set it up so only one person had access."

"You?"

"Why not?"

Justin looked back toward the forest. "Because I said no."

Everywhere else in the country, fifteen-year-olds were considered adults. Ben was eighteen and still treated like a child.

Miguel's daughter, Kayla, touched Ben's arm. Her look told Ben not to push it. But it made no sense to Ben for them to stay disconnected. Ever since the tide wall attack, the only news came through automated drones and a few passing travelers.

Justin and Miguel said they'd take first watch. Kayla pulled Ben toward their sleeping bag. They crawled in. Ben let her use his arm as a pillow. He breathed in her hair and closed his eyes, let his thought drift to the others.

He jerked up. Kayla said, "What's wrong?"

Ben was afraid to give power to his words. Still, he said, "Something's…happened. Evelyn…"

"What are you talking about?"

"At the ranch." Ben was already out of the sleeping bag when Miguel asked what he meant.

This wasn't the first time Ben's twin sister, Evelyn, had communicated with him. He'd known the second she gave birth at two in the morning, even though he was asleep at Kayla's. When they were little, a searing pain shot through his arm when she'd fallen from a tree and broken two bones. But this feeling was the strongest he'd ever felt. "We need to go back."

"Absolutely not. We're over the perimeter. If anything spots us—"

"She's in trouble."

Justin shook his head. He'd never believed in their connection.

Miguel assured Ben everything was fine. "We're running four sentries." He pointed to responder, which would alert them if anything was wrong.

Ben wanted to say sentries without real weapons, another one of his father's brilliant decisions. Last month they had a chance to get hold of some ballistics from a passing caravan, but turned them away. The group only had knives and bows.

Kayla pulled him down. "They'll be okay," she said.

Ben wanted to run back to the ranch, but he lay down beside her, told himself Evelyn was home with her husband, George, and their baby. She was probably worried about him. That's what the feeling was, nothing more.

Justin woke Ben four hours later to switch watch. His father said to wake them in three hours.

Ben did as he was told and they broke camp before the sun rose. Miguel led the way. It was cold and wet, their ponchos damp from the mist. Christmas morning on the hunt, instead of opening presents under the tree.

Suddenly, the crunch of snow and twigs. A lone blacktail deer. Ben took aim, knocked the ten-pointer down with a direct hit to its vitals.

Their fathers dressed the deer. Ben and Kayla found branches large enough to strap it to. Even with the weight distributed between the four of them, the bark dug into Ben's palm. They plodded through the forest. Everyone was quiet, the only sounds were of breathing, the squelch of mud beneath their boots. It was a little past nine when they made it back to the ranch, the houses a few hundred yards around the bend.

Ben felt the searing pain. Evelyn was in trouble. And the baby.

Ben dropped his end.

"What's the matter with you?" Justin said.

"Stay with them," Ben told Kayla.

She said something, but Ben was already running down the trail, bow in one hand, arrow in the other.

The closer he got, the stronger the pain. Ben flew out of the trees, got behind the wooden privacy fence to catch his breath.

Thirty-three families lived on the ranch. Most were crammed into the dozen single-story shacks. Ben heard the low groans of a man. He peeked out, saw Thomas in the middle of the dirt road. A pale yellow creature straddled his stomach. It pulled ribbons of red from Thomas's chest. Another abomination lay a few feet away, the hilt of a knife sticking out of its throat.

The thing was hideous, nothing like Ben had ever seen in person, but identical to the drawing a gypsy boy had passed out to a few of the kids. The family told stories of flesh-eating monsters wiping out entire communities on the fringe.

Ben slowed his breathing, nocked an arrow, took aim at its sleek, hairless head.

Voices filtered through the trees. The grotesque beast turned. Ben loosed the arrow. It drove straight through its skull. Kayla screamed. Her father threw his hand over her mouth. Those things were everywhere, peppering the field, each one devouring a body on the ground.

Everyone got behind the fence. Justin and Miguel counted the arrows. Fifty plus between all of them, knives if it got down to it.

Ben peeked through the fence. The door to Evelyn's place was open.

Justin took hold of his son's shoulder, but Ben shrugged it off and crept around the corner. Twenty feet ahead in the tall grass was another creature. This one was older, a deformed mess that'd been allowed to mature, long bloody snout and clawed hands, slits of wrinkled flesh for ears.

Ben drew the bow and let the arrow fly, punctured its heart. Others took notice, started hop-running, but Ben just kept focused on Evelyn's porch. Kayla, Miguel, and Justin loosed arrows.

Justin screamed at Ben to get down, but he stood motionless, eyes locked with a fat-bellied beast waddling toward him. The twang of Kayla's bow was immediate. The breeze of the arrow zipped past Ben's head. He closed his eyes and heard the guttural cry.

Ben moved past the creature with the arrow through its eye, prayed that wasn't George's flesh hanging from its mouth. The front porch was littered with body parts.

Evelyn and George stayed in the back room on the left. The door was barely open, an overturned dresser behind it.

Ben slung his bow over his shoulder, pulled out his knife as he moved down the hallway. He looked in, saw Evelyn on the bed, a mewling creature crumbled on the floor, licking the blood dribbling down the comforter. The left side of its head was smashed, bits of broken glass sticking out. Ben finished the job, nearly cut off its head.

Evelyn's eyes were on Ben, her stomach torn open. Ben went to her, careful not to touch her wound. She spoke slowly. "The closet."

Ben walked over to the door. Evelyn said, "It laughed."

Ben turned the knob, found his one-year-old nephew curled up in a blanket.

Justin's scream pierced the shack. Ben went to the door, saw his father fighting off a creature. Ben unslung his bow, took aim. Clean through its open jaw. Kayla and Miguel backed in. Everyone fired arrows at the creatures coming full speed.

One hit the porch step. Ben rushed the shot and missed. The thing tore into Miguel's stomach. Miguel drove the blade through its spine. Kayla pulled her father inside. Justin shut the door, helped get Miguel onto his back. The slimy red noodles of intestines started to spill out. Justin clamped his hands onto his friend's guts.

"Guess they're not just stories?" Miguel said. He tried to fight through the pain.

Ben pulled back the curtain. The creatures were gathering around the house. Their beady eyes gleaming at Ben.

There were too many.

Ben shut the curtain, looked down at the red pool spreading along the floor. A low beep began echoing through the ranch.

"What is that?" Kayla asked. She covered her ears. The beeping was getting louder, more frequent.

Justin went to the window. "They're…backing away."

The beeping amped up. It ripped through the morning, forced Ben to his knees. He saw his father's mouth moving, but couldn't hear anything but the beeps. Finally, Ben took his hands off his ears, saw the herd of yellow monsters moving toward the massive black and red Way transport hovering in the clearing. A huge metal dish spun on top of the vehicle's roof. Fifty plus creatures circled around it as it landed. A long metal ramp slid out and the creatures filed in.

The beeping faded. The dish stopped spinning.

Two Disciples in silver suits exited the vehicle. The back gate lowered and six teenage boys in red uniforms walked out, stood at attention in front of the Disciples.

The Disciples were armed with plasma rifles, the boys in red had electroprods hanging from their waists.

The smaller Disciple barked instructions. "We need this place clean by nightfall."

The boys broke up into three teams and spread out. Ben heard Lucas crying in the other room. He told Kayla to get the baby. Justin pulled Miguel's remaining arrows from his sheath. Kayla came out with Lucas. Ben told her to go out the back, head for the trees, and never stop. Kayla started to argue, but she saw the Disciples gun down two boys trying to drag their mother's body inside their house.

Ben looked at Justin. "You know this is your fault."

"You really want to have this talk?"

Ben loaded an arrow, stood by the door. If they got the Disciples first, they stood a chance. "I'll take the one on the left."

Justin nodded. Kayla bent down to give her father one last kiss. But there wasn't time. The Disciples were coming.

Seventeen Soldiers

August 1, 2072

Cassie said goodbye to her mother and headed down the main tunnel. It was completely dark after the first turn. Her hands fumbled along the cold concrete until she saw the sliver of sunlight shining under the hides she'd draped over the entrance to keep it hidden.

The pail of rocks sat beside the curtain, proof Cassie hadn't emptied her last run before going to sleep. She'd carried in forty pails to bury Charlie. They couldn't risk doing it outside. If the reports were true, Controllers were close.

Cassie placed her ear to the crack and counted to twenty, didn't hear a sound. She slipped out into the light and knelt behind the bushes, waited while her eyes adjusted. There was no one around but the birds chirping down the mountain.

Quietly, so Vanessa didn't hear, Cassie took the pail and scattered the rocks just inside the entrance. The outside of the hides were covered with dirt and branches. Cassie smoothed them until they blended in with the mountainside, then started down the trail. Her stomach grumbled because she hadn't finished her breakfast, saved the last bits inside her pockets.

The blue sky above ran into the wall of gray filth hiding the metropolis below. Cassie nearly tripped, told herself to stay focused. It was time to prove she could take care of her mother.

It'd been five days since the bearded man ran up this trail. His encampment had been overrun. Controllers came hard and fast, obliterated almost everything and everyone. The man said they captured a few leaders for questioning. After hearing this, Justin ordered the evacuation. Vanessa had to stay behind because of the deep gash on her thigh, but Justin didn't want a thirteen-year-old girl left here. His son, Ben, said he'd stay with Cassie. Over the next two days while everyone prepared for the exodus, Ben taught her the rules of the forest, gave her the skills to keep her and her mother alive.

Cassie slipped on her spidersilk gloves, flexed her fingers and let the strange, translucent material adjust to her hand. The gloves were so light she barely felt them on her skin. She wondered if maybe Charlie thought he put them on, if that's why they were still in his back pocket when she found him face down, most of his legs chewed to the bone, the fatal bite of a vipercoon across his palm.

It took a few minutes to get down to the valley where the critters roamed. Cassie took out her bear bone knife. The blade was made of the same material as the gloves, nearly indestructible and undetectable, able to slice through almost anything. Ben made her promise she'd give it back to him when she returned to the group.

Cassie crept to the edge of the clearing and started digging until she hit wood. She pulled out the box, opened it, saw the rope and a stick. Staying close to the tree, Cassie set the trap, used her last piece of breakfast jerky as bait. With rope in one hand and the knife in the other, Cassie backed up and hid behind a large oak.

The forest was quiet, Cassie's breathing louder than anything. She remembered Ben's words and melted into the tree, stilled her body. If she didn't move, she wouldn't be attacked. All she had to do was wait. And wait. And wait until she finally heard the soft thumps across the grass. A giant white rabbit stopped at the raised end of the box, turned its head side to side, its blood red nose twitching up and down.

The rabbit put its head to the grass and reached out, its paw still inches from the jerky. The rabbit pulled back and glanced right then left, paused when its black eyes got to Cassie.

Cassie held perfectly still, told herself it was a regular rabbit. It was only going to run. But even if it did attack, she was ready.

The rabbit turned back to the box and disappeared inside. Cassie yanked the rope and the box fell, thumped back and forth as the rabbit bucked.

Cassie walked over, dropped her knee on the box and prayed the sides would hold up to the kicks. A savage gnawing came from the front of the box. No question it was a White Widow, same kind that bit her mother.

Ben had explained the name was all wrong, how the White Widows had been spliced with a recluse. Human flesh disintegrated the second it came in contact with the venom. That's why they'd cut the fist-sized chunk out of Vanessa's leg.

The box thumped harder, teeth scraping wood. Cassie feared the rabbit would break through before it tired.

But fear wasn't going to help now. She straddled the box, raised the back end and drove the knife inside, striking meat. The rabbit hissed and bit at the blade. Cassie pulled back and stabbed again.

The rabbit kept fighting, but Cassie couldn't wait, the Widow's self-destruct gene releasing venom with any major wound. She got off the box and reached inside, took hold of the rabbit's bloody throat and slammed it to the grass.

The Widow's back legs flailed as it snapped in Cassie's hand. The glove prevented the teeth from penetrating, but not the pain. Cassie laid the knife across its throat and pressed down hard, the severed head hanging by a thin strip of furry skin.

Cassie held the rabbit by its rear legs, its polluted blood pouring onto the grass. Once drained, she buried the trap and headed to the stream.

She cleaned the rabbit in the water. A low rumble filled the sky. Cassie didn't see anything, but knew it was a jetpack. She grabbed the rabbit, hurried along the stream until she reached the edge of the lake. She hid and saw eighteen men in black landing. They spread out in each direction, pulsing plasma rifles in their hands.

But only one filled her with dread. A Controlling Force Agent headed down the path that led to their cave. Cassie dropped the White Widow, stayed low, crept along the trail, and scrambled up the mountain.

The agent reached the switchback just below the entrance. There was no one to yell for, no Brandon or Willy hiding with their AK's. Cassie pressed herself against the pine tree and slowed her breathing.

The agent had on the standard black armor, visor, jetpack, and gun. The tiny bulges of flesh poking out around his filtration mask were the only hints he was human. His black boots crunched the trail as the soft sea-green light of his rifle's lifescanner fanned through the trees.

Cassie was half the agent's size, but that didn't matter. Her father proved that when he took out Colonel Hayden and all the others. Her father gave his life for the revolution. Cody Bradford was a hero to the cause.

Ben had told her all agents had amplifiers, to never assume otherwise. Cassie slowly bent forward and picked up a rock the size of a large pine cone. With her back against the tree, Cassie counted off each footstep.

The agent appeared on the other side of the tree and Cassie slammed the rock into his cheek. He crumpled to the ground with a loud oomph.

Cassie kicked the rifle away from his hand and pulled her knife. He wasn't moving except for the soft rise and fall of his back.

She knew what she was supposed to do, but she'd never used the knife on a person before. Ben told her hesitation would get her killed. Agents were the enemy. They were predators.

Cassie thought of the millions who'd died at their hands. She dropped on the agent's back and plunged the knife into his neck. A warm spray pelted her forearm.

Blood covered the leaves and pooled in the dirt, a sign that'd be hard to cover. Her only hope was to get a head start, so Cassie flipped the agent to the edge of the trail. She eyed the agent's pockets and started unbuckling his utility belt when a muffled voice came from his helmet. "Check in, 447. I repeat, check in."

Cassie pushed the body and sent it tumbling down the side of the mountain. In the distance, one jetpack came to life, then another. Cassie picked up the rifle and ran.

After rounding the bend, Cassie scrambled behind the bushes and under the hides, scattered rocks into the darkness. The tunnel became pitch black, no light coming from the living area up ahead. Cassie felt her thumping heart and slowed to a walk. She used the lifescanner to see where she was going.

Cassie paused outside the open door to the living area. With her finger on the trigger, she stepped to the side and cleared the left half of the room. Nothing but empty tables and desks, the mound of rocks covering Charlie's body, the tunnels to bedrooms behind it.

Cassie moved to the other side of the door and a shadow flashed in front of her. She screamed when something slit her cheek.

"Oh God! Cassie?!"

The blood covered her fingers. The cut didn't feel deep. "Mom?"

The kerosene lamp turned on. Vanessa's face was white, the bandage around her thigh a deep red. "What were you thinking? I could've killed you."

Cassie held up the rifle, fought through the pain. "We have to go. Now."

Vanessa looked at the gun, backed into the pile of blankets against the wall. "You didn't…"

"We have to go, Mom. Now."

A blinking red light appeared at the top of the rifle. They must have found the agent. Now they were tracking the gun.

Vanessa touched her daughter's cheek. "You have to leave."

"No, we can make it. I only heard two jets."

"Look at me, Cassie. I can't go with you."

Cassie's chin quivered. "Yes, you can. Now, come on." Cassie reached for her mother's arm, but Vanessa pushed her off, lost balance, fell against the wall. Cassie started for her, but Vanessa pointed at the far tunnel and told her to go.

"I don't even know where they are."

"It doesn't matter. The group's no longer safe. Someone talked."

"You don't know that."

"How do you think they found us?" Vanessa straightened her back. "Go back to San Angeles. The city is swarming with people. You'll find ones like us."

"No."

Vanessa took the rifle from Cassie. "Head down the mountain, toward the ocean. Stick to the shadows. Move at night."

"I want to stay with you."

"Go to the book pile," Vanessa said. "Bring it to me."

Cassie did as she was told. The book was worn, the cover faded. *We the Living.*

"You carry your father's story. Share it with everyone who will listen." Vanessa opened a metal container, pulled out the forty-five. "There are two boxes of ammo. Be smart."

Cassie tried to say something, but Vanessa told her to wait as she undid her necklace, the set of silver wedding rings dangling at the bottom. "Don't let this die here."

The rush of a jetpack descending came down the main tunnel. Vanessa shook her head. "If they find you, run. If they trap you, fight. But never let them take you. Always save a bullet."

Vanessa kissed the tear on her daughter's cheek and pushed her toward the exit.

The sound of heavy boots started down the tunnel. Vanessa raised the rifle, took a deep breath then stepped into the passage. The pulsing electric bursts filled Cassie's ears.

"Run," Vanessa whispered. "Run."

Twenty-Third District

March 31, 2074

Matt Longley left behind the blue skies over the City of Light and drove into the toxic ash of the Districts. He'd been a Disciple for less than a month and wasn't used to passing through the gates without so much as a thermal scan. His years of training were finally paying off, but all the perks could end with this final sweep.

The Inner Blocks loomed ahead, each a crumbling city in itself. Matt drove by the abandoned factories, everything covered in black, the air too thick to see the tide wall. To see where homes once stood.

Matt had been instructed to double-check the District sensors for signs of malfunction. Reports said the Underground Rebellion was still moving undetected. Security needed to be tightened. In two days, the Preacher and his sons would be making an appearance at the tide wall. Matt wasn't the only Disciple doing final sweeps, but he was the most ironic choice.

On the surface, Matt's years in The Way were exemplary. He didn't flinch during the rounds of torture or when they forced him to strangle his own dog. And when Matt placed his plasma rifle to his father's forehead, as commanded, he would've pulled the trigger. That's what his father had told him to do. No one was above the resistance.

Matt's credibility was holding everything together. Without it, the coup would evaporate, and the underground tunnels would be pumped with enough gas to kill every living creature. So when Matt veered off his ordered course, he knew the risks, but this was the last chance he'd get to save the brother he'd only learned of six months ago.

Everything would have been so much easier if Isaac's name hadn't been mistakenly attached to one of Matt's evaluations. Unknown family members were usually redacted, but the details were all there, the younger brother who'd been adopted years before Matt had. Isaac Pollinar was the only person who shared Matt's blood, the only connection to biological parents neither could remember. Matt couldn't allow Isaac to die, he had to bring him into the Underground's inner circle.

The East Sector was off limits. Matt stuck to the side streets and angled toward Union Central. He parked his hovercar against the stairwell, jumped out, passed the empty elevator shafts, and took the Rapid. It zipped straight to the District's Hub.

Eyes peered from the shadows and doorways. Matt kept his hand next to his plasma pistol as he moved quickly through the security arch. He stuck his left wrist out for scanning and pretended to ignore the warm tingling on his skin. How could anyone believe these new scans were safe?

A year ago, the line for the Direct Rail would've wrapped around the corner. Now, there weren't more than a dozen people, the only ones strong enough to venture outside their rooms.

A Controlling Force Agent walked the line. Matt cleared his head, calmed his breathing. He flashed his wrist again, even though his Disciple uniform gave him clearance to anywhere in the Districts. The agent nodded, asked if he could be of any help.

Matt said no and continued down the cement hallway. The lights overhead flickered. Blackness, then flashes of light, red scribbles of graffiti.

"There's some nasty stink down there," the agent called out. "I'd watch your boots."

The Direct Train pulled up, every window painted black. Matt waited for it to disappear in the tunnel before he jumped down onto the tracks. His foot splashed in something, but he refused to look to see what it was, just entered the Old Number Three shaft. Red sensors were spaced every thirty yards. Each blinking light encased in glass. Matt checked the first few until he was completely out of the agent's sight. He switched off his GPS tracker knowing he could blame it on radiation interference if it came up in the brief.

The steel grate had rusted more than last time, making it harder to budge, but Matt finally slipped through and flicked on his P7 light. The walls dripped sewage runoff. Some of the stone bricks looked ready to crumble. Isaac's room was on the left. Matt had moved his brother here when they started the sweeps.

Broken vials crunched under Matt's boot. The caps were bright orange. Someone had been here recently. Matt unclipped his holster and drew his pistol.

The door slid open. Isaac's beard had grown, but it still couldn't cover the patches of pale yellow skin, the high forehead and sloping nose they shared. Isaac's eyes lit up. He clapped Matt on the shoulder, pulled him in. He told Matt it was good to see him. Isaac's pupils seemed to be squeezing out his irises. The kid was only fifteen, a year younger than Matt, but he looked so much older.

"You thirsty?" Isaac asked. He walked over to the plastic jugs lining the floor. Some were filled with piss and it was taking Isaac too long to figure out which ones were which.

"We don't have time," Matt said. "Come on, you have to get dressed."

"Yeah, yeah, I know. I know. I just, uh…" Isaac kept staring at the jugs and scratched at the back of his neck.

This wasn't the first time Matt had seen someone electro-juiced. Dealers cooked it with radioactive waste. Isaac got hooked after The Great Flood, after his foster parents had been washed out to sea. Matt thought he'd gotten his little brother clean. That was the deal.

Matt unzipped his satchel and tossed Isaac the stolen Disciple uniform. From the inner lining of his own jacket, Matt pulled out a skin splice. When Isaac finished dressing, Matt took his wrist and applied the splice. Matt studied it from a couple angles, couldn't tell the splice apart from Isaac's skin.

Isaac ran his finger over his new flesh. "So mine won't read at all?" He scratched his neck again.

"As long as you don't start picking at it." There was another broken vial on the ground. Matt didn't say a word, just shook his head.

"I know, I know, I messed up. I didn't mean to. I, uh, just found them. Buried in one of the walls. Someone must have been running from agents or something. I tried to hide them." Isaac's eyes filled with tears. "I'm sorry. I know I shouldn't have. You just have no idea what it's like down here."

Matt watched his brother try to calm the shakes. Every rational cell of Matt's brain told him to leave Isaac, that electro-juicers could not be trusted. But the same question that had been plaguing Matt for months kept popping up in his head. What if their lives had been reversed? Matt had been adopted by two loving parents. Sure, they'd involved him in a conspiracy plot that would, in all likelihood, get him killed, but it was better than being raised by the fiends who'd fostered Isaac, used his body to help meet the rent. And Matt didn't want to lose another family member to the Way.

"I need to know if you can keep it together," Matt said.

"Fine, fit, perfectly capable."

"I'm not kidding."

"Oh fuck off, I'm fine."

"Yeah…" Matt headed for the rusty grate.

"I'm sorry. Come on, bro." Isaac grabbed Matt's shoulder, spun him back. "We're family. You can't leave me."

Isaac stopped scratching and looked at Matt with his pleading yellow eyes. Reluctantly, Matt nodded. Isaac ran over and picked up his black backpack. Matt stared at the bag until Isaac slipped it off and unzipped it.

"Go ahead, look," Isaac said as though Matt had asked him to pull down his pants and prove he wasn't a girl.

Matt glanced in the bag. All he saw were clothes and some water filtration tablets. He told Isaac to stay close.

It was dark by the time they got outside, hardly a soul on the streets, even though curfew wasn't for another hour. Matt told Isaac to get in the hovercar.

A few minutes later, they were at the bottom of the massive ruins of concrete and dirt, the first District wall. Isaac kept checking the side rearview mirror. Matt shut off the hovercar and hoped Isaac was just being paranoid.

Nick's coordinates beeped red on Matt's locator. The entrance was just on the other side of the wall. "Are you going to be able to keep cool?" Matt asked.

"Of course I am," Isaac said. He couldn't stop looking behind them though, kept scratching his neck.

Matt yanked the sheet of soggy cardboard and uncovered a hole just wide enough to walk through. Matt kept his light off, ran his fingers along the dirt to guide them. He didn't want to see any flood victims half-buried around them.

On the other side, they were greeted with the trees and muck of an overgrown residential zone, long since abandoned. The slick, black tide wall loomed over everything, darker than a moonless night. If it hadn't been for the blinking emergency lights and anti-aircraft gun on top, it would have been possible to pretend the wall didn't exist. But the huge cannon slowly swept back and forth, reminding Matt that if he got caught, his death would be the least of his worries. His father and Jordan, the sweet girl who'd been assigned as his live-in, would be publicly executed, their severed heads broadcast all over the globe.

Matt told Isaac to hurry up. The locator said their destination was thirty yards northwest, but it wasn't accounting for the steep slopes covered in vine. When they finally arrived, all they saw was a lonely oak. Isaac asked if they had the right coordinates. Matt said yes, but he knew the Underground was constantly in motion, especially headquarters. He feared they'd been discovered, forced to flee, or worse, destroyed.

Isaac tried to kick the oak tree, but his foot went straight through. The Underground's holograms were getting better.

Matt stepped through the image and knelt. Even though he was taking Isaac into the Underground's Inner Circle, he still covered the code as he punched it in. He lifted the steel hatch and they climbed down the stairs. Matt's feet hadn't even touched the ground when he heard:

"Stop right there!"

Slowly, Matt looked over his shoulder. Nick Fuller blended into the shadows, black jeans, black jacket, scarf up to his chin. Like Isaac, he was only fifteen, but Nick looked like a man, shaved head, thin goatee. He waved his pistol at Isaac. "This your brother?"

"Yeah…" Matt said.

"And you're vouching for him?"

"Of course he fucking vouches for me. Now, can I please get down off this damn ladder?"

Nick lowered the gun, and Isaac hopped off. Nick said he meant no offense, but he had to ask. Isaac chewed the inside of his cheek and shrugged.

They followed Nick down the tunnel. Matt had lost his bearings, but they seemed to be heading for the tide wall. Isaac's teeth kept clicking over and over and Matt told him to stop. He hadn't planned on taking Isaac this far, but he wanted to see if Isaac was going to be a problem. Plus, Nick wasn't known for his patience and hated newbies, especially this late in the game.

Isaac's face was white and sweaty as they entered the gutted restaurant. It must have fallen into a sinkhole after The Great Flood. The windows were covered, every door barricaded, tents and sleeping bags along the walls. A bald man in his twenties stood atop the bar, spoke just loud enough that the hundred or more people crowded below had to lean in to hear.

"There is nowhere else to go" the bald man said. "We are literally against the wall."

A fat guy grabbed Matt's hand. It sent a burst of electricity up his arm. Everyone was now holding hands.

"Those of you with ties to the Blocks, you're our hope, the only chance we've got." The bald man walked up and down the bar, took a long look at every face. "Think of how many friends and family have been taken and killed. How many have died for The Way."

Matt saw a few of his old friends. Their faces had lost the baby fat, but he recognized everyone. It was like he'd been transported back in time. Growing up, they'd spent endless nights playing revolutionaries in his parents' basement. Now it was real.

Cassie, a thin blond with dreadlocks and two silver rings dangling from her neck, headed their way. Matt didn't know her from childhood, but wished he had. He talked with Cassie every time he stopped in, but not since he'd been assigned Jordan. Whatever connection he and Cassie might have had appeared long gone. All business, Cassie held out her hand. "I need your screens."

There was no point in trying to explain how he felt about Jordan, that he didn't know if he could trust her or ever tell her the truth. Matt just handed over his screen, told Isaac to do the same. Cassie walked over to the command center and swiped Matt's chip over the inputs. Videos of their trip to the headquarters filled a large monitor on the wall.

Isaac asked where the pisser was. Someone shushed him, but a scrawny kid with a face covered in tattoos pointed to a bucket.

"Don't look at me," Matt whispered. "Go around the corner."

Isaac pulled his sleeve down over his fingers before grabbing the bucket and walking away.

Cassie waved Nick over. She pointed out two strange shadows following Matt's hovercar on the way to the tide wall.

"We can bring down the rulers, we can open the eyes," the bald man said. "People will say life's not so bad in the Blocks. You have your races and your drink, but we are sobering up. People all over the world are gathered just like us under the earth. And soon we will rise."

Cassie enhanced the monitor and Matt saw the choppers. Nick turned to him for an answer, but Matt hadn't seen anything on the way here.

"It's got to be a mistake," Matt said.

Cassie shook her head. "There must be a tracker."

The alarm blared and Nick yelled, "Block the doors!"

Panicked bodies scattered. A few followed orders and jammed furniture in front of every entrance.

Matt took off around the corner, found Isaac leaning up against the wall. Tears rolled down Isaac's cheeks, stretched in an awful smile. "I didn't have a choice. You understand…"

"Why?" Matt asked.

"Because they're always going to win."

Matt threw his hand around Isaac's throat. "Do they know about me?"

"No," Isaac said. He leaned into Matt's grip. "But they will. They'll know all about you. The snake in the bubble." Isaac's eyes widened. Matt didn't have time to turn, just heard the particle buzz and watched as Isaac vaporized.

Cassie holstered her pistol, grabbed Matt's arm, and yanked him down the hallway. The world felt like it'd stopped spinning. Everything sounded a mile away in Matt's ears. Cassie shoved him through the door and into the wall, cracking his head hard.

"You have to get out of here," Cassie said. "Now!"

Matt tripped, stumbled toward a set of stairs. He turned back and saw Cassie sealing the steel door. Only her eyes in the tiny glass window. Muffled particle beams and explosions said agents had breached the command center. Matt pressed his face to the glass and saw Cassie hunched over cranking a metal wheel. Water sprayed with each turn. The sprays turned to gushing streams until an avalanche of sea came rushing in. Matt had no choice but to run as the water seeped under the door and rose up the stairwell. He threw his shoulder into another hatch and climbed out into the woods. As he slipped into the arriving agents, he cleared his thoughts, pretended he'd just arrived. The Underground's Inner Circle had sacrificed everything so Matt could finish this, but as he pictured his friends floating under the earth, Matt wished he'd never escaped.

Twenty-Fifth of December

December 25, 2076

John Langley stood perfectly still on the platform, afraid the cameras would home in on any nervous shifting. A woman asked him if he had the time, but John didn't trust himself to speak. He simply pointed at the screen overhead. The Glass Train was already three minutes late, but John was in no rush. He'd waited ten years for this, plotted and schemed, sacrificed almost everything. He'd lost his wife, most of his hair, and now maybe even his son.

It was hard to know what was real anymore. John had been living two lives for so long he questioned his every thought. Was it his or the other John's? He felt amorphous, fluid. He wondered if he even had a skeletal system. Tammy's death should've broken him. He still woke most mornings thinking she was in their bed. Then he'd remember the night the Controllers came, back when they were still made of flesh and blood. It was the one time John allowed himself to cry. The outside world only saw his stoic façade. They only saw the patriotic father who'd enrolled his son into The Way Training Program the day after they'd killed his wife.

Matthew did what he was told. He obeyed his father, promised to infiltrate The Way. He vowed to die before revealing the secrets of the Underground. It was a lot to ask of a young boy, but John was convinced it was the only way to end this once and for all.

The Glass Train pulled up and the door hissed open. John filed in with the others and took his seat. They were heading to the City of Light for the new Preacher's coronation. As a Disciple, Matthew would be in the ceremony. He'd procured John's ticket, which he'd had encoded last month. It was the first pseudo-contact they'd had in over two years, since the raid on the Underground, which killed Nick and all the others. John still remembered them as children running around their house, shooting water pistols.

Cyborg Controllers patrolled the cars of the Glass Train. Their metal limbs glimmered, unlike the dull gray sky passing by above. Passengers stared at their laps, their wrists embedded with electric ticket codes.

At a Controller's mechanical request, a young woman offered her palm. John turned toward the rusted carnage of some dilapidated skyscraper. The crowds gathered in the streets, everyone moving toward a giant video screen. No one looked happy, but it wasn't every day The Way offered a coronation. Citizens were required to celebrate.

John looked ahead. The blanket of ash was coming to an end. He couldn't remember the last time he'd seen blue sky, except on TV. Tammy used to tell Matthew stories of the sparrows she saw as a little girl, how they'd take off into the never-ending blue. John had seen where Tammy grew up. He knew she was lying, but he loved to see Matthew's face light up when Tammy talked about clear rain.

A Controller reached for John's wrist and jerked him from his memory. John offered his palm, tried to calm his pulse. He had plasma charges strapped to his left leg, a detonator sewn into the lining of his jacket. He needed to seem at ease. The Controller scanned his flesh, then moved on to a guy in a purple jumpsuit two sizes too big.

Towering gold spires sprouted in the distance, spikes radiating under the glittering sun. An old woman stared until tears streamed. Her husband held her close. It was as if they were just some couple going on a picnic.

John had seen the City of Light on the news, but a screen couldn't replicate this beauty. Fountains, monuments, statues of the Preacher overlooking the square. A pond they passed actually had real ducks.

Everything led to the seven towers circling the Cathedral of The Way. Three hundred feet high, marble columns, stained-glass masterpieces, created on the backs of the people.

John pictured the explosion, a billion flaming flecks floating and swirling into the brilliant blue sky, but the fantasy was interrupted by a gurgling gasp. The Controller had its claw wrapped around a skinny guy's throat. The Controller lifted him out of his seat, the guy's feet dangling like some dying marionette.

"You'll…" the skinny guy croaked before the Controller crushed his windpipe. The side door slid open and the Controller flung his body, but the wind whipped it back into the glass of the train. It cracked down onto the rails. Feet and shins snapping, splattering the underside of the car bright red.

John felt his eyes twitch. It lasted less than a second, but a man in a red uniform took notice. Everyone else focused on the bloody clumps stuck to the bottom of the train, but this guy wouldn't take his eyes off John.

John centered himself, thought only of the sunlight shining through the walls. He'd activated his neural blocking chip to keep his secrets safe, but the man in red sensed something. John knew it was no time to crack. He offered a smile.

Two kids mashed their faces against the glass as the Cathedral came into full view. Majestic. Massive. Only John knew that like an iceberg, the true vastness existed below the surface. The Red Battalion, hovertanks, plasma rockets, and enough cold fusion reactor rays to bring Heaven crashing down in a fiery heap.

The train pulled to the unloading deck, and John made sure to keep his distance from the red uniform. Still, he could tell he was being followed. Matthew was standing tall in his Disciple cloak. John hurried over and the man in the red uniform angled toward the walkway.

"Hello, Father." Matthew's face was expressionless, his eyes cold.

"Matthew," John said. He noticed a striking blond with even better posture than his son. She flashed an odd smile, which unnerved John, but he bowed his head. "And this must be Jordan."

Her brilliant blue eyes studied John's face. "Hello, Father. I'm so glad we finally meet."

"Yes, it's long overdue." John had worried Jordan would be here. He'd hoped to have a few moments alone with his son. He gave Jordan a hug, surprised by her strength.

"We should hurry," Matthew said. "I need to get you to your seats." He ushered them down the stairs, Jordan staying two feet behind them both. They joined the throngs spiraling down the silver ramp and spilling out onto the esplanade, where the reflective pool stretched to the steps of the Cathedral.

But first they'd have to pass under the security archway, red lasers scanning each well-dressed citizen. The women wore hats that looked like postmodern sculptures of the solar system. The men wore angular suits that shimmered and sparkled in the sunny afternoon. An older woman told her husband she thought they were underdressed.

John noticed another member of the Rebellion walking with the crowd. John never made eye contact. They'd all said their final goodbyes during the pact.

John squinted, wiped his sleeve across his forehead. He'd never been in such brightness. He looked over and realized Matthew was gone. He spun around twice but didn't see Matthew or Jordan anywhere. He tried to stand still, let others pass, but a Controller was suddenly behind him pushing.

"Toward the gates. Toward the gates."

John eyed the cyborg security guards at the archway. There was no way he'd make it through with the detonator and plasma charges.

Five feet to the arch. The red laser sliced through a woman with incandescent glass horns sprouting from her blazing red hair.

Three feet.

"Arms at your sides," the cyborg guard announced. "Step forward at a normal pace."

The cyborg security guards were polished to a blinding sheen. They had plasma rifles, charged and ready to destroy.

Two feet.

Designer suits and dresses, hands and leather gloves pressing against John, his back and elbows. Someone asked what the hold up was. John considered reaching into his jacket for the detonator. At least there'd be an explosion, a small strike for the Rebellion. But someone shoved him forward. The archway and lasers were inches away. Once he triggered the alarm, he'd be mowed down along with all those around him. If he could hit the button, these people would belong to the cause, not simply slaughtered like lambs.

John's fingers slipped inside his jacket and snaked around the detonator, his thumb sliding to the small metal button. He'd tested it last week in an abandoned, burned out warehouse. He angled away from the guards and toward a woman in a light pink robe. Wrinkles spread out from her eyes and the corners of her lips. She reminded him of Tammy, the woman who had set this all in motion. Maybe he'd see her on the other side.

His thumb, slick with sweat, started to slide off the button. A hand grabbed his shoulder. He tried to regrip the detonator, but saw the laser about to hit his chest.

"He's with me," a familiar voice said. Matthew brought John's hand out from his jacket and led him and Jordan from the archway. Two cyborgs blocked their path.

"All guests must be scanned."

Matthew pointed at John's chest. "His heart. The valves have telefiber connectors."

John nodded. "It's true."

But this clearly meant little to the steel assassins. Luckily, a human Controller approached. John couldn't remember the last time he was relieved to see a living Controller. The Way had made the transition because cyborgs stuck to protocol, never questioned orders, and suffered zero psychological effects. They couldn't be compromised.

The human Controller asked what the problem was. Matthew explained. The Controller pulled out a D9 scanner and pointed it at John's heart. John breathed deeply and the Controller waved them through. They passed two gigantic screens overlooking the esplanade, where ticketless citizens could watch the coronation. John, Matthew, and Jordan entered the Cathedral.

A few of the Disciples' assigned companions were gathered by a marble pillar. Jordan's face lit up as she walked over to greet them. Matthew pulled John to the side and reached inside John's jacket. He pulled out the detonator, kept it hidden in his gloved fist. Metal crunched. His son's hand was no longer human.

"This is over," Matthew said.

"What? No."

"You're clearly incapable, and this is my call."

John started to protest, to demand he change his mind. John was still his father, after all, but the look in Matthew's eyes said not to make a sound. This was no longer the little boy who used to beg Tammy for piggyback rides or for John to read him one more bedtime story. This was a man who'd buried more people than John would ever want to know.

"Is everything okay?" Jordan asked.

"Yes, just help my father to his seat."

As Matthew walked beneath the rows of golden statues, Jordan led John to one of the pews. He sat next to the aisle and felt like a fool. For months he'd wondered if his son had been compromised, if he'd been broken. But it was John who'd lost his edge, a useless old man forcing back tears.

Red light filtered through the stained glass windows. The black flying buttresses overhead looked more like the bars of a cage than painted oak. The guests, including the President and other world leaders, craned their necks as the choirboys took their places next to the altar, their hands folded in prayer, their tiny bodies draped in golden robes, just like the one Matthew had worn all those years ago.

The church was practically humming in anticipation. The Preacher hadn't made a public appearance since his first born son died over a year ago. His health had deteriorated, and there were rumors he wouldn't be able to attend today's coronation. But then the organist pressed the first key and the monstrous instrument with its gleaming crystal pipes slowly rose into the air above the altar and out over the pews. The choir's soft, angelic voices wove together like threads of the finest silk and soared through the rafters, where microphones transmitted the glorious melody over the esplanade and into homes and city squares around the globe. Floating cameras captured the procession of the Disciples in their ceremonial red robes. Everyone stood and leaned to catch the first glimpse of the Preacher and his son, Geoffrey, both dressed in glowing white robes with dark red stoles draped over their shoulders. The stoles were embroidered with the seven stars.

As they started down the center aisle, Geoffrey, a chubby stump of a kid, held his chin high and nose even higher. He'd just turned fifteen, and looked like he was in a perpetual state of smelling spoiled meat.

John kept his eyes on the cyborgs surrounding the altar. The AR implant in his left cornea clicked down the seconds until the Underground would have control of the electronic signatures. Every cyborg would be temporarily immobilized by a magnetic freeze. It would last five minutes if they were lucky.

The Preacher had to tug Geoffrey to keep him from racing ahead. John figured the floating cameras were broadcasting with a soft filter to hide the walking corpse. The Preacher's gray, wrinkled skin dripped from his cheeks and neck. The tall silver hat seemed to threaten the structural integrity of his spine.

How easy it would be for John to wrap his hands around that pathetic neck and crush his windpipe. Wasn't that the entire reason he was here? The Preacher was only ten feet away and getting closer. How could John allow the last ten years to just pass by? His son, Matthew, had lost all innocence, not to mention a hand. And they'd both lost Tammy. All because of this vile zealot.

John reached into his pants pocket and ran his thumbnail along the seam. He'd hidden a second detonator even though he knew he'd never have time to use it if the first one failed. He never imagined Matthew would've taken it away.

A cherub-faced choirboy stepped to the center of the altar. His falsetto carved through the Cathedral as John drove his thumb through the stitching. He heard the thread pop as he fumbled for the button. The Preacher turned and looked right at John, who didn't understand why until a blinding pain shot through his neck. Jordan was suddenly on top of John, his face smashed against the pew. He heard the congregation shuffling before a buzz rippled through his body and everything went dark.

# # #

Heels clicked against concrete. It grew louder, then soft. Loud and then soft. Someone was pacing. John struggled to open his eyes. A single, naked bulb hung from the ceiling. The stone walls were slick with blood. John figured it had to be his. He could taste it in his mouth. A blur flew towards his face and snapped his head back.

John had been hit before, but he'd never been punched awake. The fist felt hard, too, almost like steel. John expected to see a cyborg; he didn't expect to see his son.

Matthew walked over to the shiny blades hanging on the wall. Each weapon looked specially designed to inflict a unique brand of torture. The hatchet had tiny curled teeth on one end. John imagined one good swipe could rip off a man's back like rabbit skin.

Something was buzzing overhead. John couldn't tell if it was the light bulb or just his ears, but then he saw his reflection. It was one of the floating cameras from the Cathedral.

A child's voice squawked through the intercom. "No, the one on the left."

Matthew walked over and pulled down the club wrapped in barbed wire.

"Yes, exactly," the voice said.

Geoffrey, it seemed, was calling the shots. John was too weak to turn, but he figured the boy and his father were watching behind a one-way mirror, enjoying this like a perverse little play, son slowly filets dear old dad.

In a strange way, John was grateful he was in Matthew's hands. If anyone deserved to do this, it was his son.

Matthew swung and John tried to block the barbwire club, but his wrists were handcuffed to the wooden chair. Something rattled in his mouth. He thought a piece of the club had broken off, but his tongue told him it was a tooth.

The chair had spun, so John could see Geoffrey and the Preacher sitting behind regular glass, Jordan standing beside them, a beautiful imperial guard. They had no reason to hide their faces. What surprised John was that there didn't seem to be any cyborgs with them. He wondered if the magnetic freeze had actually worked.

Geoffrey was sitting in a high-back chair, which rose twice his height. This pudgy child would soon be the most powerful ruler in the world, but at this moment, Geoffrey looked bored, scraping the armrest with his thumbnail

John wondered how long he'd been down here. Matthew rubbed his shoulder, clearly sore from pummeling his father. John spat blood and the tooth out onto the floor.

Matthew leaned against the wall. He said, "I believe he's conscious."

The fat, little teenager stood. "It's about time." Geoffrey started for the door, but the Preacher grabbed his arm. Geoffrey shrugged off his father's pathetic grip and the door buzzed open, the light switching from red to green.

Geoffrey threw open the door and stormed into the little room splattered with globs of flesh and blood. "Hit him again."

Matthew looked at John with a silent apology before slamming the club against his father's bicep, the end of the club cracking hard on the armrest.

Geoffrey giggled and stepped into John's line of sight. "We're just getting started." Geoffrey looked up at the floating camera to address the world. "This man has desecrated our sacred grounds. He has committed treason against our countries and against The Way."

As Geoffrey continued to rattle off the charges, John strained to lift his leg. Both were chained to the ground, but he stretched his fingers and finally felt his thigh. He knew the plasma charges weren't going to be there, but he had to try.

Matthew swung again. The sound was awful, but strangely John didn't feel the pain he expected, just a glancing thud on his arm. His body must have already gone into shock.

"Not even this man's son is willing to stand by this terrorist," Geoffrey said.

Matthew swiveled his hips, extended his arms, and really stepped into the next crunching blow. John closed his eyes, braced for impact, but again, he mainly felt the vibration. Suddenly, his left arm could move quite freely. Matthew's last shot must have dislocated it or shattered every bone. It was the only explanation John could think of, until he looked down and saw the wooden arm of the chair split in two. Matthew walked back over to the wall of blades, so John couldn't tell if his son realized what he'd done. Was it an accident? Or was it something else entirely?

John wasn't in a position to ask. Matthew placed a wooden mallet in Geoffrey's hands.

"What the hell is this? Get me a blade or those daggers," Geoffrey said.

"All in good time," Matthew said. "You don't want to ruin the fun."

"Right." Geoffrey straightened his back for the camera then took a solid whack on John's kneecap.

John screamed in pain. The shock hadn't numbed him at all.

Geoffrey shuffled about and taunted the old, broken man bleeding in the chair. Geoffrey told the camera to really watch the next one then reared back with all of his weight before twisting and driving it into the next swing, eyes closed for the home run.

John threw up his hand, caught the middle part of the mallet and tried to jerk it away. Geoffrey's eyes popped open and he frantically gripped his end, locking the two of them in tug-of-war.

"Let go," Geoffrey grunted, his face as red as the stains on John's shirt. With both hands on the mallet, Geoffrey roared.

Matthew's gloved hand shoved a plasma charge into that fat mouth. The belt came next, securing the charge. Geoffrey's fingers clawed at the metal strap wrapped around his head. He tried to pull it off, but Matthew laughed at him and kicked him to the ground.

The room filled with the sound of muffled banging, the Preacher pounding on the window, looking to Jordan for help.

Matthew unlocked his father and helped him to his feet. "It was the only way."

John didn't think he could walk on his own, but then the light above the door buzzed green. Jordan held it open, a small detonator in her outstretched hand. "Father."

The Preacher screamed blasphemy, shouting for his guards. Geoffrey scrambled to his feet, fingernails sliding across the metal strap.

John limped to Jordan and took the detonator, the floating camera following him and his children into the viewing room, the door shut behind them.

The Preacher faced John, his ridiculous hat on the floor, a wild glare in his eye. A cornered animal with nothing left. He lunged for the detonator and screamed, "He's the Chosen One!"

Although he was injured and old, a newfound power filled John. He collided with the Preacher, smashed his face to the glass, John's bloody forearm crushing his neck.

"He's my son!" The Preacher struggled in vain, shouted again. "He's to be the Preacher!"

John pressed the button, the explosion shaking the room, the glass splattered red, cracked from shards. "He's no more."

The Preacher fell to his knees, but John felt nothing for him.

Matthew helped his father to the exit, but turned back to the camera and said, "Citizens of the Americas, you are now free. Do with that what you will."

In the hallway, Matthew checked John's injuries, apologized for not letting him know the change in plans.

Jordan stepped from the viewing room, blood dripping from her hand. "Come on, I have the access codes."

John used his son for support and followed Jordan down a flight of stairs and another long hallway. There was a security keypad and retinal scanner. She punched in the code, then held a detached eyeball up to the screen. The light flashed blue. Jordan threw open the blast doors, and John saw the Red Battalion's stockpile: the hovertanks, long-range thermal missiles, subsonic cannons, volcanic reactors, and the seemingly endless supply of plasma rifles, particle grenades, and P3 charges, not to mention the fifteen thousand cyborgs.

The Underground now had an army.

27 Generals

December 25, 2076

Prior to the liberation, Jordan Longley had never been on a Transport. Now she practically lived on one, about to finish her fiftieth sortie in the last six days. She was supposed to be on her honeymoon with Matthew, but there could be no time off. Instead of lying on the beach sipping cocktails, she was fortifying her husband's army.

The light armored bus rumbled through the deserted trash-strewn streets of the District. Jordan rode shotgun, on the lookout for potential recruits, as images from the past week flooded her mind – a slow-motion slide show of the people she'd killed, the ones she couldn't save. Some were Controllers, but most were citizens wearing their silver and black. A lot of them just kids. The memories Matthew couldn't modify.

Jordan sat up straight. She checked the streets, re-gripped her plasma rifle.

Elias, a Disciple turned driver, said, "Everything cool?"

"Yeah, we're good. Nothing on my side."

"One more sweep. This is it for today. Then home."

"Good." But Jordan had learned not to get her hopes up. They'd started with thirty-six generals and had already lost a fourth of them. And even if they made it back to the City of Lights, there was no telling where Matthew would send them next. Each District crawled with loyalists who were prepared to die.

They drove into the shadow of Inner Block Four which had been built bigger and badder in its resurrection. The message to the "terrorists": You will never win.

It was a message the loyalists heard loud and clear. On her first sortie in Block Fifty-Three, Jordan had been stupid enough to just walk through the front door. She found a group of men claiming they wanted to join. They recognized her immediately, went after the price on her head. If it hadn't have been for Elias, she'd never have made it out.

Elias was all business, his dark eyes darting between the road and the screens. He was eighteen like Jordan and had been in the same Camp, but they rarely talked. Not about him saving her. Not about what she did to the Preacher. Not about Savanna, Elias's live-in, who became one of the Rebellion's first casualties when he caught her attempting to report them.

The Transport slowed to a crawl as it approached the intersection, a practice they'd started after the first ambush attempt. Elias pointed out Jordan's window, down the shadowed road to the Block's main entrance. "Something's going on down there," he said.

Even with her upgraded vision, Jordan couldn't see more than a few hundred feet. She turned to the Transport's screen and tapped into the Block's cameras, stopped when she got to the group of people gathered around the benches just outside the entrance. They appeared to be shouting. Jordan turned on the speakers in her helmet. Frightened voices filled her ears. These people needed help.

"Look, Elias. We have to get them."

Elias pointed to the route pulsing on the dash. "No, we're steering clear of this."

Jordan tapped the side of her helmet. "I hear them. They need help."

Elias shook his head. "We don't have enough room. And we have orders."

Jordan saw there were too many people and not enough men, the ones Matthew wanted as warriors. But she also heard a baby, a mother pleading for a ride. "Screw the order. We'll get as many as we can." Jordan hit the e-brake and the Transport jerked to a halt in the middle of the intersection.

"What the hell, Jordan?"

"We'll be in and out."

Elias scrolled through the camera feeds, three miles of Block Four on the left, a strip of grass and the aqueduct on the right. Nothing appeared out of the ordinary except the two dozen citizens crowded around the benches. "All right, but this is on you."

Jordan got up and grabbed the handle of the cockpit door. "We swing by, load them up. In and out, just like that. It'll be tight, but we'll be fine."

Elias shook his head, but waved her out. "Hurry up."

Jordan lowered the visor on her helmet and entered the back of the Transport. She didn't know any of these men, didn't want to give them any temptation. Every seat was taken, 32 males, as young as 10, as old as 30. A few sat up straight, most of them white as ghosts. "I need five men that know how to use a rifle."

Seven raised their hands. Jordan took them all, brought them to the rear of the bus and passed out the weapons. "I want the three of you covering this door, and you three covering the front. Open fire at serious threats. Be wary of anyone in silver or black." Jordan pointed at the man with the bushy mustache. "You're with me. You help any stragglers, rush everyone in."

Everyone nodded their heads like they knew what they were doing. She told them, "Get set. Next time we stop, the doors will pop open. You protect this Transport."

Jordan returned to the cockpit, closed the door behind her. Elias waited until she was back in her seat. "I don't like this."

Jordan nodded down the street. "Noted."

They had gone close to a mile when Jordan could make out the citizens waving their arms by the benches. Jordan lowered her audio, muffling the screams, in case shots were fired.

None of these citizens wore silver or black. They were jumping up and down, arms flailing. Jordan opened the door, stopping suddenly when she saw the woman with the baby. The woman was violently shaking her head no. Something was definitely wrong.

Jordan said, "Get us out of here."

"What? We're here now."

"JUST GO!"

Elias looked beyond the benches and his eyes widened. "Oh shit." He punched the accelerator and headed for the end of the street.

The first missile blasted the bench. Body parts thudded against the side of the Transport. Jordan lost hold of her rifle just as the second missile struck the ground in front of them. Elias angled for the middle of the street as they picked up speed.

Something hit just outside the Block's entrance. As the Transport drew closer, Elias asked what it was. It wasn't a missile. Jordan turned up her audio, the plummeting screams and *Blam!* a child smashed onto the windshield. Bodies rained down, cries interrupted mid-scream as flesh splattered the street and smacked the Transport. Jordan checked the cameras that viewed the back of the Transport, saw there were only a few dents in the roof. Most of the recruits sat gripping their seats, but her seven stood by the doors, guns ready.

Jordan activated the intercom, said, "It's going to be okay."

Matthew came over the Connect. *Get out of there now! They're filing in from the back. You have less than two minutes.*

Jordan thought, *They need us. We can't just leave.*

Matthew said, *Elias get off that street. Immediately. That is a direct order.*

Jordan looked out the window. A line of men stood along the Block's roofline. They stood on the ledge with their hands up. Controllers appeared, moved in and fired. The men plummeted, became one with the street.

Elias kept his speed, headed for the end of the Block.

"Elias, stop. We can't let this happen."

"No way. Orders."

Jordan clicked off her Connect, put her gun to his head. "Stop now!"

"Jordan, don't do this."

"They're running them off the roof. Take me to an entrance!"

Elias told her that'd be suicide. A wide-eyed boy thudded five feet in front of them. Elias swerved but they still felt the crunch.

Jordan, get out of there! Matthew must have overridden her Connect. He'd never sounded so frightened. *It's a trap!*

Jordan paused, took her gun off Elias. They had already lost several Transports, the Controllers torturing every survivor, making a game show out of it, guessing how long a person would make it before ending their own life. As much as she wanted to help the people in the Block, she had a duty to protect those already in her care.

Something thwacked against the roof, collapsed it, screams exploded from the back. Elias turned the wheel hard and got the Transport as close to the grass as possible, bodies flinging forward and landing a few feet in front of them.

Jordan felt like she was about to puke, not just for the sight in front of her, but for what Matthew had done to her, taking her from a fast-tracked live-in to the ultimate traitor.

Elias said, "Jordan, up ahead!"

The end of the street was plugged with vehicles, men pointing their weapons at the Transport. A flood of armed citizens poured from the Block, the flashing lights of Controlling Force Agents flying up behind them.

Jordan told Elias to head for the fence separating the street from the aqueduct.

Elias said, "We won't make it."

The vehicles up ahead were stacked five deep, no way they'd bust through. "Over the fence!"

Elias turned the wheel, popped onto the grass, blasted through the chain-link. The edge of the aqueduct was a few feet away, the tires spinning in the mud as Elias tried to correct. The Transport shot forward, its back wheels still spinning, drifting over the edge.

Elias gave up the wheel and covered his face. Jordan held onto the dash. The Transport busted through the railing, slid down the concrete and slammed onto its side in the sludge. The windshield had cracked and Jordan kicked it out on her second try, foul blackness pouring into the cab.

Elias unbuckled and splashed down beside her. Jordan told him, "Take them out the other end. Don't stop."

Jordan clicked on the intercom and commanded her seven to gather everyone at the back. She told Elias, "You lead these people out."

"You're coming with us."

"No. Tell Matthew I'm sorry."

Jordan, no! Retreat as one down the aqueduct. That is an order!

A wave of opposition crested the hill. They were mostly citizens, only a couple cyborg Controllers. Matthew had warned her not everyone would accept change. To some they'd only created a martyr when they killed the Preacher, a saint when she ripped out his eyeball to access the armory. Jordan now saw the reasons why. For many, life in the Blocks was only worse. It'd only been six days and already there were food shortages, riots, corpses rotting in the streets. The news replayed the new Preacher's ordination in D.C., an unknown kin brought forth by the Controllers, the Chosen One who'd crush the loathsome Rebellion.

Jordan raised her plasma rifle. "Do not come any closer, or I will shoot!"

The opposition opened fire first. Jordan hid behind the Transport, chucked a plasma charge. A blue light ripped across the hill, temporarily immobilizing both the cyborgs and the people. As Elias and the recruits slogged through the aqueduct, Jordan blasted the cyborgs, watched them spark and collapse.

Elias and the recruits still had a hundred yards to the wall, but the immobilizing effects of the charge would only last another five seconds.

Jordan reached inside her jacket and squeezed her one and only disruption grenade. "Last resort," Matthew had told her. She'd expected it to be heavy, considering what it was capable of, but it was so light she feared she'd crush it like an egg.

She peered around the side, saw the final traces of the blue light. A cyborg was already raising its pistol. Jordan pressed the detonation code with her thumb. Three seconds. She looked back at Elias and the others crawling through the grate.

Jordan, please. Come on, we'll go on our honeymoon. Don't do this.

"I hate the beach."

You can still run.

No, I can't.

Jordan heaved the grenade, watched it arc through the gray sky and land in the middle of the crowd. She stepped out from behind the Transport, ready for everything to end, when a stream of children, dressed in colors of the Way, sprinted through the crowd.

So young and filled with rage.

"Oh God…"

The End

CAST OF CHARACTERS

(Warning – Contains Spoilers)

Ben Adams, the son of Emily and Justin who fights creatures raiding the ranch, is part of the resistance movement in the mountains, and becomes one of the leaders of the Underground Rebellion.

Brad Dreschner, is a Controller who retires to his estate in the Hills where he provides homes to needy teenagers.

Brian Jaworski, Todd's older brother who is a Controlling Force Agent that married Emily in hopes she'd give him a child, and then ends his career responding to an acid attack.

Cassie Bradford spends her life living in the mountains and tries to save her mother, Vanessa; escapes to the city and is part of the Underground Rebellion.

Claire Wells, Tammy's younger sister who lives with Brian Jaworski's aunt, Mrs. D., in the Hollywood Hills.

Cody Bradford, a toddler when his dad is assassinated, spends his childhood in a Way Camp, is a National guardsman who rescues Vanessa Salazar, fathers Cassie and avenges his father's death.

Colonel Hayden gives the final order to the prison, and reunites with his nephew, John Longley, and Cody Bradford.

Deborah Bradford watches her husband assassinated, has her son, Cody, taken from her and is forced into a mental health ward of the hospital where she meets Maria Salazar.

Derrick Procter, the new boy in town that Gabriel befriends.

Doug Fuller, a National Guard lieutenant battling La Causa; becomes a Captain trying to save his wife and son, Nick, during The Flood.

Emily Adams/Jaworksi/Potter, a victims' rights attorney who marries Justin after the death of her husband, Brian; meets her brother-in-law, Jeremy, who helps them escape to a small ranch where they raise their children.

Enrique Salazar and his wife, Maria, try to come up with money for their newborn, Vanessa, go to the DMV to get Maria's license renewed, and get food from Father Potter.

Eric Norvak, works as the Preacher's assassin and visits John Longley's biological mother.

Father Terrance Potter, the Catholic priest who pickets the Reverend, breaks the law by helping Enrique Salazar, and becomes the spokesperson for fellow inmates.

Frank Hollister, the cousin of Kaiden, a Disciple that convinces him to join their side.

Gabriel Kingston, the son of Wayne Kingston, and the nephew of Enrique and Maria Salazar. Gabriel is a conflicted teenager who rebels against the system.

Greg Williams, an officer who speaks at John Longley's class and encounters Vanessa Salazar at a sterilization clinic.

Jeremy Adams, the teenager who was recruited by the Controllers after avenging his sister's death, is betrayed on an assassination attempt, goes on the run but comes out of hiding to see Justin and his pregnant wife, Emily.

John Longley, adopted as a young boy and is a high school teacher who marries former student, Tammy Wells, adopts Matthew Longley, visits his uncle, Colonel Hayden, and attends the Preacher's coronation.

Jordan Longley/Newell, lived in a Way camp until she was selected as a live-in for Disciple Matthew Longley. Matthew convinces her to join the Rebellion and they are married the day after they liberated the City of Lights.

Julio Ortega, goes to the DMV with his sister, Maria Salazar; gets attacked when he tries to buy bleach.

Justin Adams, the teenager who avenges his sister's death, stands up to the Preacher, has a love affair with Emily Jaworski before marrying her, is reunited with his twin brother, Jeremy, and fights creatures alongside his son, Ben.

Kaiden Hollister, a self-absorbed teenager who struggles with life in the Way Camp but eventually becomes a Disciple.

Kent Hollister, a news reporter, is the father of Kaiden, and husband to Tammy Longley's younger sister, Becky.

Loralei Morrison/Cooper lives at the Dreschner residence after her parents are killed. She later goes to work for Dr. Cooper, and marries his son, Steven. Their baby, Matthew, came with a heavy price but makes an impact on the world.

Maria Salazar struggles to pay for her newborn, Vanessa, and goes to get her license renewed.

Matthew Cooper/Longley, adopted at five, visits his great uncle, becomes a Disciple to infiltrate the Way, is a crucial part of the Rebellion, and takes charge of a very large army.

Miguel Guerrero, a Controlling Force Agent who responds to Julio Ortega's attack, then escapes to the ranch community with the Adams' family.

Nick Fuller loses everything in The Flood and becomes part of the Underground.

The Preacher, Kenneth Murphy II, becomes ruler of The Way at a young age, increases its power and gets rid of any threats, loses his firstborn son and attempts to coronate his second, Geoffrey, when he meets his half-brother, John Langley.

The Reverend, Kenneth Murphy, founds The Church of the American Way and is accused of merging with the State.

Robert Edgefield, a high school junior in John Longley's class who later struggles to make weight.

Steven Cooper, the son of veterinarian, Dr. Matt Cooper. Steven married Loralei Morrison and together they have a son, Matthew.

Tammy Longley/Wells, a student who marries her high school teacher, John Longley, and adopts a child.

Todd Jaworski, borrows Brian's gun as a teenager, is drafted into the National Guard, and fights against La Causa.

Troy Edgefield, a correctional officer who takes his brother, Robert, to the vet, works the last day of the prison, and is challenged at the orphanage by John Longley.

Vanessa Salazar is just a baby when her parents take her to the DMV; as a teenager she reports to a sterilization clinic, is rescued by Cody Bradford, marries him, and gives birth to Cassie Bradford in the mountains as part of the resistance.

Vincent Morrison served in Iraq with Walt Jaworski who later helped Vincent become an analyst for the Controllers. Vincent's wife, Laura, is very close with Walt and his sons.

Walt Jaworski, the father of Brian and Todd Jaworski, is a Controlling Force Agent just doing his job.

REVIEW

If you enjoyed these stories I hope you'll take a moment to write a quick review. As an independent author, word of mouth and reviews are incredibly helpful. Whether you leave one star or five, honest feedback is truly appreciated. And, if it is a one star review, be sure to leave your address so it'll be much easier for me to hunt you down. Thanks!

ACKNOWLEDGMENTS

I owe special thanks to the following people:

Anthony Szpak, an incredible editor I'm very fortunate to be working with. I'm glad to say I've already got him hooked for the next three projects, but plan on turning to him as long as my stories keep his interest.

Krisserin Canary, Dave Thompson, Meg Rottman, and Larry Watkins who critiqued this collection several years ago. Many of the stories are new and they've all been reworked, but if it hadn't been for the four of you, there's no telling what this would look like.

Karl Dominey and Eugene Inozemcev for the invaluable feedback and support. Thanks for being the first friends I could trust this to and having the unlucky position of telling me what sucks. If anyone doesn't like the book, I blame it on you guys for being too kind.

Mom and Dad for encouraging me to read, letting me escape in books, and instilling a love of words. It's a shame some of my stories are too much for you, Mom, because working with Dad and having him do the final edits has been pretty awesome. Love you both.

SPECIAL THANKS

Thanks to Don Currie, whose conservation sparked "30-Day Program," and to all the readers and reviewers for their support and encouragement.

Steve Tullius	Dianne Bylo	Princess
Mary Nyeholt	Susan Cowling	Glenn Cantillo
Jodi McMaster	Deborah Sastroredjo	Paul White
Shanna Cushing	Haven Strange	Randy Jackson
Rebecca Dotson	Michael Inguagiato	Alexis Cassidy
Jasmine Thompson	Sol Rodriguez	Tracy Sanderson
Cheyann Reagan	Karen Bell	Todd Barselow
Fran Lewis	Michael Poorman	Lorraine Gonzalez
Lori Spier	Kim Trotman	Monique Ridenour
Kathy Cunningham	Suzy Wilson-Uilelea	Marie Hensche
Janice Cipriano	Jason Stanley	John Holland
Michala Tyann	Sarah Smith	Diane Taylor
Fred Hughes	CS Zimmer	Sandra Boyle
Declan Garrett	Kyle Katai	Jyllian Roach
Mark Matthews	Houston Stout	Dianne Bylo
Michelle Gillhouse	Brian Esquivel	Susan Cowling
Rich King	Kristin Moody	Daniel Teach
Olivia Hillcoat	Shannon Ovalles	Stephen Perigo
Linda Moore	Melissa Bruce	Teresa Turner
Maria Schockling	Chris Nicholson	Theresa H
Cianna Reider	Glenn Hedden	Annemieke
Shelly Grininger	Nova Reylin	Tori
Josef Hernandez	Nancy Morris	Nicole
Angela Rae	Sam	Diane Watzek
Mike Tullius	Angela	

For new books, giveaways, and updates, visit
MarkTullius.com

DETHFEST

FLAMETHROWER OMNES MORIMUR DETHROS

An Interactive Adventure

You've got tickets to the metal festival of the year. Get ready to rock. And try not to die.

An Anthology

15 Horror Stories about each of the bands that played the Dethfest tragedy.

Download Your Free Copy

Includes the first two chapters and one death scene
from each of the first seven books in the Try Not to Die series.

Nonfiction

MMA

Exploring the
Motivations of Fighters
100 gyms
23 states
400 interviews

Brain Health

Facing fears of
dementia from
repetitive blows to
the head.

Jiu Jitsu

Current Project
A coffee table book
featuring Mark and
his family training
around the world.

Listen to the Books

You can listen to several books in the Try Not to Die series, short horror stories , suspense novels, or nonfiction. Find your next listen at your favorite retailer or www.MarkTullius.com

Time for a Decision

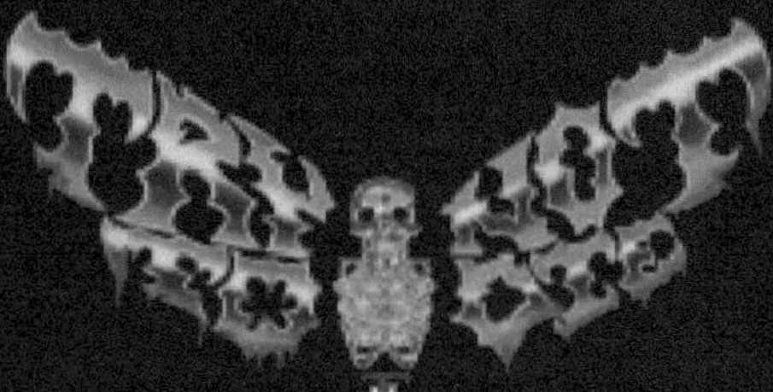

Which books do you want to die in?

On Slashtag – Jon Cohn

In a Dark Fairy Tale – Evan Baughfman

In Arcranium – Daemon Manx and Mark Towse

At Meadow Spire Mall – P.W. Feutz

At Summer Camp - Caitlin Marceau

In the Tournament of --- Wes Levine

Between the Worlds - Nicolas J.H. Alvarez

In Brownsville – Jay Bower

Horror

90 Short Stories

Connect with Mark

Mark enjoys sharing his passions on social media. Check him out on IG at https://geni.us/TulliusIG

In addition to Instagram, you can also check him out on Tik Tok at https://geni.us/TulliusTikTok

And on Facebook find him at https://geni.us/TulliusFB

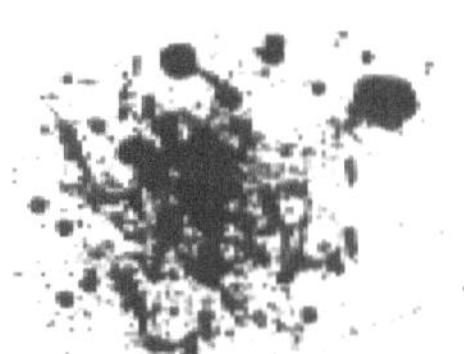

To watch Derek the Demon, book reviews, podcast clips and more. https://geni.us/TulliusYouTube

Connect with Try Not to Die

The Try Not to Die series has its own social media pages. Check them out on IG at

https://geni.us/TryNotToDieOnIG

In addition to Instagram, you can also check them out on Tik Tok at

https://geni.us/TryNotToDieOnTikTok

And on Facebook find the series at

https://geni.us/TryNotToDieOnFacebook